C9999000143749

D1429175

John Burke was born in Sussex and brought up in Liverpool. During the war he served with the RAF, REME and on attachment to the Royal Marines during the liberation of Europe. He started one of the first science-fiction fan magazines in Britain, *The Satellite*, and had several short stories published before winning an Atlantic Award in Literature from the Rockefeller Foundation for his first novel, *Swift Summer*. He is now a full-time author and has had more than 140 books published. He has five daughters and two sons and lives in south-west Scotland with his wife.

DEATH BY MARZIPAN

When high-flying businesswoman Brigid Weir is thrown out by her employers, she plans revenge in no-holds-barred memoirs, and recklessly chooses as ghost writer a figure from her past who may still have his own grudges to bear. Trouble is inevitable once word of the project leaks out. But a different kind of trouble arises in the theft of treasures from her Scottish Borders home, and art expert Detective Inspector Lesley Gunn is barely on the scene before another crime demands her attention — the discovery of the body of one of Brigid's ex-husbands in the grounds of her present husband's estate . . .

JOHN BURKE

DEATH
BY
MARZIPAN

Complete and Unabridged

ULVERSCROFT
Leicester

First published in Great Britain in 1999 by
Robert Hale Limited
London

First Large Print Edition
published 2001
by arrangement with
Robert Hale Limited
London

British Library CIP Data

Burke, John, *1922 –*
    Death by marzipan.—Large print ed.—
    Ulverscroft large print series: mystery
    1. Revenge—Fiction 2. Scottish Borders (England
    and Scotland)—Fiction 3. Detective and mystery stories
    4. Large type books
    I. Title
    823.9′14 [F]

    ISBN 0–7089–4344–6

Published by
F. A. Thorpe (Publishing)
Anstey, Leicestershire

Set by Words & Graphics Ltd.
Anstey, Leicestershire
Printed and bound in Great Britain by
T. J. International Ltd., Padstow, Cornwall

This book is printed on acid-free paper

1

It was a Friday afternoon when she came back from lunch to find her office door locked. Personal belongings from her desk drawers were propped against it in a large carrier bag. The two partners were waiting for her in Sandy Cameron's office. They weren't going to risk her confronting them separately.

'Will somebody tell me just what's going on?'

They told her. It was as if they had rehearsed the piece and shared out the lines like a comedy duo. Only it wasn't funny. She was fired, and they wanted her off the premises this very moment. A financial settlement would be communicated to her by their lawyers the following weekend.

'What the hell am I supposed to have done?'

They told her that as well, though she had guessed already. Word of her meeting with Alastair Blake had somehow been leaked, and they weren't going to wait for explanations. No chance of her extracting crucial data from the computer to take with her.

'You'll be hearing from me,' Brigid said as

she left. 'That's a promise. And you know I keep my promises.'

In the taxi bouncing and lurching along the Edinburgh streets to her flat she saw nothing, sitting too tense and choked to cry. It was years since she had cried about anything, anyway.

First thing Saturday morning she rang Blake's home number. That devious fat sod must have been behind the leak. Nobody else could have known about their meeting. Nobody else could have had any motive for ensuring that if she wouldn't dance to his tune, she'd get no chance of leading a dance anywhere else.

'Bridie. Great to hear from you again, so soon.' He was always hearty and booming, much given to putting his arm round your shoulder and sharing his insincerity in gin-laden gusts. This morning there was an additional gloating undertone. 'Been thinking things over?'

'Yes indeed. What sort of cheap revenge d'you call this?'

'Revenge? Why should I want revenge on anybody?'

'Just because I turned down your offer — '

'No hard feelings, lassie. None at all. On my oath.' He paused, then said: 'You havnae been having second thoughts, maybe?'

'No, I haven't. But I did want you to know . . . ' She floundered, and hated herself for it. Her swift reactions were legendary, but now she wasn't even sure what she did want Alastair Blake to know. 'I'm not going to let this rest. One way or another, you'll be hearing from me.'

'I look forward to that. Best of luck, Bridie.' He sounded intolerably smug. And she hated being called Bridie or lassie.

No use chasing anybody else until Monday morning. She was impatient for it to come. Before word got round and the stories got twisted, she had to tell her own story and wait for a good offer to come in. There were plenty of high flyers who had reached their present executive positions on her recommendation. They owed her. It was time to collect.

But on Monday morning she learned that word had already got round. Not just that: it had been vigorously *sent* around. She ought to have known. She had been in the thick of it long enough, and watched it happen to others. Now, like so many of those others, she found herself the last one to learn that she was on the skids. They were all polite, all eager to invite her to lunch and have a good chat one day soon: but not *too* soon.

'Why not take a sabbatical?' one creep said urbanely. 'You deserve one. And it's not as if

3

you *have* to work. I'm sure the laird'll be delighted to have more of your company.'

The bastards. After all she had done for so many of them.

Seething her way through a few moments of tumultuous thought, she phoned the office and asked for Sara.

'Who is that speaking?'

'Brigid Weir.'

'I'm sorry, Miss Weir, I'm afraid I can't put you through.'

'What d'you mean, you can't put me through? Is Sara there, or isn't she?'

'I can't put you through.' And the line went dead.

Sara wouldn't have been where she was if it hadn't been for Brigid. That evening she rang the girl's home number. All the admiration and warmth had gone from the usually obsequious voice.

'I've been asked not to talk to you, Miss Weir.'

'Asked?'

'Well . . . told.'

'Who the hell do they think they are? You've been with me for three years, why the hell shouldn't we talk if I feel like it?'

'Miss Weir, they think you were thinking of taking me and Ian with you when you quit.'

'Who said I was quitting?'

4

'They think — '

'Thinking's not usually their line of business.'

It was true, of course, that she had considered taking two out of her team with her when she chose to leave — which had certainly not been in order to join Alastair Blake. But they'd have had no reason to jump to conclusions about her possible departure until the thwarted Blake had fed them a load of malicious gossip.

'I'm sorry, Miss Weir,' Sara was saying, 'but there's really no point in talking. I'm sorry. Really I am.'

Another phone was put down.

Now it was time to consult her solicitor. Or, rather, not so much consult him as tell him precisely what she wanted.

And while all that was being set up, how would she occupy herself? A sabbatical? Bloody impertinence. She would love to have everything wrapped up and be presented by tomorrow lunchtime with a tasty carry-out of the heads of Sandy Cameron and his sidekick. But these things took time.

Time for action — for a sortie they didn't expect. Sometimes she had been accused of devising strategies off the top of her head, without careful consideration. But she had always maintained that it was better to make a wrong decision than to dither. Most of her decisions, even the wrong ones, had turned out successful in the end.

By Tuesday evening she had decided on her next move.

Sooner or later she would be back in the rat race. They couldn't do without her. She was the most skilled selector of top-grade rats in the Edinburgh marketplace. But for a while she would have time on her hands; and that was something Brigid Weir couldn't bear. She had to have something to occupy her.

So she would write her memoirs.

Once the idea was conceived, she could see the whole future: a book, serial rights to one of the papers where she had good contacts, interviews on TV, maybe a series of programmes tied in with the book. Maybe even putting something exclusive her step-daughter's way, to show she really did mean well towards her. Tell the world how the market worked, how the headhunters worked, and what happened to the heads when they had been turned by flattery and money.

And, of course, by women. The prestige wives, the kept women, the family destroyers, the predators. She knew so many names.

Hadn't there been an 18th-century courtesan who sold chapters of her memoirs at a high price to the men who featured in them and wanted them suppressed? That was a tempting idea. But the first thing was to get the words down on paper.

Brigid Weir settled herself in front of the screen and began to put short sentences down at her usual speed. Start with her first big coup, the poaching of Colin MacWilliam from Kinloch Systems and delivering him to the office high above Heriot Row where he now looked down on the world. She remembered every last little detail, including a few that MacWilliam would probably prefer to forget.

After five pages she sat back, fidgeted a moment, and then went to make herself a cup of coffee. She stared down from her own high window on to the oily undulations of the Water of Leith and its cargoes of plastic cups and crumpled lager cans; five minutes later was still staring unseeingly while her coffee grew cold.

She had been one of the first to see the potential of these conversions within old wine warehouses in Leith, and had bought in before prices soared. Looking down from her eyrie was usually a soothing, rewarding experience. Today she was too much on edge to appreciate the view, the sunshine, or her own thoughts.

Things would sort themselves out as she

got into the swing. She had heard of writer's block but didn't believe in it. She didn't believe in insurmountable obstacles anywhere, in any profession. But she certainly didn't like what she had written so far. It was not much different from the headhunting appraisal she had written of MacWilliam at the time. For a book, more colour was needed; more depth. She sat down again and began to insert a few personal features she had omitted from her original report, bringing the man himself alive on the page. Still there was something lacking.

She had been too clinical in her approach for too long, stripping things to the bone. That had been an essential part of her job, simplifying things for top personnel managers who found it difficult to cope with too many psychological complexities at a time. This present venture needed a different technique.

It might be a good thing to have someone else with whom to mull over ideas until they bubbled into life.

This was a field in which she was not at home. But there were always ways on to uncharted territory. Shifting managerial types and whizzkids about the board, tracing the routes from one boardroom to another, she had boned up on so many different skills and professions, mastering their intricacies and jargon in half the time it would take anybody else. Whatever the challenge, she had always known where to respond and who to use.

Suddenly it came to her. Of course she knew who it had to be.

Did she dare? What would he say? Would *he* dare?

First things first. Get the deal set up before taking the chances. Two years ago she had headhunted a publishing executive from one specialised house in Glasgow and delivered him to a conglomerate in London, chucking out a languid, puzzled ex-Etonian in the process.

Murdo Cowan owed her a favour. She phoned him and overrode his welcoming platitudes by saying bluntly that she was writing a book.

'You're thinking of a textbook on managerial consultancy? Could be interesting.'

'No. A bit of autobiography, and some studies of leading individuals in the field.'

'Individuals? Could be dangerously personal.'

'I'm still kicking ideas around.'

'And thinking of kicking a few old enemies around? Could be some nasty legal problems. Depending on just *who* . . .'

She heard his faint hissing intake of breath. He would of course take it for granted that he was important enough to feature in anything she wrote. Let him stew.

She said: 'Murdo, if you'd rather I approached some other publisher, just say so.'

'No, good heavens, no. After all the time we've known one another . . . '

Even on the phone the tremor of his disquiet was obvious. Too many rival publishers would rejoice at the chance of seeing a chapter about Murdo Cowan over which he had no editorial control.

Not that she had any intention of letting him exercise control over anything she wrote.

'Another thing,' she said. 'I was thinking I needed — what d'you call it, a ghost?'

'You, Brigid? I wouldn't have thought so. Though I suppose you'd find the detailed work difficult to fit in with your usual ferocious schedule.'

Clearly word of her downfall had not yet reached the London publishing world. On Sundays they all read the literary review pages, not the paragraphs tucked away in the business supplements.

'Someone to act as a sounding-board,' she said smoothly. 'Just someone I can bounce ideas off.'

'God help her, the way you're likely to serve 'em.'

'You're suggesting a she?'

'Melanie Parkes. Just up your street. She's

collaborated on a couple of top sellers for us. Really good at digging into the feminine psyche, if you know what I mean.'

'I don't fancy another woman in on my psyche. I'd prefer working with a man.'

'Could be a bit embarrassing.'

'Not for me.' Maybe for her collaborator, though. She had always known the top man in any field — that was what she had built her reputation on — and in this case she had every reason to know who that man was. It would be interesting to see him after all this time. And interesting to see what his reaction would be. 'From what I hear,' she said, 'Gregory Dacre's the top man.'

'Well, yes. We've used him a number of times. But he can get very quirky. I'm not sure he'd be quite what you're looking for.'

'I'll make him what I want him to be.'

'I ought to have a word with our sales team and work out just how many copies we can be sure of shifting.'

'Get Mr Dacre in on Friday,' said Brigid. 'I'll fly down and we can sort out a basis for working together.'

'Friday? Rather short notice. Depends on how he's fixed.'

'He can get to you easily enough from Norwich. He *is* still living there, isn't he?'

'You know a bit about him, then?'

'A great deal. Oh, yes, indeed. A very great deal.'

After past experiences with Brigid Weir, Cowan knew when to stop arguing. 'I'll see how our senior editor is fixed, and she can set up a meeting. She'll be able to suggest a general approach, and she'll be the one to see your book through the press. Though of course I'll be on hand if you need any extra weight. And we could have lunch together after you've made up your mind.'

She wondered what sort of chapter she might make out of Murdo Cowan and whether, if he did become her publisher, he would fight to cut all the snide bits out.

There were likely to be snags and stormy scenes ahead. But overcoming snags had always added spice and excitement to any of her undertakings so far. Not to mention out-and-out stormy scenes, when the adrenaline really began to flow.

There was nothing more to be done here in Edinburgh for the moment. Time to spend a couple of days at home. For a brief spell she could switch from being Brigid Weir to being Lady Crombie, while waiting for the answer to her question. But not — the word still rankled — not anything as protracted and inoffensive as a sabbatical.

A breathing space, that was all. And the

breathing wouldn't be all that leisurely.

Would Greg be capable of facing her again, and facing some of the revelations she must inevitably bring out into the open?

Would he dare?

2

Should he dare?

Greg Dacre's first impulse had been to turn the job down. Did Brigid really think that after all this time she could condescend to him, toss him scraps from her table? He didn't need her. And he didn't suppose she would really be willing to tell all the truths that were needed if her book was going to be any good. She hadn't been all that good at telling the truth in the past. Why should he suppose she had got any better?

He wasn't put off by the possible troubles there could be with other people and companies. Once word got out that Weir the Wheeler-Dealer was letting her hair down, there were bound to be twitches of terror in the business and advertising fraternities. There might even be threats or hurried attempts at bribing her into silence. She would know that as well as anyone. The threats could reach out to her collaborator as well; but it wouldn't be the first time he had found himself saddled with the blame for interpreting what the nominal author of the book had told him. He had learned to cope.

On one project he might have been alarmed by the activities of shadowy little men from M16, if they hadn't been so absurd. During his work on the memoirs of a Soviet spy with a mistress in Moscow and one in Manchester, the spooks had prided themselves on keeping him under the most sophisticated covert surveillance; until the day when he walked up to one of them in the street with a sheaf of typescript, and said: 'Here's the latest chapter. It'll save you trying to get through my computer firewall.'

In his time, Greg Dacre had been not just a Soviet spy but a rock star, an Olympic athlete, and an international faith healer. He even, for a few months, immersed himself utterly in the character of a highly respected brothel keeper and was offered a number of free perks which from professional integrity — or sheer funk — he declined. So it came as no great surprise to be offered 'a substantial advance and a generous percentage on royalties' — the meanings of 'substantial' and 'generous' to be thrashed out with his literary agent — to take on the *persona* of a tough female headhunter. He had good reason to know just how tough she could be. But hadn't it occurred to her that of all men he was the one best qualified to know her weaknesses, too?

He came down by train from Norwich to Liverpool Street — some folk said 'up' to London, but Greg had long ago come to regard London as down from almost anywhere — and took a taxi to the Clement & Cowan office block.

★　★　★

Brigid was already there, sitting facing the door as if to challenge him the moment he appeared. 'So you decided to come.'

'Just to find out what precisely the deal is.'

'As I told you in our phone conversation, Mr Dacre' — Penelope Vaughan-Smith, spikily upright behind her desk, didn't like authors or anybody else taking up the running before she had even fired the starting pistol — 'Miss Weir . . . or do you prefer to be called Lady Crombie, Lady Crombie?'

'Professionally I've always been Brigid Weir. That will be the name on the book.'

'Of course. Right, Mr Dacre. Miss Weir wants to throw out a few ideas and see whether you're both on the same wavelength. It'll be my job to act as interpreter, you might say, if necessary.'

'You might say that,' said Brigid, 'but I think Mr Dacre and I speak roughly the same language.'

16

Greg was not so sure of that, but stayed silent. He studied Brigid as she spoke, and knew that she was aware of this. Had she dressed and made herself up with extra care for this meeting?

In her late forties now, she would stay beautiful for at least another two decades. Her lips were thin but finely shaped, ready to smile when that was needed in a negotiation. Tiny puckerings in the corners, though, were not laughter lines. She was as relaxed as a tigress deciding in leisurely fashion which limb of its prey to gnaw next. There was even a hint of a tiger's stripes in her hair, a deep bronze with two swathes of dark brown carefully sleeked back from her high forehead. Her pale blue eyes, quite out of keeping with that tawny mane, were lazy but watchful. The grey two-piece was less a business suit than a stylish pelt, shaped tautly over her breasts and high at the throat. She knew how to make any man conscious of her sinuous body within those expensive clothes.

For fifteen minutes they discussed the general thrust of the book-to-be. It was noticeable that although Brigid sounded crisp and confident, explaining the ins and outs of professional appointments, headhunting, forays into venture capital, takeovers and covert monopoly deals, and the sort of man

17

who could make a fortune and lose a fortune, she was giving no individual details away. Not yet. Not until she was ready, thought Greg. Of course that was how she must always operate. All the same, he sensed from little shifts in her tone of voice and the tempo of some remarks an underlying desire for vengeance.

He had spent part of yesterday on the phone consulting friends in the City and on a financial weekly. They gave colour and an additional dimension to what he, like anybody regularly reading newspapers or catching a passing reference in some TV money programme, already knew about Brigid Weir.

The title of the organisation within which she had performed so ruthlessly was Excel-Con. An expanded version on its letter heading in smaller type defined this as Executive Link Consultancy. They charged high fees for running management courses and corporate motivational weekends, notoriously the most searching in Scotland and some way down into England. Discarded victims had protested that the experience was more like a battle course than a business executives' programme. At the same time ExcelCon was rumoured to assess the worth of people sent on such courses, and either recommend their expensive promotion within their current company or try luring them away elsewhere.

And somewhere, somehow, Brigid had blundered. It would be interesting to see how frank she was prepared to be about that aspect.

Miss Vaughan-Smith was out of her depth. She shifted uneasily on her chair, wanting to assert herself but not grasping enough of the subject to know where she could interrupt.

At last she risked it. 'I'm sure this is the sort of thing where you'll find Mr Dacre helpful. Getting things into a shape the general public can understand.'

That had taken quite an effort. At the moment Greg Dacre was not in her good books. Not that Clement & Cowan were exactly noted for good books. Hyped biographies and the ghosted autobiographies of illiterate fashion models and sportsmen, yes; but few of any outstanding literary merit. The accountants who dominated the group had their eyes on swift, substantial returns from the latest crazes and celebrities rather than on less substantial long-term rewards for quality and creativity. Penelope Vaughan-Smith would probably spend only the usual six months here before flitting off to some other publishing house, where she would tell

19

everyone what utterly grisly people she had left behind.

Right now Greg wasn't sure what her toothy snarl implied. It could be a lingering reaction to his most recent letter denouncing her editorial subversion of his punctuation. She had a habit of spattering commas like fly-droppings all over a page, saying, 'I'm sorry, but that's our house style.' Or maybe she was still peevish because some weeks ago he had turned down her offer of another ghosting job, not even bothering to get in touch personally but leaving it to his literary agent. He was eager enough for a continuing income, but not desperate enough to put a gloss on the memoirs of a repellent Cabinet Minister who had recently lost his seat: the man's self-justifications would be more suited to a work of fiction than an honest autobiography. Or maybe Miss Vaughan-Smith — Greg could never imagine anyone getting round to calling her Penelope, let alone Penny — disapproved of the way he was sizing up the other woman in the room. She must sense that she herself, with her bony shoulders and muddy complexion, was never likely to attract that sort of rapt attention; or that kind of income.

Greg had often observed how very sexy money could be. Really rich men could be really ugly and still attract beautiful women; and not always because of the plushy lifestyle they had to offer. And rich women themselves somehow gave off a scent which had nothing to do with expensive perfumes. Money itself was the great aphrodisiac.

'Mr Dacre does have a reputation for empathising with a congenial subject.' Miss Vaughan-Smith continued with her grudging effort to set Greg up as one of the company's prized writers. 'For bringing out the real person.'

Brigid made a faint inclination of the head in Greg's direction. 'It must have taken quite some time to develop such a talent.'

Miss Vaughan-Smith began to sense something between the two of them which had not been confided to her. Her long face drooped a resentful inch longer. She switched tactics. 'Perhaps we can settle terms here and now. Have to go to our contracts department to be finalised, of course, but I'd like to establish the basics: the advance, dates for a synopsis, some specimen chapters, delivery dates and so on.'

Brigid Weir eyed her up and down in an appraisal which briskly wrote off Miss Vaughan-Smith's narrow head as not worth the hunting; or, indeed, any other part of her anatomy. She said: 'Before committing

21

ourselves, I think Mr Dacre and I ought to have a personal discussion to make sure we empathise — that was your expression, wasn't it? I suggest we break for lunch.' She wasn't suggesting it at all: she was commanding it. 'And then if I find we can get on *nowadays*' — the emphasis baffled Miss Vaughan-Smith even more — 'Mr Dacre can come and spend a few days at my place to finalise our working timetable.'

'Stately home in the Borders?' said Greg.

'You've been checking on me. Yes, stately home — sort of. Fewer distractions than the flat in Edinburgh.'

'Either of them is a long way from here.'

'All the better. Fewer distractions,' Brigid said again. Smoothly she added: 'Would you like to bring your wife? Or do you find *her* a distraction when you're working?'

It was Brigid's way of finding out what had been happening to him in recent years. At the same time her tone of voice implied that personal attachments would be regarded as a nuisance.

The truth was simple enough. 'I don't have a wife any more.'

'She's dead? I'm sorry.'

'Not dead. Just not in my life any more.'

'Ah. Like my husband.' Blandly she added to Miss Vaughan-Smith: 'Husbands in the plural, actually. Two of them gone, one still functioning.'

Miss Vaughan-Smith had had enough of this. It was her office, she was used to authors and suchlike being deferential. 'Perhaps,' she said, 'it would be a help if I joined you at some stage. I could manage to get away for a few days in a case like this.'

'Very thoughtful of you, but I don't think Mr Dacre and I need a referee. We'll fight it out between us.'

Greg wondered how close she was to adding — *Just as we always used to.*

'And as to the money,' he said, 'I'll have a word with my agent before I leave.'

Miss Vaughan-Smith's face fell even further. She hadn't really hoped, had she, that just for once she would be able to fiddle things all her own way instead of being wrestled into submission by Kate Hadleigh?

★　★　★

At lunch, they ordered and then sat in silence for a few minutes: not so much an awkward silence as one of mutual assessment as they took up positions, each waiting for the other's gambit.

'Well,' he said at last.

'Well,' she said. She waited for the ritual of

wine sniffing and tasting and pouring to be completed, then made the first move. 'So you haven't married again. Or did you marry and then find that that one didn't work either?'

'No. I haven't remarried.'

'I thought there was some ravishing blonde around at one stage.'

'I didn't know you still kept that keen an eye on my career.'

'The sort of glossy magazines I have to skim through to keep an eye on my clients — you appear in them occasionally.'

'Very occasionally.'

'She looked rather gorgeous.'

'It was just publishers' publicity. You know how it is.'

'I do indeed.' She paused as the melon and Parma ham were set in front of her. 'And you've got at least a glimmering of what *I've* been up to and what we'll be writing about?'

Greg nodded. 'What gets me,' he said, 'is that when your headhunting is so blatant, why do top people allow it to happen? Why risk sending their best men on such dangerous campaigns, knowing the chances of them defecting?'

'A lot of the book's going to be about just that. Don't expect me to trot out an easy synopsis off the cuff.'

'But you really do want to tell all? Give

24

away all the secrets, how the big shots make their decisions, how they work behind the scenes, switching men and women to and fro at ever-increasing salaries, collecting their own dues, recommending someone and damning someone else?'

'And put flesh on the bones of the contestants, yes. Lots of flesh. And then strip it off for everyone to see.'

Who would trust her after these revelations she was bent on making? Or had she decided she was no longer interested in being trusted?

Abruptly she was the one doing the questioning. She ate in quick, small mouthfuls, skilled at formulating crucial barbs to launch at her companion when his own mouth was full and he had to gulp before coping with the answers.

'Do fill in the gaps between those occasional pictures and paragraphs. How have things been for you?'

Put flesh on his bones . . . so that she could strip it off layer by layer . . . ? She had always been good at getting down to the raw nerves.

'It depends,' he said warily, 'on who I've been at any given time.'

It was almost like facing an interview for a job. Which, he supposed, was really the way she saw it. Only he was not a desperate applicant. Just as she could choose not to employ him, he could choose at any minute to walk out. Just as she had walked out, way back.

Without boasting or trying to ingratiate himself, he summarised his career crisply and impersonally, as if sketching the outline of somebody else's biography.

She hardly needed telling that he had worked with little hope of advancement in that sombre little Edinburgh educational publishing house in its cramped cobbled square, while more ambitious colleagues headed towards London to make a name for themselves. It had always been a source of argument and bitterness between them. Brigid had left in a fine flurry of rage before he turned his own footsteps towards London and discovered his own real talent. The Edinburgh firm had sold out to a conglomerate, and it was a matter of accepting a transfer to the London office or wandering round Edinburgh looking for something else.

The shake-up shook many things into a new pattern for Gregory Dacre. Editing a clumsy autobiography commissioned by his new employers, he began to sense what the man was really trying to say, and found in himself a talent for becoming another person, and then a whole sequence of other people: not so much impersonating them as assuming their identity. Quite unlike the bossy Miss Vaughan-Smith, always wanting to impose her own straitjacket upon a variety of other people, he didn't assert himself, but coaxed the truth out of his collaborators. Even when he had become a respected name in the profession, his own face was never on the cover or even the back flap of a book. But he had become sufficiently sought after to justify his name appearing on the title page, usually in the form of 'as told to Gregory Dacre' or 'with Gregory Dacre', as if he were some sort of detergent additive. There came a time when people felt privileged if his name was suggested as their ghost. He didn't suppose Brigid would regard him quite so respectfully.

Yet she was famous for her intuition in choosing the right man for the job. And she was the one who had insisted on Cowan approaching him.

Just what were her real intentions?

He would find out, not from her but through her. He had become a more skilful dramatic interpreter than any actor. He didn't just play the part: thinking himself deeper and deeper into it, he virtually *became* the character. When working on that Soviet spy's autobiography, he had thought and become the man himself, in spite of original distaste for him. Usually it was a man. But several women had gushingly said that he understood them.

That wasn't something he would risk reporting to Brigid.

'I can't believe,' she said over the poached salmon, 'that you've been entirely celibate all these years. Come on, Greg, if we're going to work together — '

'It's your autobiography we're going to write, not mine. Just when and where do we start? And when you tell a pack of lies, how much am I allowed to put right?'

She fidgeted for a moment, uncharacteristically unsure of herself. Then she stooped to pick up her briefcase and took out a few pages of print-out which had obviously been left ready to hand. There was an unusual timidity in the way she handed them over to him, as if at the last moment she might snatch them back. 'My first sketch of an opening. I know there's a lot of polishing to be done . . . I can see faults in it myself, but . . . '

It was a familiar situation. They always made lame apologies, hating the idea of anyone else casting a critical eye over their efforts.

'Let's just have a quick look, shall we?' said Greg soothingly.

'Would you excuse me a minute?'

Of course she couldn't bear to sit and

watch him while he read the few pages. This was where he ceased to be regarded as a potential employee and began to take charge. It had happened so often before. He had never expected it to happen with Brigid.

She was back in ten minutes, talking fast before she had even sat down. 'I don't expect you to rush into an immediate judgment. Not off the top of your head. Have a look through it before we next meet. Tell me what you think when you've had time to digest it.'

He already knew what he thought. It had taken only a few minutes to get the flavour of it. Too detached. Stodgy. Some provocative facts were there, but there was no life in it. No real people. Not even Brigid herself.

Over the coffee he deliberately refused to offer her the few stopgap assurances which, in spite of what she had just said, she was waiting for. Quite a new sensation, keeping Brigid dangling.

Just for the hell of it, he returned to the attack. 'What I don't understand is why these organisations who send their top people on those courses don't realise they're likely to lose them. I mean, with you sitting there picking out the likely ones — '

'Like a vulture?' Her smile this time was quite unforced. She was so pleased with herself.

'I can't believe they could be that gullible. Running risks like that.'

'If they sometimes lose a good analyst or administrator to a competitor, they can afford to be philosophical about it, because' — she studied her coffee cup as if her palate had suddenly sharpened — 'sooner or later they'll acquire somebody better. From the same source. They rarely send anyone on those courses that they're genuinely worried about losing. It's usually only dubious folk from the Marzipan Layer.'

'The what?'

'That's a new one on you? Bright middle management types. Sometimes getting too cosy. Not uncommon for us to get a tipoff from the top floor that they wouldn't mind this one or that one getting a bad report, or being nudged somewhere else. But there are others who are just about ready for something more ambitious. Nobody in that middle segment, the Marzipan Layer, is ever quite safe, one way or the other.'

'But the prizes for coming out of the marzipan into the icing on top of the cake are considerable?'

'You're getting the hang of it.'

'I shall look at some folk I know in the publishing world through new eyes.'

'On that subject,' said Brigid, 'I wasn't

impressed with that Miss Vaughan-Smith.'

'Publishers' editors are all pretty much the same. They love to try telling you how to write, and then alter what you've written because they don't feel they're earning their salaries if they don't meddle.'

'What sort of salaries?'

'What you might call the Digestive Biscuit Layer.'

'You do pick the terminology up fast, don't you?'

There was still that question which kept popping up in his mind. 'Why have you decided to spill the beans now? I mean, won't it make it difficult for you to get another job later? Or are we going to stick to fairly uncontroversial material?'

'No,' she said, 'we certainly are not.'

'In which case — '

'We'll deal with each case as we come to it. And bring out all the facts, whatever they may be.'

Or whatever you've decided they should be, he thought.

He said: 'Isn't this going to get dangerous? Somebody might get hurt.'

She was smiling to herself this time, far away in some daydream of settling old scores. 'That's the whole idea, Greg. So let's not waste any more time, right? You can fly up to

Edinburgh with me this evening, and we'll drive to — '

'This evening,' he said, 'I'll be seeing my agent, to sort things out. Then I'll go back to Norwich to pick things up, and drive to Baldonald House first thing Monday morning.'

The lines in the corners of her mouth tightened. 'Driving up? So you can make a quick getaway if you can't stand me? Like last time?'

That was a more twisted interpretation of the facts than he would have thought even Brigid capable of.

He wondered whether the victims she was surely lining up for the book would eventually wish they had never been in her debt.

How many of them had she slept with? Or had she scrupulously avoided any entanglement of that kind?

He looked at her as the sudden bright reflection from a waiter's tray skimmed across her face, and went on wondering.

And she looked searchingly back at him.

3

When Kate opened the door of her flat to him, she wasn't putting on any pretence. Or, indeed, much else. She was wearing only the flimsy floral dressing-gown he had given her last Christmas, not even bothering to knot the sash.

'First things first,' she said.

In bed with her it was as easy and uncomplicated and fierce as always. Yet somehow each time was always the first time. He marvelled at the sleek length of her as if he had never explored her before: the creamy olive skin that suggested some distant Italian ancestor still lurking under that very English voice and self-assured, almost arrogant face; those steady nutbrown eyes and those full lips which in some lights darkened like purple bruises.

She flaunted herself at him before dragging him close so that it was the smell and feel of her that mattered, and in their loving battle he caught only the occasional glimpse of a writhing shoulder, the twitch of her head, a smile and a greedily opening mouth.

When they lay back, she let out a shuddering

breath and said: 'All right, now we'd better talk shop. Or do you want to get out of bed and pour us a drink?'

'No, I don't want to get out of bed.'

'Good.' Her fingers stroked his hip. 'What's the deal, then?'

He told her.

'Just a minute.' Her breath was still unsteady, but now out of disbelief. 'You're talking about getting involved with *her* again?'

'It's just a job of work. Analysing her dispassionately — '

'You're always boasting about actually *becoming* your subjects. You seriously think you can cope with this one — with *being* your wife?'

'Ex-wife.'

'Don't niggle. You believe she'll let you into all her secrets? You of all people?'

'I'm quite looking forward to squeezing them out of her.'

'Yes,' murmured Kate. 'You're rather good at squeezing the lifeblood out of your women. But don't you think that, just for once, you might be the one who gets squeezed? Suffocated?'

'It could be a big seller, if we get it right. She's got quite a reputation.'

'I'm aware of that. But didn't you tell me what a hell of a life she gave you? Left you

34

mortally wounded. And you're going to risk a replay?'

'Things have changed.'

'You reckon?' Her cheek had been damp against his shoulder. Now she pushed herself up in bed and stared wonderingly down at him. 'What on earth was it like, meeting her again after all these years?'

'Weird,' he conceded.

'No nostalgic memories? No danger of falling for her again?'

'Absolutely not.'

'The photographs I've seen of her, she still looks pretty terrific. Rather a bossy mouth, though.'

'You're dead right there.'

It was incredible that, long ago, he had so often kissed Brigid's tight, savage lips. Why had he once loved her? Or, if not loved, been obsessed by her?

Brigid's enthusiasms had been so over-whelming. She swept you off your feet with the intensity of whatever passion possessed her at any given moment; persuaded you of her intuitive rightness; until you learned to keep your feet firmly on the ground and let the tide break over you to expend itself somewhere behind you, somewhere further away.

He felt appetite stirring again. Not because

of Brigid, not that. Oh, no, not any more. It was Kate whose skin was against his, Kate whose warm right leg moved sinuously against his left thigh.

She drew abruptly away from him. 'Are you pretending I'm her? Wishing you could be back in bed with her instead of a nobody like me?'

She gasped as he cut her short with a sudden, angry plunge into her — an anger that she answered by digging her nails into his back, until the heat of their anger became the rich heat of desire. He mumbled sounds into her mouth that never became words but inflamed her into an uncontrollable dance, still in his arms and urging him to a faster, more insistent rhythm.

Until at last she had only enough breath left to sigh, lovingly: 'You're a real swine, aren't you?'

'I'm real, all right.'

Her hand strayed over his body. 'I'll say you are. When you're here, that is. It's damned dismal when you're not.'

'We've always agreed — '

'No, we haven't. You've made it clear you're not going to be lumbered, and I've gone along with it. Had to. That doesn't mean I've agreed. Just accepted, because there wasn't anything else I could do. Selfish sod.'

'Oh, Lor'. Kate ... darling ... you've always known what I am.'

'No, I haven't. When you're working, you're somebody else. I'm the mug who gets you these jobs, or sorts out the money for you. But then what? Once you've sunk into a part, I *don't* know who you are. The number of times I've lost you. Never flaming well knowing who you're going to be next time we meet.' She stared intently at him. 'Somehow, somewhere there's always that question: who *else* are you?'

And in the morning, before he set off back to Norwich, she kissed him and said: 'All right, I'll screw every penny I can get out of Clement and Cowan. And while I'm slaving away at that, you'll be nice and cosy in bed with her. I'll bet on that.'

'You'd lose your bet. After all the things I went through — '

'If that woman decides you're going to go to bed with her,' said Kate sadly, 'you'll go to bed with her.'

⋆ ⋆ ⋆

Driving across the Fens in the early morning light, Greg began to wonder if Kate was right. Not about hopping into bed with Brigid — no way — but about his ability to cope. In this silvery haze, it seemed crazy to be leaving a world whose vast skies he had come to think of as his own, and a city whose streets never failed to enchant him. Leaving such security for another tussle, and this time a tussle with someone he had never been able to vanquish in the past — how could this be a rational judgment?

He stopped for coffee and a snack on the A1 and then was halfway to the Border before traffic thickened and lorries bore in from either side. Ahead, the A1 went on towards Edinburgh. He was glad she hadn't insisted they start work in Edinburgh. Too many memories there; too many early frustrations. He turned off towards the A68, and could not help relaxing as he climbed the breathtaking miles to Carter Bar and its promise of the Scottish hills and valleys beyond. Through Jedburgh, and then a loop west into the vale of the Yarrow Water. In such surroundings he could almost believe that he was going to enjoy himself.

Baldonald House stood high on a brae above a curve in the river. He swept in between gateposts with two stags facing each other, and past a lodge with fuchsias trailing from a hanging basket.

A windbreak of larches and a dark barrier of rhododendron bushes which had long since shed their blooms shielded the frontage of the house until he was almost upon it. His first jaundiced thought was that Brigid had done very well for herself. Here was a setting worthy of the go-getting Miss Brigid Weir who had become Mrs Gregory Dacre and then Mrs Simon Pringle and now Lady Crombie.

The grey stone façade, with its two symmetrical arcs of steps meeting at a huge front door on the terrace, would have defined it as a classical manor house were it not for the addition by a nineteenth-century Crombie, under the baleful influence of Sir Walter Scott, of a bulbous stair turret at the west end and an improbable flourish of battlements. A flag with the Crombie arms fluttered within the crenellations of the tower.

Greg stopped on a wide gravel expanse more fitting for a four-horse carriage than a Renault Laguna.

In keeping with the atmosphere, a young woman came out of the turret door, walking slowly along the terrace and down the steps like a princess in a pantomime. In other ways she obviously belonged to the late twentieth century, dressed in a sleeveless, figure-hugging charcoal-grey dress and chunky-heeled shoes probably advisable on those picturesque but chipped steps.

She stood waiting for Greg to get out of his car. Her black hair was closely cropped round her head like a helmet of deepest jet. Close to, she was sturdier than she had seemed from a distance, with arms which might have looked too muscular if they had not been so beautifully shaped. An outdoor girl, one would have summed her up. When she smiled a welcome her top teeth rested a fraction of an inch over her lower lip. The welcome did not include her eyes. They were pale green and very chilly.

He introduced himself. 'Gregory Dacre. I think I'm expected.'

Her fingers as they shook hands were strong but unforthcoming. 'Caroline Crombie.'

'The Hon. Caroline,' he said.

'Been swotting us up already?'

'Just the basics,' he said.

'Lady Crombie says she's terribly sorry.' There was an almost imperceptible emphasis on the *Lady* Crombie which might have been a faint sneer or just a mannerism. 'She's had to dash into Edinburgh.'

Typical, thought Greg. Brigid's old tricks all over again. Making an appointment and then keeping you waiting. Showing up hours late with a bright, dismissive smile and an apology reverberating with an *aren't I just deplorable but forgivable?*

40

'She had a call from her solicitor about an action she'll be bringing for constructive dismissal, breach of contract, that sort of thing. And father,' Caroline went on, 'has ridden over to see the Macphersons about some fishing rights. So I've been deputed to look after you until they get back.'

'I'm sorry. I'm sure you don't need to — '

'It'll be a pleasure,' she said unconvincingly.

A young man in a waistcoat and tight trousers which must have been some kind of domestic uniform took Greg's bags and showed him to his room. At the foot of the main staircase Caroline Crombie said: 'I'll be waiting for you in the vestibule here, to show you around. But don't rush it. Do take your time.'

The view from the window of his room took in a long sweep of lawn, the stone wall of an enclosed garden, a stable block, and what looked like trays and pots of plants on trestles outside a greenhouse. Through the trees there was the glint of a stream, feeding down an uneven slope towards the Yarrow Water.

'I'm sure one of our regular guides could do this better,' the Hon. Caroline greeted him as he came down, 'but this isn't one of our open days, so you'll have to make do with me.'

41

She brushed the perfectly smooth turn of hair behind her left ear with two fingers, and a moment later made exactly the same movement. She wore no rings, earrings, or other jewellery.

'This is the morning room.'

It was huge, and smelt faintly of warm dust, heated by radiators under the tall windows. The panelled walls between the windows and beside the fireplace were hung with an uneven pattern of family portraits. 'The first Baron Crombie,' recited Caroline: 'killed at Flodden Field.' Then a succession of Lords of Parliament, a noble cousin who had been executed after the '45, and a Countess or two. Names rolled unfaltering off her tongue. She might have been the most highly trained of those guides she had mentioned.

Brigid's third husband was the twelfth Lord Crombie, descendant of a long line of Royal Keepers of the Forest, though there was little left of the ancient woodlands today. His face, like those others staring down from the walls, left little doubt of the continuing legitimacy of the line. All the men had the same heavy jowls and puffy lips, and each held his head stiffly back as if a collar were chafing his neck or he could not bear to look any ordinary mortal straight in the eyes.

And Caroline, like the men who had gone

before her, tilted her head back when addressing Greg. He doubted, though, if she had inherited that habit of stroking the hair behind her ear so repetitively and with such a little click of tongue against teeth as she did so. They were very much her own mannerisms.

The paintings on the staircase were mainly of the womenfolk. Sir John Lavery was at his most sumptuously flattering in a group of two complacent Edwardian sisters and a large rough-haired deerhound. There were celebrations of a stream of distinguished marriages. In an earlier incarnation Caroline might herself have expected just such a union; but Greg wondered what sort of husband she could hope to find round these parts nowadays.

She nodded at a portrait in the shadow of a landing. 'My mother. Used to hang in the dining-room. Brigid had it shifted for father's sake, so it wouldn't awaken memories every day.'

'And replaced it with a portrait of the — um — present Lady Crombie?'

'No, she hasn't gone that far.' Caroline allowed him the flicker of a faintly disdainful smile. 'Not yet.'

He was shown the bedroom where Bonnie Prince Charlie had slept on his way back from England, heading towards fatal Culloden.

On the dressing-table stood an anamorphosis painted on a concertina'd fan of parchment. From one direction, the slats showed a portrait of the Prince; from the other, a human skull.

'There's a similar one of Mary, Queen of Scots, in Edinburgh,' said Caroline. 'A few weeks from now this one'll be going to join it, off to Canada with some of our Jacobite portraits and relics for a big exhibition. They settled on a nice dramatic title in the papers yesterday: *Secrets of the Stewarts.*'

The Crombies had, like so many other families with Jacobite sympathies, been disgraced for a while — which Caroline quietly but uncompromisingly declared to have been no disgrace. In any case they were too important to the traditional social and administrative balance in the old Border region for their banishment to last more than a few decades.

Caroline opened a door and stood back to let Greg look in. 'There used to be a small suite of rooms for the Master here.'

'The master of the house?'

'No. The older son, always given the title of Master — in our case, the Master of Yarrow. Only in this generation there's been no son. I occupied the suite myself for a while. But after I'd left, Brigid — Lady Crombie' — in the correction there was again that whisper of distaste — 'preferred to bring the rooms up to date. Preferred something more modern.' The interior was that of an expensive hotel bedroom, leading on to a sleek modern bathroom and shower, with toilet paper matching the flowered wallpaper. 'For guests. Especially big shots coming for the horse trials, or country fairs, or whatever else she can persuade my father to put on. Had to get rid of a lot of . . . well . . . family junk, I suppose you'd call it . . . to pay for it all.'

At the end of the landing, she pointed out of a tall window with wooden interior shutters drawn back. At the foot of a grassy slope was what looked like a cobbled track.

'Our Roman pavement. Must have been part of the ancient route to Trimontium — near Newstead, as it is today.' She sounded calmly possessive, as if the Crombie line was in unbroken succession from the great Roman generals who decreed the building of roads to link their centres of civilisation.

To one side of the half landing was a small room whose door she opened with a kind of reluctance, as if unwilling to trespass. 'My father's hideaway. And that hole in the wall over there is the laird's lug, of course.'

'The what?'

'The laird's lug. Through which he could

listen in to seditious chatter in the sitting room underneath here, or in the kitchen.'

'Both at the same time?'

'It could have been confusing, yes. Like two overlapping radio wavelengths.'

She closed the door.

They went downstairs by another staircase at the back of the house, emerging into a long corridor with more portraits and a few landscapes of local forest which had since disappeared. Caroline opened the first door on the right. 'The library,' she said. 'Or it used to be. Lot of family history tomes that nobody ever looked at. A few fetched a good price. Paid for the phone extensions and the rest of it.'

One range of mahogany bookcases remained at the far end of the room, but its shelves held modern business manuals, and tables jutting from the other walls carried telephones, a fax machine, and arrays of files.

'There used to be a pretty little ebony work table there, with pewter-inlaid drawers.' Caroline nodded at a plastic and metal desk on castors, with shelves angled to take a computer screen, keyboard, and printer. 'I suppose you could call *that* a work table. Just as curious and olde-worlde a hundred years from now.' Abruptly she added: 'You're one of her exes, aren't you?'

'The first,' he confessed.

'Must seem odd.' She could be wondering just how envious he was to see what his ex-wife had achieved since they split up.

At the far end of the corridor a door opened on to the outside world. From this angle, the stable block he had seen from above now sprouted signs lettered *Refreshments* and *Toilets*.

'Another of Brigid's ideas. Ploughmen's lunches and gifts. It's only just beginning to cover the cost of converting the stables.'

'Well edited,' said Greg.

'I beg your pardon?'

'As a TV documentary, you couldn't have done it better.'

She looked him up and down, and her tone became less impersonal. 'Very observant, Mr Dacre. I do do some local television work.'

'A bit of a remote base, this.'

'I did tell you, I moved out quite a while ago. But I do come back, naturally. To see father. It's still . . . ' For the first time she was fumbling for a word. At last she said, doubtfully: 'Home.'

They went on a few paces in silence. Then, with an abrupt laugh, she said: 'Look, are you sure you know what you're doing?'

'I'm supposed to be pretty competent at my job.'

'Brigid's been very good at getting people into jobs or out of jobs. Now she's out of one herself, and somebody has to be made to pay. But maybe there'll be some who decide to pay back. She could get into a lot of trouble with her enemies, you know. And drag you into it, too. Doesn't that worry you?'

As he was about to concoct an answer, the sound of a car scattering gravel came from the curve of the main drive. The lady of the house was home.

★ ★ ★

'God, I can do with a drink.' Brigid led the way unhesitatingly into a small sitting-room which Greg had not yet been shown. 'All this dashing to and fro. Sorry I wasn't around when you got here, but I can see Caroline's made you feel quite at home. Caroline darling, do join us and keep Greg entertained. I've a suspicion that I've lost the knack of it.'

Caroline prodded at her hair. 'No, I'm really running short of time. I do have some homework to get on with.'

'Homework?' said Greg after she had gone out of the room.

'She does odd jobs on a television programme.'

'Oh, yes, she did mention that.'

'A local chat show, and news items galloping all over the landscape. They think having a real live lord's daughter on the programme gives it class.' Brigid's tone was much the same as Caroline's when uttering her own name. 'And I did do a bit of string-pulling in certain quarters.'

The young man who had taken Greg's case upstairs appeared, opened a corner cabinet, and poured drinks.

Greg watched him go as silently as he had come. 'Are the locals telepathic, or something? Materialising before you'd even reached for the bell-pull.'

'Young Drew. A good local lad from the home farm. A bit fey, like a lot of them round here. Comes up Sunday mornings and plays the pipes along the landing outside our bedroom until Hector goes out and tells him he can stop.'

'What if you oversleep? Does he have to keep on playing all morning?'

'Have you ever tried to sleep when somebody's playing the pipes outside your bedroom door? Hector can lie there for a good twenty minutes, wallowing in it. Me, one pibroch and two variations and I need to go to the loo.'

Brigid was sitting upright in what was

obviously her usual chair, with a low table near her right hand carrying a pad and gold pencil, and a coaster for her drink. A higher table with a black and gold porcelain lamp stood to her left. She was wearing a white suit and, in spite of her talk of dashing about, looked unflustered and uncreased. Unlike her stepdaughter, she did not have a hair out of place. Greg sat facing her, across a small fireplace with a log fire burning in it, welcome even on a warm evening like this.

He suppressed a yawn.

Brigid was on it at once. 'You've had a long drive. Must be tired out. We'll eat the moment Hector gets back and let you get to bed.'

'It's dangerously cosy by this fire.' He raised his glass. Reflections of the flames winked and swayed within the amber liquid. 'Satisfactory trip?'

'All in competent hands. Ammunition provided.'

'Ready to start, then,' he said, 'in the morning?'

'In the morning, yes. If you're up to it.'

'Bright and early,' he promised. He let the warmth of the peaty malt add to his torpor, then made an effort to jerk himself out of it. 'Just one thing. If you've set this up just to make me look small — '

'You wouldn't have come if you'd thought that, would you? And the book wouldn't stand much of a chance of being any good.'

'As long as we understand each other.'

'Better than we used to, maybe. We've both come a long way since then.'

He looked at a modern painting behind her head of a man in the uniform of a colonel in some Scottish regiment, and recognised the Crombie features yet again. A few minutes later a living facsimile of the portrait appeared in the doorway, in clothes which were in their own way a kind of uniform.

Lord Crombie was wearing a green tweed jacket and a brown leather waistcoat above tartan trousers, with a regimental tie clumsily knotted into his check shirt collar. He had a gingery moustache as floppy as the tie, and ginger hair which had long since retreated from his freckled forehead to form bushy outposts behind his ears. His smile as his wife introduced their guest was sincere but awkward.

'Good. Yes, good. Um — got a dram? Och, right then. Never do to . . . ' He stared at something intangible as if trying to blink away a floater in his eye, and started holding forth about what young Macpherson had been telling him. 'Can't say I'm keen, but the man's right, we only lose money on carriage driving or horse trials. Great occasions. But they're a drain. Aye, a drain.' His ginger eyebrows were two inverted circumflexes, his large lips a puzzled pout. Whatever school he had been to, or whatever officers' mess he had frequented, they had eradicated most traces of a Scottish accent apart from a resonance at the back of his throat; and occasionally a spontaneous word slipped through. 'All the same, I'm nae keen on the idea of a . . . what did he call it? A pop festival. Or a theme weekend. Now, what the devil would a theme weekend be?'

'Do sit down, Hector,' said his wife. 'I hate it when you *loom*.'

'Says there's an exhibition in Edinburgh early next month. All about country houses and the way to exploit them. *Exploit* them!' He sank into a chair and stared at Brigid with a hangdog expression. 'We'd not really want to go to that, would we?'

'I shall be busy,' said Brigid dismissively. Then she took a slow, thoughtful draught from her glass. 'I don't know, though. By then, Greg and I may need some time in Edinburgh for the background material. Might be a good opportunity for you to see what's on offer, Hector. We do need some means of raising money to sweep the mothballs out of this place.'

Greg conjured up a vision of Caroline's sour smile.

'Aye, well then . . . ' Hector thought for a moment, then made an effort to include their guest in the conversation. 'Damn ridiculous. There's the Maxwell Stuarts over at Traquair, allowed their own brewery. Jacobite Ale, they call it. All we can manage are tutored wine tastings.' He snorted. 'Much better let us start up our own distillery. Why not Jacobite Whisky?'

'You'd drink the entire production,' said his wife.

Hector fidgeted in his chair, muttered something about having a word with old Crichton, got up, and headed for the door.

'Dinner in twenty minutes,' Brigid called after him. 'And don't have too many drams before then. Remember what you were told about your blood pressure.'

The fire spluttered a gentle cough and scattered a few sparks. As Brigid reached for the poker, Greg said: 'You've found yourself a very comfortable lifestyle now.'

'And you?'

'I get by. I can pick and choose.'

'Didn't you ever risk choosing one of those shapely little creatures who used to hang around when my back was turned?'

'They never existed.'

'From what Simon used to say — '

'What Simon used to say was malicious muck. And you did enjoy wallowing in it, didn't you? Until the smell got too rank even for you.'

They studied each other across the fireplace.

'I do think,' she said, 'that we'd do well to keep that particular subject in reserve. For the time being.'

'When we do get round to it, d'you think Simon will care for being shown up in a book?'

'Probably preen himself on being such a shit.'

'That figures. The only way to put paid to Simon permanently is by wringing his bloody neck.'

'I agree with you.'

'And you used to be devoted to him!'

'I've told you, he can wait until I'm ready to deal with him. We start tomorrow morning with the real stuff.'

'The wheelings and dealings the public don't know about,' he agreed. 'More exciting than broken marriages, deceptions, divorce, and all that run-of-the mill stuff. Stale stuff. Absolutely.'

'Starting,' she said vengefully, 'with that crass little cheat who dropped me in it. I think we can make it quite exciting, Greg.'

The pale blue of her eyes was almost washed out, like the palest of inks on cream writing paper. Some job interviewers prided themselves on the discomfort they could cause by their piercing gaze. Brigid's apparent unresponsiveness could be far more disconcerting. But when someone reacted in a way which really got through to her, those eyes took on a sheen like that of opals brought to life by the warmth of rubbing against flesh. At this moment they had become alive and radiant.

'Greg.' He cringed at the affection in her voice, dredged up from a past she was persuading herself into believing. She was as good at this as she was at persuading men she met whatever she wanted them to believe. 'It had to be you on this job. I insisted on you. You're the only one I can share it all with.'

Caroline Crombie's voice echoed in his mind. *Are you sure you know what you're doing?*

4

The Conference Venue Exhibition covered the whole first floor of the Market Street Centre. Rows of trade stands displayed samples of gift-shop pencils, rubbers, bookmarks and china mugs bearing the names of stately homes, paperweights with a family crest gleaming inside, and mock-ups of glossy brochures. In discreet cubicles men and women with discreetly modulated voices offered expert advice on converting beautiful but cash-strapped castles and mansions into hotels cum conference centres, tastefully adapted for Corporate Presentations.

Detective Inspector Lesley Gunn studied the visitors strolling from one exhibit to another. This Saturday, the last day of the exhibition, had brought in large numbers of people too busy during the rest of the week. Sharp entrepreneurs assessed one another's offerings and weighed up chances of plagiarising a profitable idea. Middle managers of large companies drifted with carefully maintained nonchalance down the aisles while maintaining a slight sneer which among them was almost as characteristic as a

Masonic handshake. They checked on amenities for conferences and corporate hospitality packages, combining catering facilities with state-of-the-art lecture rooms and spacious halls for brainstorming sessions.

A third category consisted of the inheritors of noble names and noble buildings, dignified but desperate to find ways of shoring up their finances. Their tweedy womenfolk disdained to look at anything which might suggest they were interested in vulgar commerce. Such distasteful matters were left to their dejected husbands.

One Englishman with a calculatedly languid yet piercing voice was escorting a group from one display stand to another. 'We *have* found in Yorkshire and Northumberland' — he could have been delivering a television commentary on a documentary about the far reaches of Azerbaijan — 'that it pays to advertise not in the obvious tourist guides but in county magazines and selected women's magazines. Or should I say *ladies'* magazines?' He smiled and waited for their obedient smirks of gratification. 'At the same time, leaflets supplied to a range of select hotels . . . '

He was leading his flock like a guide in a stately home when one of them detached himself to greet a red-faced man glumly contemplating a teddy bear wearing a tam-o'-shanter and a kilt.

'Crombie! What brings you here?'

'Her ladyship's got some work to do in Edinburgh. Thought I'd leave her to it, and drop in here. Out of curiosity, ye ken.'

'Aye. Me, too.'

Together the two men edged away from the conducted party to contemplate a board displaying a coloured map of an imaginary estate. A children's playground in one corner led to a walled garden selling herbs, and a path wandered in and out of trees beside an ornamental lake.

'Bicycles!' spluttered Crombie. 'Good God. Bicycle hire for rides round the grounds?'

'All the rage, I'm told,' said his companion dolefully.

'We've already got a nature trail, and that does enough damage. Throwing their crisp packets and ice-cream wrappers into the shrubbery. Mind you' — Crombie showed yellowing teeth in a smirk — 'I suppose cyclists could run a few walkers down.'

DI Gunn returned to the stall to which she had been detailed to show official approval. 'Get those old buffers to guard their belongings properly in the first place,' the Chief Super had decreed, 'and we can cut down on time chasing their lost property afterwards.' He was never entirely happy with having the Midlothian and Merse CID Special Operations Unit under his wing. Its section concentrating on agricultural matters and misdeeds was something he could grasp. His remote predecessors had sought to subdue the Border reivers and their cattle raids. Today the trade was still flourishing, though sheep were now the more usual prey. Lorries came up across the Border and escaped with their cargoes down the A74 and the M6. So did valuable paintings and antiques. But Detective Inspector Gunn's highly specialised knowledge of art treasures and their likely destinations when stolen was way outside his own training. Her track record was so impressive, however, that she was an obvious choice to keep an eye on this exhibition — most especially, beside those stalls offering inducements to welcome visitors into family mansions, the one displaying surveillance cameras, alarms and safety locks to keep unwelcome visitors out.

A middle-aged woman in a Prussian blue blouse and white slacks strolled from the main door down the central aisle.

'Hello, m'dear.' Crombie gave her an awkward peck on the cheek. 'Glad you've made it. Need some advice.'

Her eyes were taking in the room in a

critical sweep. 'Best advice would be to find the coffee shop.'

'Left your tame scribe typing up what ye've done so far?'

'They don't call it typing nowadays. It's keyboarding.'

Lesley found herself watching the two of them sauntering past the wares of an olde-worlde kitchen restorer (recommended by the Duke of Jedburgh and Viscount Islay after tasteful restoration of their basements) and lingering by a spread of glossy printed booklets. She tried summing them up. Crombie had to be Lord Crombie, among whose treasures were two Raeburns, a Lavery, a couple of valuable tapestries, and a fascinating anamorphosis of the Young Pretender which she kept promising herself to visit. There was also talk of a cellar of fine wines. His wife, a lot younger, was something fierce in the business world.

'Detective Inspector Gunn, I think?'

The voice came from near her left cheek. 'Well, Sir Michael.' Sir Michael Veitch, Scottish MD of an international insurance and pensions investment group — here to advise on insurance cover for stately homes and their contents? Unlikely, at his level.

He settled the question for her. 'Two of my chaps have recommended new conference venues for our American friends when they fly over. Near a golf course, and maybe a bit of shooting. Thought I'd spend ten minutes assessing the layouts for myself. Any helpful comments, inspector?'

A year ago it had been her task to trace a Bohemian triptych stolen from Veitch's private collection. He had made flattering comments to higher authority when she retrieved it from the vaults of a dubious Glasgow gallery, and now sounded genuinely respectful.

'I'm not here to advise on anything other than safety precautions against break-ins, Sir Michael.'

'Who better? After that last experience, we've installed every device you recommended.' He looked past her and raised a hand in a brief salute. Lady Crombie's nod was even briefer. He said: 'You seem interested in those two. Ever visited Baldonald House?'

'Not yet. The Department has been considering adding some of its contents to our Antiques Register.'

'Excellent idea. When it comes to scaring villains off, I don't suppose old Hector's got beyond the notion of blasting away with his shotgun.' But he was staring at Lady Crombie rather than her husband. 'I gather

61

the lady has time on her hands nowadays. You know of her, of course?'

'Something to do with managerial recruitment.'

'The most lethal headhunter since the Papuans in their heyday.'

'Perhaps she's getting ready to retire gracefully. They do seem to be interested in the sort of thing that might expand facilities at Baldonald House.'

'The least I can do is offer them some advice, after our own experiences in that field. I think perhaps a few words from an old friend . . . ' He favoured her with his most practised yet impersonal smile. 'If you'll excuse me, inspector.'

Lesley watched him join the Crombies, and above the shuffle of visitors heard Lady Crombie's clear, hard voice. 'Pity we haven't got a real prince or princess to entomb in the grounds — or Flora MacDonald's ashes to boost the takings.' Veitch laughed, but even from this distance Lesley Gunn was sure that the polite gestures had very little friendship in them. And a moment later Lord Crombie's voice was raised in outrage. 'Let it out for weddings?'

'Any bride would love to be photographed coming down those steps, posing on the fourth or fifth from the bottom.'

'Like a bloody Christmas pantomime!'

Lady Crombie was obviously suggesting that he should keep his voice down.

★ ★ ★

Greg set the printer to run off the three chapters he had achieved during these past three weeks, with ten pages added this morning, and poured himself a cup of coffee.

Sunlight bounced off the great hulk of the Scottish Office. A streamer across the façade of a neighbouring warehouse announced the opening of yet another new restaurant. Delivery vans bumped over the cobbles, and a constant stream of artics and heavy trucks stormed along the main coast road, but all of it was eerily silent: double glazing cut off any distracting noise from outside. He watched a young man following a girl across the bridge, matching his pace to hers, and instinctively began thinking himself into the mind of the wary pursuer, building up to the brasher approach and then . . .

He wrenched himself back to reality. No eager young stalker needed an autobiography ghosted. Greg's own task right now was to become Brigid Weir-cum-Dacre-cum-Pringle-cum-Crombie.

The flat had three bedrooms, each with its own shower and a lavatory whose mahogany seats, raised with august slowness by heavy brass weights, must surely have been salvaged from some grandiose nineteenth-century hotel. Greg's room was the smallest of the three, with its own phone and a clock radio. Hector Crombie did not share the main bedroom or occupy the third. He had chosen instead to stay in one of the members' flats at the Scotch Malt Whisky Society a few minutes' walk away.

'Be less of an interruption for you two,' he had mumbled.

'And we won't interrupt your sampling of the hundred proof Speysides,' Brigid retorted.

This main room, with its wide window looking out over the streets and harbour, was more an office than sitting-room. Like the Baldonald House library it had a VDU, phones, an answering and fax machine, and shelves of files. Where one might have expected to find copies of *Country Life* or *Scottish Field* on the coffee table and the window seat, there were business supplements and appointments inserts with a few items ticked or encircled with pink highliner. 'Give you some idea of the general background,' Brigid had said after declaiming part of a chapter and then phoning for a cab to take her to meet her husband at the Conference Venue Exhibition.

Greg put his coffee cup down and browsed through the advertisements for world-class administrators capable of handling international investment portfolios within a team environment; dedicated depute unit managers with experience in brand enhancement, segment repositioning skills, re-profiling and facilitation; and an Expert required in Change Management. And what might Change Management be? He tried to imagine himself moving smoothly and skilfully through such a world, inventing new descriptions for himself. Words sprang off the page at him. A Crisis Manager . . . ? Did you have to create a crisis in the first place in order to demonstrate your skills at managing it and bringing it back under control?

Brigid had scribbled notes in margins here and there. He must ask her the meaning of 'call options' and 'a strangler'.

In the meantime the printer had spewed out its final sheet. It was time to re-read the text and see where some of this jargon might be fitted into the bare bones of the story. Not that the bones were all that bare. A certain Project Potential Assessor looked very well covered with flesh in the pictures accompanying features in the financial press. The solidity of his reasoning was acclaimed, too, because he had been one of the first to insist on the importance of tackling the Millennium Bug. The fact that he was computer illiterate had not prevented him from sounding off impressively and manipulating the nerds who were genuinely immersed in the idiom. He was skilful at deriding critics within and outwith his own organisation, ever since Brigid had identified a placement for him and shown him how to exploit the weak spots of some and batten on the strengths of others. That glittering CV of his would be somewhat tarnished, though, when his enemies and the general public read of those secret deals with an American investment bank and a software company whose auditor had blabbed figures to Brigid.

Then there was a high-flier called Declan Fraser. Greg had always, quite irrationally, refused to believe that anyone named Declan could be trustworthy. It was just one of those things. If asked to ghost the memoirs of a Declan, no matter how well paid the job, he would have refused. The character would somehow have come out perverse and shifty, whether or not he had been that in the first place. And certainly this one, successful as he might be, gave off an air of seediness which would not endear him to the reader.

Though of course this might be just Brigid's way of slanting the story.

When it came to selecting the juicier bits from the finished book, newspapers would surely pick on revelations like this. Brigid had spelled out in searing detail the way in which a global consortium based in Chicago had guardedly financed Fraser's money management company in the UK, experts in leveraged buyouts. Later Fraser, supposedly in the interests of a UK pharmaceutical company which had consulted him about raising extra finance, organised a merger which turned out to be effectively a takeover. After surviving for eighteen months with the aid of Government funding, the asset strippers moved in. The company was wound up on the grounds that, regrettably, worldwide corporate strategy meant the consortium would have to close down these operations and move them elsewhere.

Fraser might claim this as normal business practice; but some aspects, such as the undeclared conflict of interest between the backers of his company and their part in the takeover, would surely now be investigated.

Nor would Alastair Blake be too pleased when he read Brigid Weir's dissection of his climb to power.

'We'll start the book,' Brigid had said, 'with Blake. The bastard who dropped me in it. And then let's see how long *he* survives.'

Privately Greg had decided that in any sensible chronology Blake must wait until later in the book. He figured most prominently in the Fall aspect of The Rise and Fall of Brigid Weir rather than in her earlier triumphs.

Starting as a financial journalist, with a flair for smooth talk and greasing the palms of political contacts, Blake had promoted himself from nudges and winks in Royal Mile bars to more solemn briefings in expensive restaurants. Eased into partnership with a retired administration officer from the Scottish Office Financial Systems Unit who had sought Brigid's help in setting up an agency called Vinculum Placement, he had soon removed its founder and made himself supremo.

Whatever the nominal aims of the agency in finding appropriate placements for aspiring executives, Blake's own concentration was on political lobbying. Discreet lunches and dinners were set up. Officially no money changed hands. On the rare occasions when awkward questions were asked, Vinculum could invoke the inevitable social cross-currents in the constricted world of top executives, unexpected shifts due entirely to circumstances of the moment over which the agency itself was powerless, and — the stock excuse — the need to keep Government and public services in constant touch with business and enterprise elements.

Opportunist as ever, Blake had been trying to lure Brigid herself into forming a new consortium within the Government Relations wing of his agency. She was to pick a couple of her best people within her present department and bring them with her.

Greg went on staring at the Scottish Office, like a squat atomic power station with a sun roof. With this and the new Scottish Parliament, there was going to be plenty of scope for lobbying in the neighbourhood.

Definitely a late chapter in the book. But it had done no harm to get the facts down on paper while Brigid was hyped up and in a mood to talk. And some of those facts jarred discordantly against the images portrayed in the financial columns. The sexual transgressions of some were bad enough. Far worse were the fiddles, the thousands of people who had been ruined by some sleight of hand which gave their destroyers even more profit than they had contrived at the start.

Greg was beginning to believe that the brothel keeper whose memoirs he had ghosted had led a far more honourable life than any of these pillars of the City.

He heard the faint whine of the lift, and

69

Brigid's key in the lock. She looked hard at him as if accusing him of wasting time, just standing there with a handful of papers instead of pounding away at the keyboard.

It was the expression he had known way back, when she had come back to their poky little flat and virtually condemned him for not having shouldered the deputy chairman and then the chairman of that tinpot little educational publisher out of the way to make room for himself.

He said: 'Had a nice day?'

'Amateurish bumbling. Disneyland castles with pretty pictures indoors and paddling pools outside. All their ideas need a complete overhaul. Someone at the top to pull it all together.'

'And you know just the head to hunt?'

'That sort of thing's not my concern any more. But' — her eyes lit up and came fully alive again — 'at least I had a happy half-hour with my solicitor. We're going to screw those two shysters for every bawbee they've got.'

'What's their defence — rightful dismissal?'

'Par for the course. They'll make a settlement only if I sign a guarantee to honour the terms of commercial confidentiality.'

'Meaning what?'

'Meaning I mustn't communicate information to any other employer or any indivdual or outside interest regarding the workings of the agency. All the usual blether.'

'Not unreasonable, from their point of view.'

'No chance. Absolutely no chance. They don't know it yet, but every little detail's going to be in the book.'

'You're not worried about libel?' He held out the printed pages. 'I think we might need to tone down this bit where — '

'Let's get the facts down first, all raw and bleeding. Then we can debate whether any of them need cooking.'

As she riffled through the sheets he had handed over, Greg said: 'Just what does trigger you off? We've got the facts here, but not the motivation. With Blake, for instance. In the early stages did you wait to be approached, or did you sniff out what was going on and spot where you could make a few grand?'

'I seize opportunities, yes. I've got a gut instinct. As you say, I can sniff them out — the right men for sensitive, lucrative jobs. Provided,' Brigid added, 'I get my appropriate finder's fee.'

'Like that chapter we sketched out last week? That top clinical research job. Only you'd just got round to saying the man wasn't medically qualified, so — '

'But a good creative accountant.'

'Creative?'

'Let's say he knew where the blood transfusions could be set up most economically, and how to channel the supplies. He'd have made a good Dr Beeching, slimming down hospitals like the railways: getting rid of awkward things that clutter up the account books.'

'I'd have thought that nowadays, with all these inquiries going on into top-heavy administration — '

'Inquiries are just a way of postponing decisions nobody wants to make. He's covered himself by now. Until,' said Brigid, 'I choose to uncover the holes in his duvet. Or I may let him down lightly. I did get rather well paid for that bit of consultancy.'

'So it's basically money plus the tingle you get from power.'

'What else?'

'If it involved some crime syndicate, would that worry you?'

She looked at her watch. 'I think it's time for a spot of lunch. And then we'll press on.'

★　★　★

In the glass shell of the Turkish restaurant facing the Scottish Office, Brigid plucked herself out of whatever had occupied her during the morning, and concentrated on her next priority. Now, without any preamble, it was single-minded application to the matter of a man called Veitch.

'Clever in his way,' Brigid was saying. 'Damn good at assessing in venture capital the players who'll be able to keep a clear head during the white knuckle phase.' Her glee in reliving old campaigns was infectious. She was a retired general rejoicing over past tactics, rarely admitting that some victories were due more to the enemy's errors than to his own brilliance. 'I met him this morning at the Exhibition. And he really deserves a chapter to himself. How he got a knighthood. I can tell quite a story there. All about a little creep who spent years in Opposition denouncing cronyism and backstairs dealings, and when in power showed just how much he had been studying form. It cost Veitch a pretty penny in that direction to get where he is. And some even prettier pounds to finance the peerage he's expecting now. But where do you suppose all those pounds and pennies went to?'

For a few minutes they both wrestled appreciatively with their kebabs, and then

73

Greg ventured: 'Have you considered putting a few success stories in?'

'They're all success stories. How to win prizes by putting your coins in the right slot.'

'What I meant was, isn't there any example of one of your placements which has worked out for the public benefit? I mean, just for once without any backstairs fiddling? I do think we might get some variety into the overall tone of the book.'

'In the end,' Brigid overrode him, 'mine'll be the big name on the book. So it had better be the real me between the covers.'

The phrase made him laugh. On impulse he asked: 'All these men — did you sleep with any of them?'

'I don't see what that's got to do with it.'

'I'd have thought there were circumstances when it might have been quite an important factor.'

'You're not jealous, are you, Greg?'

'After all this time?'

'I've often thought we could have made a go of it, you and I. If only you hadn't been so pig-headed.'

Years ago he might have flown off the handle at the monstrosity of that. Today he simply said: 'Yes or no — did you sleep with any of them?'

She shrugged. 'When it suited me.'

'Many of them?'

'Only when it seemed necessary. Pathetic, really. Often I'd got them hooked without having to go the whole way.'

'Basically, to get what you wanted you didn't mind being a prick-tease?'

'You put it a bit crudely, Greg.'

'How else would you put it?'

Her smile was slowly becoming one of complicity, of sharing a joke. She was beginning to enjoy this line of questioning.

'It gave them a feeling of such importance. Made them feel they were in charge after all. All that old macho swaggering. For all my importance in fixing things for them, they loved to convince themselves I was still more in their power than they were in mine. So easy to let them believe that, and then do what I'd meant to do all along. Wait till they read this book, then they'll get the whole scenario.'

'You didn't ever feel you were degrading yourself?'

'Never. I've always enjoyed a good session in bed as much as a well-organised deal. You should remember that.' A slight arch of her right eyebrow suggested she wasn't sure whether he really appreciated what he had lost. 'The preliminaries,' she reminisced. 'Dinner, subdued lighting, whispering secrets and half promises . . . mounting tension . . . '

Yes, thought Greg. Thrust and brief battle of bodies and minds, and the sated withdrawal. And afterwards, the reckoning. Only so far as he and Brigid had been concerned, they had started out too poor to have much in the way of expensive dinners or subdued lighting — other than the 40-watt bulbs in that dismal rented flat, and the night-light by the baby's cot.

'Just as money-orientated, when you think of it,' he said, 'as a prostitute's bargain. Only in this case the men never quite realise whose body is being sold along with the soul.'

'Most of them were grateful for the pay-off. I was the one who saw a potential they'd never have seen in themselves. I virtually created their new persona.'

'You didn't create *me*.'

'You never gave me enough time.'

'Or maybe you just never made the time to see the potential, as you call it. Too busy with Simon's potential. Too busy edging him into that cushy number as a — what was it? — Interpersonal Strategy Consultant. Whatever that may be. Just as meaningless as the claptrap Simon could talk non-stop without any outside help. Must have suited him perfectly.'

'I always knew how to place people.'

'As a matter of interest' — he kept it as cool and level as possible — 'why *did* you ditch Simon in the end?'

'We haven't got to that bit yet. I've told you, he'll come in when I'm good and ready.'

'You're dodging something. Don't tell me there's still something I haven't been told about that two-faced little shit?'

She waved to a passing waiter and dug out her credit card. 'Time we got back and did some serious work.'

When they were back in the flat, she looked expectantly at the tape recorder, obviously rehearsing mentally what she wanted to deal with next. Before switching on, Greg said: 'Why d'you suppose you're so good at assessing men for difficult jobs but so hopeless at choosing one for yourself?'

'I've got no complaints about Hector.'

'After two disastrous failures, I suppose he must be a very comfortable type.'

'You wouldn't begin to understand.'

He shot it at her: 'Are you going to put all the bedroom negotiations into the book as well?'

'Where relevant.'

'And you think Hector's going to enjoy reading every titillating little detail?'

'Never mind about Hector. What about *you*? Are you up to getting it all down on paper? Think you can stand — ' She was interrupted by the phone ringing, and reached for it with automatic precision. 'No, your father's not here. Still up at the Exhibition.' She put her hand over the mouthpiece and flashed a grin at Greg. 'Or back in the Members' Room trying his tenth malt of the day.' She removed her hand. 'What is it, Caroline?'

The grin did not so much fade as snap off. Brigid listened, took a deep breath, and then said: 'We'll come back at once.'

'Something wrong?' Greg knew it was silly as soon as he had spoken. All too obviously there was something wrong.

'Grotesque.' In a crisis Brigid could be either flintily calm or flintily savage. This time she was calm. 'Only a few hours ago, there I was, looking at all that paraphernalia for protecting property — locks, bolts, bars, alarms and the rest of it. Too late. That was Caroline. We've had a break-in at the house. A pretty thorough job, by the sound of it.'

5

Morning mist had been slow to clear from the valley. Tendrils like spun sugar clung to the branches of trees as Detective Inspector Lesley Gunn and a uniformed constable drove in through the main gates. She hadn't expected to see Lord and Lady Crombie again so soon, this time close to. Wryly she thought what a pity it was that they hadn't had time to take any of the precautions on display at the exhibition.

The local uniformed officer hadn't expected, either, to be accompanying her on a Sunday morning to the big house. He had been the one to answer the telephone call from Caroline Crombie, and to report the break-in to higher authority. Now, assigned to back up this female plain-clothes officer, he mounted the steps to the main door in awe of the mere idea of Lord Crombie, whom he had met only once before, in Selkirk sheriff court.

'It might be a good idea if you made a long recce of the grounds while I talk to the owners,' said DI Gunn as they waited for the door to open. 'I don't yet know what we're looking for, but you must know this area and what's normal and what isn't.'

Flattered, PC Kerr was immediately on her team. He hurried gladly away from the steps.

An agitated housekeeper let the detective inspector in and led her in pursuit of the lord and lady of the house. On the way Lesley Gunn had time for only fleeting glimpses of large blank rectangles on the staircase and corridor walls.

They caught up with the Crombies on a first-floor landing. Lady Crombie was being followed from room to room by her dazed, stricken husband. He looked as if he might completely lose his way in his own household unless she was there to guide him.

Lesley introduced herself. 'Detective Inspector Gunn. I saw you yesterday, very briefly.'

'Saw us?' mumbled Crombie.

'At the exhibition.'

'Och, aye. Maybe you did. If we'd only stayed at home instead of wasting our time there — '

'But we didn't,' said his wife, 'did we?'

'If you could just show me round,' Lesley urged. 'Give me some idea of what's missing. But please try not to touch anything. We'll have to dust for fingerprints and any other evidence. Though this does look the sort of professional job where they'll have been very careful not to leave obvious traces.'

Crombie looked appealingly at his wife, who set off at a brisk pace along the landing and turned right into a long gallery. At the corner he fell behind, staring dismally at a blank space on a wall and reaching out towards a console table to touch something which was no longer there. What was left of his history had been ravished brutally away, leaving only bright, empty rectangles on the faded wallpaper and panelling. He perked up only for a moment, gazing at a painting forlorn and alone on one corridor wall until his wife came back to collect him.

'His grandfather's ghillie,' she explained to DI Gunn. 'Frankly, no masterpiece. Obviously they'd only go for the worthwhile stuff.'

'You do have . . . *did* have . . . some very fine pieces, I believe.'

'I did try to do a deal for handing the lot over to the National Trust for Scotland. Would have taken a load off our minds. But Hector and that daughter of his got very uptight about it. If only they'd listened to me!'

'The thieves might still have targeted the place.'

'Well, at least with the insurance we ought to be able to smarten this old barn up a bit.'

Lesley was taken aback by the woman's apparent indifference to what must surely be the painful family significance of their loss.

Brigid Crombie led the way into a bedroom, incisively summing up what was missing. Two antique framed maps, some silver-backed hairbrushes, and a valuable bedspread, supposedly embroidered by one of the Queen of Scots' four Marys. The thieves had evidently found it too time-wasting to remove an ornate mirror fastened between the folded shutters of two tall windows. Sunshine struck obliquely through the eastern window on to the three figures, making their reflections in the glass brighter than the nondescript pictures still remaining on the walls. It occurred to Lesley Gunn that only Hector Crombie really belonged in the frame of that mirror. His jacket cuffs were frayed, and there could never have been much of a crease in his trews; but his heavy brogues were polished to a dazzling gloss. You somehow knew that this was one task he undertook for himself every day, and enjoyed it. He belonged. The other two of them were intruders in this place.

A fourth figure swam into the glass, almost ghostly for a moment with her pale complexion and jet-black hair. She edged her way towards Crombie. In profile Lesley saw that she, too, was family.

Hector Crombie's instinctive courtesy plucked him out of the depths of his trance.

'Inspector — er — Gunn, isn't it? My daughter, Caroline.'

The young woman reached her father and squeezed his arm. At first glance Lesley would have summed her up as a laid-back, unsentimental young woman; but at a moment like this there was an immediate, visceral bond between father and daughter.

Again she thought how out of place Lady Crombie was.

Brigid Crombie might almost have picked up her thoughts. 'I'm sure Caroline has a better notion of what's missing. I'll just go and have a thorough check of my equipment in the library. I only had time for a quick look when we got back last night.'

'Unlikely to be anything of historic value,' said Caroline.

The tension between the two women was almost palpable.

Caroline sounded clear and dispassionate for the first few minutes as she escorted Lesley Gunn from room to room. But when she turned to watch her father plodding after them there was a taut anger in her whole body — anger on his behalf, for the even worse pain that he was suffering.

83

Halting before one blank space with an unlit strip-light above it, she was trying to make herself sound matter-of-fact and unemotional. 'Lady Arabella Crombie's portrait used to hang here. She died defending the house when Cumberland's blackguards came for herself and her children. They'd already murdered her husband.' She reached out, just as her father had done several times, as if to touch the painting which was no longer there, and her composure cracked. 'The place has been defiled. Contaminated. But I suppose you're used to this sort of thing. All in a day's routine.'

'No,' said Lesley. 'I never really get used to it. And I do know how it feels.'

Anyone who had ever suffered a burglary felt the same: dirty hands rooting through one's possessions and leaving invisible but indelible stains, invading feet stamping all over a home that would never again feel quite like home.

'This is our big tourist attraction. Bonnie Prince Charlie's bedroom.' Caroline tapped the glass top of the dressing-table. 'And his anamorphosis stood here.'

This was one of the treasures Lesley had most wanted to see. She had left it too late.

'Didn't I read that it was due to go to Canada for an exhibition along with the

Queen of Scots' example from Edinburgh?'

'And several of our paintings — under strict security, of course,' said Caroline ironically.

And that, too, had been left too late.

'Do you think the publicity may have directed the thieves in this direction?' Lesley theorised aloud.

'Could well have been one factor. But where could they hope to get rid of it? Don't tell me they're art lovers, anxious to keep it for their own pleasure?'

Lesley's own anger was beginning to build up. There were so many things here she would have liked to study. Perhaps that ought to have been her profession from the start — a connoisseur rather than a copper. Her skills should have made her a custodian rather than a sweeper-up after things had been snatched away from eyes that had loved them. Her superiors would not have agreed: her knowledge of the subject, along with her dogged determination, had made her unique in that special arm of the CID.

Hector Crombie caught them up as Caroline opened a door into a little snug with a bare wall, broken only by a recess like a small aumbry.

'The laird's lug,' she explained. 'So the man of the house can listen to his wife gossiping with her friends.'

'Rubbish,' growled Crombie. 'Never dreamt of using it. The only time I've ever heard anything from that room has been my wife rustling paper or being rude to somebody on the phone.'

The little room was obviously his own special hideaway. Caroline steered him towards a worn leather armchair, opened a cupboard, and poured whisky into a large crystal tumbler.

'At least they haven't stolen that,' he said. 'All the same, I'm not sure I ought to be — '

'Sit back, father. Take your time. It'll do you good. And I've brought the Sunday papers. Picked them up from the *Tam Lin*.'

She indicated the heavy wedge of newspaper and supplements on a chest in the corner, and closed the door quietly as they went out.

'What do you suppose will happen to our . . . our possessions?' She asked it in an undertone, as if her father's listening cavity might cover even this stretch of corridor, and make his pain worse. 'Shifted across the Atlantic to some millionaire's private collection?'

'Things only work out like that in films. Or television plays.'

'Don't knock my livelihood.'

'I'm sorry. I hadn't realised.'

'Oh, it's all right. I don't get into the big

dramatic stuff. Just local news, motor rallying, deer stalking, and suchlike.'

'Sometimes,' Lesley conceded, 'we hear of the private collections of Latin American drug millionaires. Some gangs steal to order. Storm in with sawn-off shotguns like that robbery at York last year. Or roll up in the small hours of the morning, their getaway van with the engine still running, not giving a damn about alarm systems because they know exactly what's required and how to get it out fast.'

'At least we didn't have a shooting match here.'

'No. And you didn't have any sort of alarm system. But they did seem to be able to pick out the more important pieces. Could be their particular field is tied in with some big crime syndicate, using art works as a means of exchange in place of cash. Wrapped up and put in bank vaults, or sold on again as collateral in big drug deals. Too easily identifiable items can't be sold at public auction. Sometimes they're taken to be ransomed.'

'You think that might apply here? But God knows where we'd raise the money.'

'You'd have to sort that out with the insurance company. They might co-operate by offering a reward, if the payout would be less than coughing up the full insurance value.'

'And how do the police view that sort of deal?'

'With heavy disapproval.'

'But if it did come to it . . . '

'You'll be contacted.'

'And they'll tell us not to contact the police.'

'While we insist that you do just that.'

'And meanwhile?'

Lesley explained the practice of notifying Scotland Yard's Arts and Antiques Squad as a matter of routine. It was likely enough that the stolen items had gone south of the Border. Or else were on their way out of the country. 'Can I use a phone? Must put out a warning to ports and airports.' And check with the Arts Loss Register's database of missing works from around the world, and enter the list of Baldonald House treasures. It all sounded very competent and reassuring when she summed it up for Caroline Crombie; but omitted any mention of the hideous gaps into which so many treasures had fallen forever.

'Perhaps we could prepare a list right now? And insurance value?'

'Lady Crombie knows more about insurance

values than I do,' said Caroline. 'It's one of her specialities. My father and I would prefer the things themselves back where they belong.'

DI Lesley Gunn had had it dinned into her that a police officer must never under any circumstances get personally, emotionally involved in a case. Calm, neutral sympathy to a victim, yes; but don't get worked up. It was no use: already she was keen to get these family treasures back where they belonged. Her resolve was stiffened when Caroline appealed: 'I'd be so grateful if you could track those bastards down.'

'We'd better start by finding out how they got the stuff out. And when we can rustle up Forensic, we must fingerprint the whole household.'

'They won't like that.'

'To eliminate them, and concentrate on prints that ought not to be there.'

* * *

Mrs Dunbar, the housekeeper, was indignant when the fingerprinting was explained to her, and Lesley commented about marks on doorjambs and the wainscoting. Mrs Dunbar and her weekly helper dusted and polished everything properly.

'Of course there won't be any fingerprints or scrapes from folk in this house. Anything would have to come from outside.'

'Exactly, Mrs Dunbar. That's what we want to establish. And no matter how hard you may have worked on them, an expert can detect finger marks and footmarks on all kinds of surfaces. We have a great range of chemical and photographic processes nowadays. Nobody can move anywhere without leaving some trace.'

Mrs Dunbar nodded, not really comprehending. For several minutes she was too flustered to make sense. She took the meaning of her position almost too literally. She was supposed to keep the house, and when something went wrong — as now, when some of it had been torn away — it was somehow entirely her fault. She was a widow in her early fifties, with greying hair pulled back into a bun, and a rosy complexion. She must have been a very pretty, buxom girl, though she had gone dumpy and had fleshy arms, with stubby fingers which looked well-worn and competent, though today they were shaking as she kept saying she was so ashamed, so ashamed.

'I don't think Lord or Lady Crombie would dream of holding you personally responsible,' Lesley soothed her. 'The best help you can give us is a straightforward summary of exactly what happened.'

'If only I knew. Och, if only I'd been more careful, if only I hadn't . . . och, I mean, that is . . .'

They were seated close to the window in Mrs Dunbar's sitting-room beside the kitchen, looking out on a small courtyard with a couple of outhouse doors in the wall opposite. Their view of a small arch opening on to the outside world was partly obscured by a hanging basket of pink and white fuchsias dangling their silent bells in the breeze, more profuse than those by the lodge gates. Through the arch was a glimpse of a narrow track snaking away into an avenue of trees.

'Where does that lead?'

'Past the chapel. And the family vault alangside,' said Mrs Dunbar reverently.

'Still in use? Regular services, I mean. Open to the public?'

'Och, no. Not any mair. Family weddings and funerals. And there's nae sign of any wedding since that o' the laird and her ladyship, and that took place in Edinburgh. In a register office,' said Mrs Dunbar regretfully.

'But it's open to visitors?'

'Used to be, on visiting days. But it's nae in

good condition, and her ladyship decided we couldn't afford the cost of repairs.'

'And the path ends there?'

'Nae, it goes on to the west lodge.'

'Sort of tradesmen's entrance?'

Mrs Dunbar did not look too happy at this blunt description, but managed a nod. 'Deliveries do come in that way.'

'Does anybody live in the lodge?'

'The dominie. Retired now, of course. Rents the lodge and helps out on visitors' days. A bit of a painter himself, so he's the right one to explain our collection. Loves lecturing people.' It was said admiringly rather than disparagingly.

'There are gates by that particular lodge?'

'Aye. But they're never closed.'

Hairs on the the back of Lesley's neck prickled. 'I noticed when I came in up the main drive today that those gates were open. Were they left open all day yesterday? It was one of the afternoons when the house is open to visitors, wasn't it?'

'They're always open. It's a Crombie tradition.' Pride and loyalty were steadying Mrs Dunbar's voice. 'Over at Traquair, they've got gates which they say will ne'er be opened till a Stuart sits on the throne again. Nae chance o' that, so they'll nae be needing to spend anything on oiling the hinges. But here' — Mrs Dunbar was now in control of herself and her material, reciting it off by heart — 'the gates stay open because the Crombies have long had the tradition of offering a welcome and hospitality to any visitor.'

'So it would seem,' said Lesley drily.

That jolted Mrs Dunbar back to reality. Before she could start on fresh lamentations, Lesley hurried on: 'Just what did happen yesterday afternoon? Right from the beginning, if you can manage it.'

Mrs Dunbar had been on duty issuing tickets, with Mrs McKechnie from the main lodge looking after the refreshment room, and Mr McKechnie acting as a guard, circulating through the main rooms. 'The dominie conducts the tour, and Rab McKechnie follows up to keep an eye on things. And he makes it gey obvious to visitors that that's exactly what he's doing.'

'You manage with just the few of you?'

'We like helping to keep the place going, for the laird's sake.'

'But surely you ought to have someone sitting in each room.'

'There's nae the money to spare. We make sure there's nothing within reach that you could easily slip in your pocket. Nothing's ever been lost.' Mrs Dunbar was not just less dithery than before, but becoming positively aggressive. 'Until now. And that wasnae slipped out under *our* noses while we were on duty.'

'And after you were *off* duty, you saw nothing — heard nothing?'

'I went round, the way I always do, after the visitors had gone and Mr and Mrs McKechnie had handed over to me. Everything was the way it ought to be.'

'Then when did you become aware of the thefts?'

'When Miss Caroline came over and let herself in.'

'Came over? She doesn't live here?'

'Not since her father married again.'

'But she still has a key.'

'Aye. *He's* always glad to see her.'

'And she was the one who realised what had happened?'

Mrs Dunbar was beginning to look unhappy again. 'Aye. And rang the laird to get him back.'

'And you'd heard nothing at all? Seen nothing?'

'Nothing.' There was an odd croak in Mrs Dunbar's throat, and her hands were trembling again. 'We wasnae expecting the laird and her ladyship back until late on the Monday — tomorrow, that is. Cook had been told she could take a week of her holiday, and as for me . . . well, there was nothing I was called on to do, so . . . '

'You had a snooze, after the coachload had gone.'

'Aye.' Mrs Dunbar grasped at this. 'Aye, that's just how it was.'

'And when you woke up. Miss Crombie was here.'

'I didnae hear her come in, but when I went upstairs I could hear her. She was so upset.' She began to sniffle, and reached for a handkerchief, crumpled and less clean than everything else in her spotless sitting room.

Leslie went off to phone a repeated request for Forensic and their photographer to get a move on. It was a Sunday, and the house wasn't exactly within easy reach. But she had a return call within half an hour, and was happy to learn that the SOCO in charge would be one she had worked successfully with before. He had helped solve the theft of two antique mirrors on the evidence of a few shreds of gilding scraped off against a van door. Just the sort of man they needed here.

When she was assured the team was on its way, Lesley went to see the couple at the main gate.

★　★　★

The curtains in the lodge twitched as she approached. By the time Mr McKechnie answered the door, his wife had settled herself on a sofa with her hands folded tightly in her lap. The sofa was too large for the little room, and too high for Mrs McKechnie, whose feet only just touched the ground, so that her lap sloped forward and there was no relaxation in those folded hands.

Mr McKechnie sat beside her and patted her knee. He was a big man, taking up more than his fair share of the sofa. His feet in their heavy black-soled shoes were planted firmly on the floor. He would make a threatening sight, trudging in the wake of visitors to the house.

'We've been waiting for you,' he said solemnly.

They might almost have been doing just that since the crack of dawn — sitting there stiff and uncomfortable, summoning up strength to face the inquisition.

Lesley sat in a chair with a creaking wickerwork seat which Mr McKechnie had indicated. She tried to put them at their ease.

'Now, I'd be most grateful for your help. Will you please tell me in your own words what happened. And if you can remember

96

exact times, so much the better.'

Mr McKechnie, like Mrs Dunbar, was proud of his position in the Crombie household. He described every inch of his progress through the house, the appearance of each room and corridor, the timing of most tourist visits and this one in particular, and his part in shepherding stragglers to keep them up with the main body. Nobody escaped his gaze. Nothing had so far been snatched since he started his patrol.

Lesley wanted to hurry him along, but adjusted her pace to his, nudging him the way he nudged those dawdlers on visiting days.

At last he reached the last details of how he would report to Mrs Dunbar while his wife cashed up in the refreshment room and handed over the proceeds to Mrs Dunbar, who kept separate cashboxes for the restaurant and the ticket proceeds.

'What would happen to the money?' asked Lesley.

'There's a safe down the cellar steps from the kitchen. Both the cashboxes go in there, along with the ledgers. Mrs Dunbar keeps the key on her bunch of keys, and the laird has one as well.'

'Was the money stolen along with the paintings and the rest?'

'Ye'd have to ask Mrs Dunbar that. But I

doubt they'd have been able to get into that safe without spending a lot of time on it.'

'And when you've handed over your particular responsibilities, that's that? You come back here?'

'We come back here,' Mr McKechnie confirmed.

Somebody, thought Lesley, must have stayed behind. Someone from the tourist coach, hiding until the main body of visitors had left and Mrs Dunbar had done her rounds: on his own while his pals were already in position in the grounds, waiting for him to open the doors from within and let them in.

'Did you notice anything unusual — anything out of the ordinary routine? Or spot anybody you'd seen before, who didn't seem to belong?'

Mrs McKechnie summoned up the courage to speak, in a highpitched whine which gave away her Glasgow origin. 'There were two coaches yesterday. One of them was late in leaving. We'd got back here before it went.'

'Was that a common occurrence?'

'It's been known,' said Mr McKechnie. 'People go strolling in the grounds and lose track of the time.'

'Or was it largely empty,' Lesley suggested, 'with nobody noticing what might have been slid into the deep baggage compartments?'

'Didn't have any chance o' noticing that. Tinted windows, ye know the thing — ye can see out from inside, but the passengers are high up and it's difficult to make out much from outside.'

'Just darkened *our* windows for a wee moment,' added his wife, 'and then it was awa' doon the road.'

'And in any case,' said Mr McKechnie, 'surely the stuff hadn't gone when the coach left? Mrs Dunbar would have done her rounds to make sure there was nobody left on the premises, and she'd have noticed.'

Lesley was even more certain that somebody must have stayed behind, hidden, waiting until Mrs Dunbar had finished trotting around and settled herself for that snooze.

But how could he have predicted that she would be sound asleep and out of harm's way when he wanted to let his cronies in?

Lesley would have liked to know more about that delayed coach, but the McKechnies had nothing further to offer.

It was time to see what the schoolmaster had to contribute.

On her way to the side gates she was intercepted by PC Kerr, looking pleased with himself. He led her to a spot near the blank wall of stableyard beside the coffee bar, with overhanging trees clustering close to the white-harled stonework. Some of the lower branches had been snapped or bent, and there were tyre marks on the ground below.

'Judging from the wheel base,' said Kerr weightily, 'I'd say it was some sort of van stood here. And footprints leading to it through the yard from the kitchen door.'

'And heavier footprints on the way back. Carrying heavy weights. Nice work, constable.'

A vanload rather than a coachload?

And all of it carried from the kitchen door — with Mrs Dunbar snoozing so close at hand?

★   ★   ★

The lane from here led directly to the west gates and lodge. To her left a partly overgrown path wove its way through undergrowth and some tangled coppices. A hundred yards on, a crudely painted board nailed to a tree said: DANGER. KEEP OUT. Beyond it was a glimpse of a huddle of stone which must be the family chapel and vault, as neglected as the coppices.

Angus Murray must have seen her coming — must have been waiting and watching, just like the McKechnies — and was ready to

100

greet her in the open doorway, below a lintel carved with a much eroded heraldic shield.

He was a short man with short arms and large hands, cropped white hair and a smartly trimmed white beard. 'A lady officer?' he said; and it was half a polite welcome and half a long practised schoolmaster's sneer. 'Please. Sit ye down. Anything I can do for the wellbeing of the community, consider it done. This is a shocking business. Truly shocking.'

Lesley wanted to waste no time in preliminary fencing. 'Mr Murray, can you give me the clearest possible précis of your movements yesterday during visiting hours and in the immediate aftermath?'

'Ah.' He settled himself contentedly in what was obviously his favourite armchair.

Equally obviously, he was a pedant who would positively enjoy showing parties of reverential tourists around Baldonald House and lecturing them in well-modulated phrases resonant with a knowledge the rest could never hope to achieve.

'Tell me about yourself,' Lesley invited.

Her old superior and hassler, DCI Rutherford, believed in attacking every witness as a potential suspect. Frighten them within a few seconds. Lesley Gunn favoured letting a witness do the talking, while she waited. Make them feel relaxed. If they were innocent and anxious to be helpful, it eased the way. If they weren't, there was so often a crucial litle clue, sometimes the unexpected bonus of a real giveaway.

Mr Murray needed no further bidding.

He lived here at a nominal rent in return for contributing 'in my own wee way' to the smooth running of the estate. He was highly regarded as a guide — 'highly regarded' was his own wee way of putting it — and also produced much useful background material 'in my own wee machine shop'.

'Perhaps you'd like to inspect it?' His white eyebrows arched like the thatch over dormer windows.

He led the way through to his office.

The lodge was small; the sitting-room necessarily small, the office a cramped space — a truly wee room, thought Lesley — triangular in shape, tucked as it was into an angle of the building. One wall carried rickety bookshelves bending under the weight of booklets, history books, and note pads. To reach the shelves you would have to squeeze round a table carrying an array of equipment. Mr Murray was in a mood to lecture again. He proudly explained the functions of his high-spec PC and his digital camera, flat-bed scanner and full-screen computer with colour printer. Retired he might be, but clearly he kept himself occupied and up to the minute. He reached past his battery of hardware to pluck a handful of leaflets from the end of a shelf, and showed how they could be mounted on small wooden boards like table tennis bats for distribution throughout the various rooms. And there were menus for the refreshment room. 'I suppose I'll have to revise all the leaflets now,' he said resignedly, but clearly looking forward to the task. 'There'll be so much missing from the house.'

It was time to move on from the background briefing to the immediate problem. 'On that subject,' said Lesley, 'what exactly was your afternoon like, yesterday?'

'Very busy. Busier than usual, but then, the season's just livening up. We had to cope with two coachloads of trippers. Though of course one mustn't call them that, must one? Let's say visitors, shall we, eager for contact with a more gracious world than their own, yes?'

She could imagine the boom of his pedagogic voice as he condescended to the shuffling herd of people who had paid their money and put themselves in his charge — a more respectful and responsive audience than his school classes could ever have been.

They went back into the sitting-room, and he held forth again. His story confirmed the overall timetable established by Mrs Dunbar and the McKechnies.

'And there was absolutely nothing out of the ordinary?'

'Nothing that I observed.' And then he said: 'Except for the van being still here rather late.'

'The van?'

'Well, I took it to be the usual van from the Eskdale meat and game supplier.'

'Delivering on a Saturday afternoon? Is that usual?'

'Now you come to mention it' — Murray made a steeple of his fingers and looked very earnest — 'I wouldn't have thought so.'

'In any case, why would it have been delivering to the house? Lord and Lady Crombie were away, and the cook had been taking a week's holiday. That I do know.'

'Quite. But it may have been because yesterday was so busy. The refreshment room may have run out of food.'

'An emergency delivery of lamb chops or game pâté when it's nearly closing time? You say it was still here rather late.'

'Aye.'

'Whereabouts did you see it? Near the refreshment room, or the kitchen yard, or — '

'I didn't see it. Not while we were looking after the visitors. Not until it was leaving. And that was long after I'd come back here.'

'It went out through those gates?'

'Aye.'

'And you're sure it was the tradesman's van?

'It was white, that's all I saw. I assumed it was the butcher from Eskdale. Only . . . ' He paused, looked even more earnest and anxious to be helpful. 'Now I come to think of it, I didnae notice any lettering on the sides. The usual delivery van has the butcher's name and phone number. Mark you, I had only a wee glimpse, through that window.' He nodded towards the side window, half obscured by a grey lace curtain. 'I wasn't expecting anything to go past that late in the afternoon.'

Lesley made her way back to the house to check on this piece of information with Mrs Dunbar and the McKechnies.

She found the two women bustling up and down stairs with plates of cold meat and bowls of salad. Lord Crombie tried to flatten himself against the wall to let them pass, but was too hefty to manage it easily, and edged to one side as Lesley approached.

He stared at her, trying to place her in the middle of his abject miseries. Then he said: 'Ah. Yes. You'll be joining us for lunch?'

'That's kind of you, but I think you'll have a lot to talk about. On your own.'

'Nonsense. Where else would you eat, anyway? There's nowhere round here for miles, except the *Tam Lin*. You'll have to make do with scraps, though. No cook until this evening. Not expecting us back.'

'No, really, I wouldn't dream of — '

'I'll not have you starving. An empty stomach won't help you in your enquiries.'

He was doing his best to be jovial about it. She could not possibly refuse him.

Food was laid out in an improvised buffet on the long table in the main reception room. Brigid Crombie looked surprised at Lesley's presence, but then caught her husband's eye, and decided it was a perfectly reasonable arrangement. If the master of the house did not contemplate sending the detective down to the servants' quarters for a snack, she was content to agree with him.

'Thank you, Mrs McKechnie,' said Hector Crombie. 'You've worked wonders.'

'Thank you, Mrs McKechnie.' His wife's version of gratitude had a tinge of making it clear that for one person at any rate it was time to get below stairs.

Lesley hurried to intercept her at the door.

'Mrs McKechnie, can you clarify one little point? How long was the butcher's van here yesterday afternoon?'

'The van? I didnae see any van.'

106

'You weren't running out of supplies in the refreshment room? Phoning for an urgent delivery?'

'We work things out better than that,' said Mrs McKechnie starchily. 'Rabbie would no' ha' been asked to make any deliveries yesterday afternoon.'

Then whose van had been driven past the west lodge late that afternoon? And what was inside it? Gloomily Lesley thought that although she couldn't yet answer the first question, she was pretty sure of the answer to the second one.

The SOCO was waiting for her in the hall when she made her excuses and left the lunch table early. 'Shouldn't take long to make a selection between the overall prints and those of the residents and staff. Then we can whizz 'em off to the Index.'

And if they were lucky, the National Criminal Fingerprint Index would trace a parallel with any known villains who special- ised in this particular line.

If we're lucky, thought Lesley without any great optimism.

6

All through the makeshift lunch Hector
Crombie remained silent apart from the
clumping of his feet as he plodded about the
room with a plate in his hand, glancing at
spaces on the walls and then forcing himself
not to look. Brigid ate with the quick,
dabbing skill of one accustomed to balance
plate and glass at cocktail parties without
interrupting either the flow of conversation
or the intake of nibbles. Caroline had
positioned herself by the window, staring
moodily out.

Detective Inspector Gunn had politely
distanced herself from the others, but Greg
was sure that she was unobtrusively sizing
them all up. He tried making his own
private assessment of her. Although she was
a plain clothes officer, her dark blue jacket
and skirt, white blouse and blue stockings
had the trimness of a uniform. Her hair
was short and as closely fitting as a light
brown helmet. There was nothing of the
heavy-footed copper in her: her hips swayed
very gently, her grey eyes were sharp but
unthreatening as she glanced at him,

presumably trying to fit him into the *dramatis personae*.

In the end Greg had to break the silence. He was no part of this. Brigid had brought him here; it was to Brigid that he would make his adieus.

'Look, perhaps I'd better leave. You won't want me hanging around while — '

'You're staying.' Brigid interrupted her eating for only a few seconds, without even dropping a crumb. 'I suppose we'll have to wait until tomorrow. Give you time to do some sleuthing, eh, Inspector Gunn? Then we can get back to the book.'

Greg thought that this at any rate might provoke some comment from her husband. But he was far away in some sad twilight of his own. Then suddenly he came awake, staring at his right hand as if aware for the first time of another loss. Something was undoubtedly missing.

'Dammit, we haven't got anything to drink. Caroline, do go down to the cellar. Bring up a couple of bottles of claret. Plenty of stuff to choose from.'

'No,' said Brigid sharply. 'It's not worth the bother. We don't want to start drinking at this time of day.'

'We certainly do.'

'For goodness' sake, Hector. Help yourself

to a whisky and be done with it. The rest of us can manage. Don't bother with the claret, Caroline.'

Caroline turned away from the window, put her empty plate on the end of the table, smiled briefly at her father, and went out of the room.

There was an awkward pause, a silence even more oppressive than it had originally been.

DI Gunn said: 'Lady Crombie, I realise you still haven't got over the shock of this theft. But in preparing my report to our experts in the field I really do have to sit down with you and sort out precisely what has been lost, and what individual items are worth.'

'I thought I'd made it clear to you that my stepdaughter knows more about the history of the different pieces.'

'She gave me the impression that you would know more about the financial implications.'

'She did, did she?'

'I do need your help,' Lesley Gunn persisted. 'About the running of the house as well. Who does what, who comes and goes, anything suspicious or out of the ordinary — anything that will give us a lead.'

'I wasn't even here when it happened. I was in Edinburgh.'

'Even so, you must have ideas about . . . well . . . '

Their attention was distracted by Caroline arriving with two bottles, each carried carefully in a wine cradle. She opened a cupboard and took out glasses while her father slowly drew the cork from one bottle.

'Not much choice, really,' she said.

'Hm? What?'

'You said there was plenty of choice. Not many bottles in the racks, actually.'

'They've taken the wine as well?'

'Most of it. Or have you been running stocks down? You did say the whole wine tasting programme had been a flop.'

Her father looked confused. 'Maybe. Yes. But I thought there was plenty left.'

He wasted no time in any act of sniffing and swirling the plum-red liquid around in the glass, but took a long gulp.

Caroline sipped and made a face. She bent over the label. 'I thought you were supposed to have some noble vintages down there.'

Brigid looked over her shoulder. 'That's a *premier cru*. What's wrong with it?'

'Tastes like something you'd knock back on some Italian hillside when you were too sun-drunk to notice.'

'All tastes the same to me,' confessed her father.

'Are you sure you weren't taken for a ride by that grotty little wine snob?' She studied the label again. 'Or has someone been topping these up from a tanker?'

'Tastes perfectly good to me,' Brigid insisted.

Her husband had another slurp. 'Dacre, what d'you make of it?'

Greg knew very little about wine, but was ready to put on a reasonable performance. As the ghost of a qualified vintner, he swirled the wine gently, held it up to the light, sniffed, and took a sip, then a larger gulp.

'It's a bit on the tart side,' he admitted.

Brigid glared at him. 'Since when have you been . . . '

There was a sound of tyres on the gravel outside. Caroline went back to the window.

'Oh, no. It's a coachload. Turning into the yard.'

DI Gunn joined her and looked out. 'You're open to the public on a Sunday?'

'Saturdays, Sundays and Wednesdays in the season. Forgot all about it, with this flap going on. Why on earth didn't Mrs Dunbar think of it?'

Hector Crombie tipped the bottle towards his glass. 'Damn-all for them to see. Half the things in the booklet are missing.'

Brigid helped herself to another slice of

cold roast duck. 'We'll have to put up a notice. Closed until further notice.'

Caroline hurried out of the room.

People were already walking towards the stable block to buy tickets and be tempted into the gift shop or the refreshment room. It was a pattern all tourists took for granted, part of what holidays were about: coach trips, pac-a-macs, pubs, souvenir shops and stately homes.

'They'll be trampling all over any evidence there might be.' DI Gunn set off after Caroline.

McKechnie strode in. 'We've only just realised, your ladyship — '

'Yes,' snapped Brigid. 'So have we. Do get out there and turn them away. And then we'll have to notify the tourist offices. Closed until further notice,' she repeated.

★ ★ ★

Lesley Gunn caught up with Caroline, who was being freezingly polite but firm with the coach driver. His passengers had paid their money for the tour, they had been told that the historic Baldonald House was on their itinerary, and he wanted to know why he'd been allowed to get all this way without being told the place wasn't open.

113

Lesley stood to one side while the Hon. Caroline apologised in a haughty way which managed to make the complainant feel somehow guilty of something himself, without knowing what it was.

When he had finished reluctantly shepherding his passengers back towards the coach, explaining but grumbling along with them, Lesley stopped him before he climbed up into the driver's seat.

'Was it one of your parties which came here yesterday afternoon?'

'No, that it was not.' He climbed on to the second step.

'As Miss Crombie has explained to you, there has been a serious crime committed here. We need to question anyone who may have been on the premises, or near them, at the time.'

'And who might you be?'

She held her warrant card up to him. 'Detective Inspector Gunn.'

'You're not accusing me or one of my mates of . . . look, d'ye see us carrying a whole load of pictures and that kind of thing out under the eyes of a whole load of passengers like this lot?'

'If you or any of those mates of yours think of anything you've noticed, not just this weekend but a week or two ago, that might tie

114

in with what's happened, we'd be glad of the information.'

'Aye,' he said, sliding across to his seat and making the door hiss and clank shut.

Lesley turned back to Caroline. The two of them watched the coach depart. Lesley said: 'Miss Crombie, you were the one who discovered that things were missing?'

'That's right, yes.'

'Were you expected here yesterday?'

'Expected?'

'You don't live here full-time, I believe?'

'Not any longer. I have a pad in Linlithgow. Handy for Glasgow and Edinburgh, but a good escape from either of them. I do come back here often enough, though.'

'To unwind?'

'To see my father, and see how he's getting on.'

'But,' Lesley repeated, 'were you expected yesterday? I mean, I understand Lord and Lady Crombie had been in Edinburgh all week. Hadn't they notified you they'd be away?'

'We don't consult one another every hour of the day, or even every day of the week. I just felt like coming down after a hectic recording session, and I came. That's the way it is, nine times out of ten.'

They went back indoors. Lesley headed for

115

the phone to check with the butcher whether he had in fact been delivering yesterday, in spite of assurances from people on duty that he had not. Someone might have overlooked a last-minute arrangement to deliver something. Everything had to be checked.

It was Sunday, and the butcher's answering machine was on. Just as she had finished recording a message for him, there was a click, and a man's drowsy voice said that he'd just heard what she was on about, and no, of course he'd never been near the place. Never did on a Saturday. And this particular Saturday, his van had been to and from the fête at Langholm all morning and afternoon. He sounded as if it had been quite a celebration, and he was only just recovering.

★   ★   ★

While the panic over the coachload was being dealt with, Greg meandered at a loose end along the corridors. Ahead of him on the second floor he heard Brigid's voice, and slowed down rather than catch her up. He had heard it all too early that morning, just after the first wail of the bagpipes as young Drew fulfilled his duties, and Brigid had howled: 'Not this morning, for God's sake.' Now her tone of voice was just as

116

exasperated: 'Do stop *prowling*, Hector.'

Greg waited, then resumed his own prowl, like a ghost thinking himself not into a living author but into the persona of some past Crombie who had been Keeper of the Forest, home after despatching a few outlaws and showing mercy to a poor serf caught poaching.

'Dacre!' Hector Crombie's gruff voice came out of the snug like a command from a loud hailer. 'Do come in and have a dram.'

Greg was about to make a polite excuse, then realised there was no need: there was nothing else he could contribute to anyone else in the household. He went in and sat down, while his host poured considerably more than a dram into a large tumbler.

'Well, what d'ye make of it all?'

Greg wondered if he could insinuate himself into the mind of a master criminal, planning the coup and carrying it out, and finding somewhere to hide out while arranging for distribution of the loot. Ghosting the memoirs of an art thief, where would he begin?

'I haven't a clue what could have happened,' he confessed. 'It must be one hell of a blow for you.'

'Aye. Not just the value of some of the things. No collector myself, ye ken. Just

117

inherited the stuff. Perhaps my wife's right: the insurance'll come in handy. But there are some things . . . ' He coughed, grunted, and took a large swig of whisky, coughing more loudly over that and reaching for his handkerchief in a pretence that the drink had made his eyes water.

'Personal connections,' said Greg.

Crombie nodded. 'That portrait of my wife. My first wife. Brigid hung it in a rather dark corner. I didn't go out of my way to . . . well, no point in getting maudlin. All the same . . . ' He took another massive swig and fumbled for words, none of them coming easily. 'Dammit, it *belonged* here.'

There was a rustling sound which Greg thought at first came from Crombie's throat. Then it grew louder: a fitful spattering against the small window at the end of the snug. Rain was beginning slowly, but even as they talked it swelled from a whisper to a tattoo on the glass.

With the glow of Highland Park warming his throat, Greg was courageous enough to prompt his host. 'This place means a lot to you, sir. Will your daughter be able to take over in due course?'

'She's a capable lass. Och, if maybe she could have found the right partner and the two of them . . . hm. But she'll have to sort

118

things out for herself. Or with a good friend. I fancy she has one she can rely on. That's what I'm hoping.'

Greg felt that one of them was getting fuzzy from the drink. He didn't follow the line of reasoning. 'Some man she's . . . well, nowadays they call them partners, not husbands or wives?'

'No. Brigid's daughter. Such a douce lassie. Such a pity.'

A chill stabbed down Greg's back. 'You mean Ishbel?'

Hector was embarrassed. 'Oh, damme. Of course. Forgot.' He reached for the bottle and topped up both their glasses. 'You're the father, aren't you? Damn thoughtless of me.'

'What about her? What's Ishbel got to do with it?'

'Pity she had to fall into that wretch's hands.'

'Who?'

'Sorry, old chap, I'm no' very good at explaining things, am I? My wife's second husband. I mean, the one that came after you and before me.'

'Yes, I know. Simon Pringle. But you're not saying he got up to something — not *again*? Not with Ishbel?'

'Such a shame. Things were going so well,

until then. Damned impertinence. Coming and hanging around here, pretending he had some rights. Coming between her and Caroline. When the two of them had been such good friends. So close. She was like another daughter to me. And when the two of them were here at the same time, it did brighten this old place up. Until that vermin Pringle got to work on her.'

Greg drained his glass and stormed off in search of Brigid. She was in the library, unhurriedly turning over the pages of the Sunday business supplement. She seemed unperturbed by the comings and goings of the detective inspector and Caroline. By the look of it, the library had been untouched. Greg could only suppose that the intruders had been specialists in the art field. No ordinary thief would have passed up the chance to take the VDU and its associated hardware, which would be so easily and profitably disposable.

He wasn't that madly interested. All he had to say right away was: 'What's this about Simon and Ishbel?'

'Oh, God. Hector's been getting dewy-eyed, has he?'

'You let Simon take over our daughter? You were married to him, and you let him — '

'At least he didn't marry *her*,' she said

120

stonily. 'Just had it off with her. Par for the course.'

'But how could she have let him? How could *you* let it — '

'All right, you shouldn't need to be told. You knew Simon. Your dear old mate. He got up to his old games. Sly innuendoes, snickering gossip, and of course the terribly understanding friend so ready to listen to one's troubles. Only not with me any longer. That had ceased to amuse him. No challenge any more. So just for the fun of it, it had to be my daughter.'

Something tightened in Greg's stomach. A terrible pang clutched him. '*Our* daughter? Ishbel?'

'So you do remember her.'

'Don't be so bloody stupid. What about *me*?'

'What about you?'

'I'm her father. You should have let me know.'

'But you hadn't been her father for a long time. You were too busy being somebody else. Very successfully, I'll say that.'

'But what the hell were you doing? What *did* you do?'

'I suppose I was away too often, expanding operations here and Glasgow and London. It was a long time before it dawned on me that

121

he was sniffing around Ishbel. He was incapable of not cheating on anyone close to him.'

'And when you did find out?'

'I finished him,' said Brigid with lethal quietness. 'Divorced him, threw him out.'

'And the job you'd found for him?'

'The firm had been having a rocky few months. I recommended a company doctor and told him what to look for. Took a few months, with Simon wriggling and twisting. But I had him out. Forever.'

'And Ishbel?'

Brigid was so tense, so close to choking in silence as he had been a few moments ago, that he was almost tempted to reach out and take her hand. But there was too vast a gap between them.

'The stupid little thing took pity on him,' said Brigid at last. 'He came sniffing around her again after I'd married Hector, putting on his sad, misunderstood act. And she believed it, and moved in with him.'

'And after your own dose of Simon, you still let it happen?'

'If you'd been around, you think you could have stopped it? But then, you hadn't been around for a long time, had you?'

'I thought we'd agreed on that. Just one thing we did agree on. Better not to complicate things. You wanted Ishbel under *your* wing. Or under your foot. Clean break, that's what you persuaded me was the best for Ishbel. It wouldn't have done any good for me to reappear at intervals and — '

'You didn't make the effort to do any reappearing, did you?'

'Clean break, that's what you insisted on,' he repeated.

'And you let me get away with it? What sort of father does that make you?'

She hadn't altered. In any argument with Brigid, it was heads you lost, tails you lost.

'You were always somewhere else,' she raged on. '*Somebody* else. In America or Moscow or God knows where.'

'You didn't like me to start making a success of things on my own, did you? More fun to go on wallowing in all that crap from Simon.'

'Not all of it.'

'Just the bits it tickled your fancy to believe.'

'He could be amusing. Until one got down to it and found out what he was really like.'

'By which time it was too late.'

'What about *you*?' He remembered all too well how her voice levelled out rather than being raised when she had something scathing to say. 'He was supposed to be your friend. You'd known him for years. Why didn't *you* stop him before it was too late?'

'By the time it dawned on me what he was up to, it was too late.'

'And I wasn't worth the effort?'

'Not by then. If you enjoyed sniggering with him and egging him on, then no, you weren't.'

'Did you ever love me?' She might have been an interviewer throwing a key question at him.

'I suppose I must have done.' It was all he could bring himself to answer.

'Until . . . ?'

'Until I found out who you really were.'

'Oh, no. No.' Her voice was even lower and more intense. 'You never did find that out. That's what you're supposed to be doing now. Only this time you're getting paid for it. Are you sure you've got the guts to go ahead with it? Really collaborate?'

'I thought that's what we've been doing anyway.'

'I mean really collaborate.' Her opal eyes were azure with excitement again. 'I mean really get down to it. Get our own back.'

'On whom?'

'On treacherous bastards everywhere. The ones who buggered things up for me — and the one who buggered it up for both of us.'

In spite of the glossy veneer, she was still the same Brigid Weir deep down inside. She still felt herself, as she always had done, the ill-done-to centre of an outrageous storm, buffeted by winds of stupidity and misunderstanding which only a woman of her calibre was talented enough to survive.

'And me?' he asked.

'Haven't you ever wanted to get your own back on slimy Simon?'

'So you did notice at last that Simon was slimy? That's not the way you used to talk about him. Used to have such great fun, listening to him belittle me and cuddle up to you and lie to you. And of course one of the things about Simon is that he not only likes cheating on a friend — or a wife, eh? — but has to make sure the friend finds out. For him that's the biggest thrill of the lot. Just as when he simply had to let me know he was at it with you.'

'I was wrong.' How had she managed to utter those words?

'A bit late to discover that.'

'You ought not to have let him get away with it.' She was petulant again. 'He was your friend. You introduced us. You ought to have known.'

Greg laughed out loud. First the grudging admission, then the hasty attempt to switch the blame. 'And after that, *you* ought to have known. Where is he now? Where's Ishbel? Where are they?'

'From what I've heard, living in squalor in Portobello.'

'From what *you've* heard? Haven't you tried to follow up? Do something for Ishbel?'

Before Brigid could answer, Caroline came in with another of the Sunday newspaper's voluminous sections, this time the books and media supplement. She flapped it towards Brigid like a matador provoking the first attack.

'I thought you were keeping your memoirs under wraps till they were well and truly ready for publication.'

'So I am.'

'Someone appears to be in a hurry to spread the gladsome tidings.'

Brigid snatched the paper, skimmed a few paragraphs, screeched 'The stupid bitch', and threw the crumpling sheets across the room.

Greg picked them up and sorted out the relevant page.

It was a typical literary gossip column, once headed *Pen in Hand* but in recent years translated into *Words in Process*. The offending paragraphs were in the usual know-all style.

Penelope Vaughan-Smith, bestseller-hunting acquisitions editor of Clement & Cowan has acquired quite a shiny scalp for her New Year list. Ruthless headhunter Brigid Weir — better known to the Scottish huntin', shootin' and fishin' set as Lady Crombie of Baldonald House — is taking a sabbatical from the world of high finance and low dealings to write her memoirs. Penny Vaughan-Smith promises white-hot revelations. 'Chapters I've seen so far,' she raves, 'are going to scorch the fur of some very fat cats indeed.' Bidding for serial rights is already intense.

'She hasn't seen any chapters,' raged Brigid. 'What the hell is she playing at?'

'Playing at what they've slipped into that last sentence.' Greg knew the scene well enough. 'Issuing hefty hints and hoping for an auction of serial rights.'

'Before they've even seen a word?'

'You often get a better deal that way. Get money in the bank before they find out the revelations aren't up to much.'

'These are damn well going to be up to a lot. A hell of a lot.' Brigid stormed towards the phone. 'When I've had a word with — '

Before Greg could utter a warning, Caroline anticipated him: 'I don't think publishers' offices are a hive of industry on a Sunday.'

'That dreadful woman. *I'm* the one who'll decide when we tell the world, and when serial rights or any other rights are on offer.'

'But now,' said Caroline, 'aren't you worried there'll be some attempts to stop you? Your intended victims have been alerted. They may decide to get at you before you get at them.' She sounded none too displeased.

Brigid said: 'I'm going to London.'

'You can't just rush off like that. Not with all this other business to attend to.'

'I'm not just going to hang about waiting to make a phone call tomorrow morning. God knows what time that woman and the rest of them condescend to saunter into their offices on a Monday morning.'

Caroline tried again. 'You can't just — '

'You heard me. I'm going to London. Take them by surprise and knock hell out of them. Caroline, while I get things together, do me a favour — check train and plane times this evening and first thing tomorrow morning.'

Greg heard the rain on the window intensify, drowning the sound of the two women's footsteps as they left the room; and drowning the sound of another woman's feet as she came in and took their place.

Detective Inspector Gunn said: 'And how

128

exactly do you fit in here, Mr Dacre? A relative of the Crombies?'

'No, I'm working with Brigid — Lady Crombie.'

'In what capacity?'

'I'm her ghost.'

The neat, rather demure little face tightened into official disapproval. 'Mr Dacre, this isn't a time for jokes. I have a serious investigation to carry out.'

'Yes, of course. Sorry, but it's true. I'm working with her on her memoirs. We call it ghosting, in the trade.'

'Ah, I see. And where were you when this burglary took place?'

'Miles away. In Edinburgh. With Lady Crombie.'

'Indeed.' Her clear, unfaltering eyes were considering questions she wasn't too sure of asking. Not yet, anyway. In the meantime she was obviously adding him to her store of local eccentrics. 'Working on these memoirs?'

'Exactly.'

'An alibi which Lady Crombie will undoubtedly confirm?'

'Good God,' Greg exploded, 'why should I need an alibi? You don't suppose I could have had anything to do with this business? I'm a writer, not a housebreaker. Wouldn't know where to begin.'

The young woman sighed. With a face and graceful cast of the head like that, it could have been a gentle, romantic sigh. But it wasn't.

Brigid walked back in.

'Inspector, I'm afraid I have to go to London. Urgently.'

'Lady Crombie, I do need you here. There are so many things you'll need to clear up for me.'

'I wasn't even here when this outrage took place.'

'I'm aware of that. But you must see that as one of the most responsible people in the household, I do need you on the premises to check each bit of evidence I can collect. It is, after all, your home we're talking about.'

'Yes, but something has cropped up.'

'When will you be asking for the insurance claims investigator to come and assess the problem?'

It was said so quietly, but Greg enjoyed watching Brigid being so effectively knocked off balance.

'I've . . . er . . . got it on my pad to ring when I get back from London.'

'They'll be a bit peeved if you don't notify them at the earliest possible opportunity.'

'One of us has to go.' Brigid changed plans with her usual impetuous speed. 'Gregory, it'll have to be you.' She had only called him Gregory when she wanted to lay down the law. 'That young woman's got to be stopped. And Murdo Cowan's got some explaining to do. Think you can handle it?'

Greg contemplated the prospect of tearing a strip off Miss Vaughan-Smith, and was sure he would be delighted to handle it.

'I'll leave you a phone number,' he said to DI Gunn before she could raise any objections. 'My literary agent. Kate Hadleigh. She'll know where I am at any time of the day.'

Or night, he thought; and caught Brigid's eye, all too capable of detecting a telltale resonance in his voice when he as much as uttered Kate's name.

But what the hell had it got to do with her anyway, any more?

7

The *Tam Lin* was a white-harled inn at a lonely crossroads above the unhurried Yarrow Water. In earlier centuries it had been a welcome refuge for drovers and other travellers seeking shelter before being snowed in. Once there, they didn't worry too much about the snow, unless it lasted long enough to cut off all supplies from outside.

Today it boasted electricity, but there was still an overhang stacked with logs against the danger of winds or the weight of snow bringing down the power line. At one stage the landlord had been conned by a glib salesman into installing piped music in the bar, but after the speakers had three times been unobtrusively removed by regulars as skilled and sly as any Border reiver, he allowed talk or companionable silence to prevail.

Beside the fireplace was a framed copy of verses from the ballad of Tam Lin, and above the fireplace a primitive oil painting of the Queen of the Fairies emerging from her bush of broom, half obscured by a more recent glass case containing a massive salmon which had somehow found its way here from the Tweed.

The inn's two letting rooms were generally occupied by fishermen or walkers. DI Lesley Gunn found the accommodation pleasantly neutral: it would have been too far to travel daily from HQ, and there was no question of accepting hospitality from the Crombies. Her bedroom was at the back of the building, overlooking a tiny yard which the proprietors had never ventured to call a car park. Her Vauxhall Astra was the only vehicle there this morning. Come lunchtime, there would probably be a couple of Range Rovers and maybe a muddy estate car with a family touring the region, making sour jokes about Scottish drizzle but revelling in the quaintness of the natives, and assuring themselves that they weren't frightened of their teeth being fractured by the local oatcakes.

All through the night there had been more than drizzle: late summer rain had been beating against the windows and striking booming bass notes from the downpipes. When Lesley drove in towards Baldonald House on the Monday morning it had slackened, but the hills were still shrouded in a lingering haze, and trees dripped great splashes of water and soggy leaves on to the top of her car. Halfway up the steps to the main door of the house she could hear the hoarse chatter of the burn, like a steady stroller being forced suddenly into a headlong rush.

There was another car, a Volvo, parked close to the steps. Lady Crombie already had a morning visitor. He was standing with her on the first-floor landing as she rattled off grievances about the loss the family had suffered, occasionally making an attempt to interrupt but each time yielding to Brigid's catalogue of woes.

He was glad to welcome the newcomer as Brigid introduced them.

'Now, Mr Abernethy, here's someone who can vouch for everything I've been telling you. Detective Inspector Gunn . . . Mr Colin Abernethy, from our insurance company.' As they were mumbling the usual 'How d'you do', she went on with heavy emphasis: 'Detective Inspector Gunn is the police expert on works of art. I'm sure if you want any confirmation of the value of the works in question, she'll be able to put you on the right track.'

'Mm, yes. Very helpful.' But Mr Abernethy's eyes were wandering. 'No window locks?'

'On this level? No one would be likely to shin up the side of the house in full view of — '

'In full view of anyone who was awake, and standing in full view of *them*? No. But would there have been anybody around at that time? Anyone who might have raised the alarm?'

Against the background of Brigid rattling through a list of the staff and the routine on a visiting day, Lesley found herself conjuring up a vision of men carrying paintings down the back stairs and out of the side door towards the shelter of the stableyard, where the van was waiting. And Mrs Dunbar was snoozing in her housekeeper's room — and they had humped things past without waking her?

Could someone have doped her tea?

Mr Abernethy was saying: 'And the downstairs doors? Deadlocks?'

'We'd been at an exhibition that very day, considering what safety devices to instal.'

'A bit late, Lady Crombie. But first of all, can you supply me with a list of items missing, purchase prices, and current valuation, so that I may compare them with the schedule on your policy?'

'Don't be rididulous. These things are family heirlooms. You don't think we've kept receipts from centuries ago?'

'At some time you must have had a reappraisal of the current values.'

'I imagine that you'll have all that on your files from when we took out the insurance. I think it was renegotiated eighteen months ago.'

Yes, thought Lesley, it probably was: around the time when their hostess became Lady Crombie. That was something a woman like the new lady of the house wouldn't have overlooked.

As they went back downstairs, Mrs Dunbar fussed out of the dining-room, looked at the stranger, and then looked around as if anxious to flee.

'You have complete confidence in your staff, of course?' Abernethy spoke with insulting loudness.

'Been with the family for years.'

Lesley said: 'Mrs Dunbar . . . '

'I was just on my way to . . . I, er, if I can just get past . . . '

'Mrs Dunbar, did you actually drowse when they were carrying things out, right past your door?'

'It's dreadful. I don't know what came over me. I'm so ashamed.'

'All right, Mrs Dunbar.' Brigid waved peremptorily. She was obviously keen to go on establishing her claim for a quick insurance settlement. 'Let's not go on about it.'

Mrs Dunbar gulped. 'Your Ladyship, could you spare me a minute?'

'Later, Mrs Dunbar.'

'It's important, ma'am. I wouldn't ask but . . . ' She looked apprehensively at the other two, seemed about to make a bolt for it after all, but then spluttered: 'It's about Saturday.'

Lesley tensed. 'Is it something I ought to know?'

'Please, ma'am, I'd rather have just a word. Before it's too late.'

'Too late?' Brigid strode past the assessor and the detective. 'Oh, for goodness' sake. All right. Leave this to me for a moment. We'll get back to work as soon as possible, Mr Abernethy.'

When she had gone, Abernethy turned to Lesley. 'What do you make of it all, inspector?'

'The open days are part of the problem. Visitors swarming all over the place. Plenty of opportunity to work out the lie of the land under cover of visiting trippers. The staff is too small to operate efficiently. None of them properly trained to look out for suspicious behaviour. At the same time, it's not the sort of place where you'd want a constant surveillance operation by some security firm. Men in blue uniforms with big belts and big necks.'

137

'A few more personal security installations would have been advisable, though.' Abernethy might well owe his employment to the invaluable qualification of a natural air of permanent scepticism about the whole human race. A light snuffle added at key moments could indicate to the claimant that the entire claim was suspect, and that in any case recompense for stolen items could never amount to even half what was hoped for. 'We might consider offering a reward,' he said reluctantly. 'At the thought of a handout, there's often someone who'll risk cheating on his associates.'

'I must go and see what time we can expect Forensic. Give me a shout if you come across anything interesting. But *please* try not to touch anything or brush against anything until our folk have been over the place.'

Abernethy continued on his way with a pocket database. His fingers stabbed at it, questioning it more aggressively than he had so far dared to question Lady Crombie.

In the large sitting-room, Mrs Dunbar's voice was raised in a squeak of terror.

'Come in, inspector.' Caroline stood in the doorway. 'I think you'd better hear this.'

A television screen flickered in the corner, incongruous in this panelled room with its old, well lived-in furniture. The sound must have been turned down: the prevailing sound was still that of Mrs Dunbar wailing, with occasional snappish punctuation from Caroline Crombie. Hector Crombie sat well back in a corner, like a teddy bear dumped in an armchair to stare beadily at what was going on.

'Do stop that noise, woman.' Brigid added her own reproof to Caroline's. 'Tell Inspector Gunn what you've just told us.'

'Oh, please, Your Ladyship, not the police. I ken it was stupid, but the police . . . I mean, please . . . '

'Stop snivelling and tell her.'

Mrs Dunbar gulped again, looked at Lesley as if preparing to fend off a physical assault, and then croaked out a few words.

'Speak up,' Caroline commanded.

'Well, miss . . . inspector . . . it was like this. That afternoon, the moment we'd finished and the coaches had gone, I did only a quick check round. Lord and Lady Crombie being away in Edinburgh, and nobody needing me, I left the house. No more than an hour or so, honestly it wasn't.'

'Left it? To go where?'

'Och, I'm so ashamed. I never thought I'd be so — '

'To go where?'

'To spend some time with . . . my . . . with a gentleman friend.'

'Nearby?'

'Over Ettrickbridge way. I went upon my bike. No more'n fifteen minutes ride.'

'And this . . . gentleman friend. A local man?'

'Nae, just staying in a wee cottage there. Renting the place while he does some work round here.'

'What kind of work?'

'He's a tree surgeon.' Mrs Dunbar could not resist sounding a little bit perkier, rolling the words admiringly round her tongue. 'Working up in the woods for Forest Enterprise.'

'So, while visiting your friend, you were away for how long, did you say?'

'Just an hour an' a bit. That's all it took us.' She caught her breath in a fleeting moment of reminiscence, then glanced sheepishly at Caroline. 'I got back only just in time, just before Miss Crombie showed up.'

Caroline said furiously: 'You'll have to go, Mrs Dunbar.'

'Miss Caroline, I'm so sorry, so very very sorry, I . . . '

'I'm surprised you didn't invite him in. Have it off with him down in the kitchen, or up in the fourposter, or . . . or . . . '

'That's enough,' said Brigid Crombie. 'I'm the one who decides whether she goes or stays.'

'No.' Her husband's gravelly voice was quiet but powerful. 'She'll not be thrown out. She and her folk hae been here nearly as many generations as mine. And we've made plenty of our ain mistakes. She's been gey silly, but I'll no' be letting her go after all these years.'

'Oh, sir.' Mrs Dunbar thrust a wet, crumpled handkerchief even more vigorously into her eyes. 'My Lord . . . '

Lesley said: 'Of course this may affect the whole timetable of the robbery. And the people who organised it. I'd be obliged if you'd let me have the address of this friend of yours, Mrs Dunbar.'

'Oh, miss . . . officer . . . please, I don't want him dragged into it. He couldn't have had anything to do with it.'

'Couldn't he?' said Caroline.

'His name, please,' said Lesley. 'And the address.'

Wretchedly Mrs Dunbar said it was Mr Ross — she did not give a Christian name, and one felt that even in his arms she would still call him Mr Ross — and he rented the cottage by the brig where the forestry folk's firebreak began. Before Lesley could ask for

141

more lucid guidance than this, Caroline snatched a folded map from the bookshelf and opened it out.

Her father said: 'I think you can go now, Mrs Dunbar.' It was a decisive end to one matter, and the beginning of another. 'And Caroline, m'dear, isn't it time for your programme? We don't want to miss it.'

This was presumably the programme Caroline had been working on at the time of the robbery. Watching the pictures come to life on the screen, Lesley had to agree that the daughter of the household had a pretty impressive alibi. The final editing, as she had explained, was wrapped up on the Saturday morning, after which she had had a late lunch and then driven here — to find the place looted. Not that Lesley had ever imagined Caroline being involved in the theft of family treasures which obviously meant so much to her. But she watched the programme with the rest of them, attentive for the slightest nuance which might trigger her interest.

The round-up began with motor sport along forest roads, and then a feature on deer-stalking. Hector settled down to watch, making it clear that he'd be offended if everybody else didn't do the same.

Automatically Lesley concentrated on sizing up the presenter. Caroline had done a voice-over for the motor rally, but was very much on screen for the deer-stalking item. Her voice became instantly more intense, lilting with enthusiasm.

She spelt out the difference between the old tradition of encircling for shooters, and the skill of individual stalking. It had once been customary for sportsmen to locate deer and then form a tight semi-circle known as the tinchels, driving the quarry towards a narrow valley or a man-made enclosure, the elrig, where the guns were waiting to shoot them down. Then in the nineteenth century came a new, subtler sport. It was found to be more exciting, and a lot more demanding, to use primitive instincts and skills to approach the quarry stealthily without frightening it off, and kill it with one clean shot instead of loosing a whole fusillade.

A professional gamekeeper and a keen amateur stalker demonstrated the technique. Caroline then went through the same sly approaches, followed by the zoom lens of a cameraman perched uncomfortably motionless in a tree. Each of the professionals had got within a hundred yards of the stag before it became aware of them and bolted. Caroline, like a sleek cat easing her way through the undergrowth, paused, advanced a cautious paw, froze again, and then reached out with the other forepaw. She got within fifty yards before the stag sensed her and bounded away.

At the end of the programme, Lord Crombie stared admiringly up at his daughter. 'We must have a day out together, when we've got this other damn business settled.'

Lesley said: 'None of those animals actually got shot?'

'You'd have liked to see some bloodshed?'

'No, but I gathered that the whole idea was to finish things off with one accurate shot.'

'It was a programme about stalking technique, not marksmanship. A lot of viewers would have protested if we'd shown them an actual killing.'

'Mm. Very impressive. Well,' said Lesley, 'I think I'd best be off to see this gentleman friend of Mrs Dunbar's.'

'Pathetic,' said Brigid. 'I'd leave him be, if I were you.'

Caroline reached for the remote control, and the screen went blank. 'I still think Dunbar ought to go. She's let us all down.'

Her father began grunting an objection.

Lesley left them to it, and headed towards the hall.

The cellar door was open, with a feeble light filtering up from below. She peered down the steep stone steps. A clinking sound rose from below. Young Drew was down there, carrying out another of his regular tasks. When she went down to join him, he looked startled for a moment, but in control. This was part of his own world. He was carefully taking four bottles of whisky from a rack against one wall and putting them in the compartments of a sturdy wicker basket.

'Stocking up for the day?' said Lesley.

'That's right, miss. It's a dreich day. I reckon His Lordship will want to keep warm.'

'He favours one particular blend?'

'Two BNJs,' said the lad. 'And two single malts. He likes a choice.'

Against the longer wall a terrace of wine racks looked like small caves in a hillside. Most of the openings were empty.

'The burglars helped themselves here, too?'

'No, miss. That's the way they were.'

'The laird isn't a great wine drinker?'

'There were some tastings, a year or so back. But they gave them up.'

'And never replenished the stock.'

'No, miss.'

Lesley slid a bottle from its opening, and turned it carefully in her hand. She remembered working with Sir Nicholas Torrance in his Kilstane tower house, and remembered his reverence towards good clarets and a great Chablis. This sample in

145

her hand looked like a good château bottling; but the label was peeling away at one corner, and even in this muted light she thought it looked odd. The picture on the front was a typical château, and the lettering suitably restrained in dark brown print. Yet it was almost too neat.

She was getting suspicious about everything and everybody. Time to be on her way.

Young Drew waited for her to go back up the steps before following and putting out the light.

Emerging, Lesley found Lady Crombie watching her speculatively.

'Looking for anything special, inspector?'

Lesley hadn't the faintest idea what she was looking for. Off the cuff she asked: 'You used to have wine tastings, but I gather you gave them up.'

'It doesn't work out here in the sticks. We tried a series of tastings tutored by an expert, but he charged too much, and there weren't enough people attending the evenings.'

'A long way to come, especially if they had to drive home afterwards?'

'Exactly. Hector had been persuaded to lay in a large stock for his cellar, and for a while he tried running it off his own bat. Turned out to be drunken parties rather than tastings. And his cronies usually finished up back on the hard stuff.'

'It did strike me that there was something fishy about the labels. You don't suppose he would have tampered with them, if he felt so contemptuous of the whole thing?'

'That's outrageous.'

'Lady Crombie, I do have to follow up every possibility. And then rule out anything I can possibly rule out.'

'You can rule that notion out, for a start. That's not Hector's style. But he wouldn't have a clue if he'd been supplied with duds by some shyster wine merchant.'

'Who did supply the wines?'

'Some firm in Edinburgh. Hector will have some receipts somewhere. If he hasn't mislaid them.'

'I might follow it up in due course. It's hardly a priority at the moment.'

'I was about to say that,' said Brigid tartly.

Lesley settled back in her Astra and headed for Ettrickbridge.

★ ★ ★

There were few cottages on the winding road, and it was easy enough to find the one Mrs Dunbar had described.

There was nobody at home.

Next stop, the Forest Enterprise office in

the woods. Even before she drew up outside the neat wooden hutment, Lesley felt she could predict the answer she would get. No, no tree surgeon by the name of Ross worked for them or ever had worked for them.

She would have to find the name of the agency handling the few self-catering properties in the area, and see if a cheque or a credit card could give a lead on Mr Ross. It was unlikely. Anyone who had taken the time to win Mrs Dunbar's favours, learn from her exactly when the family would be away, and keep her occupied over that crucial period, would have been careful to cover his tracks.

Yet how could he have predicted when, even within a space of weeks, there was a possibility of the owners being away? How far ahead had this thing been planned? How long would he have been prepared to pleasure Mrs Dunbar before giving the signal for his mates to move in on the house?

By the time Lesley got back to Baldonald House, the rain had stopped. Lady Crombie approached the car on the drive and waited for Lesley to get out, shoes squelching on the water-logged gravel.

'Just been down to discuss clearing out stocks in the refreshment room,' she said. 'Until we know whether we can get back to the old routine, no point in letting food just sit there.' She strolled on to the grass. 'And how did you get on?'

Lesley told her.

'Might have guessed.' It was as though the matter no longer concerned her in the least.

The burn roared as they approached.

Lesley wondered how someone so direct and determined as Brigid could be so vaguely wandering across the damp grass on a drab day like this with no apparent goal. Perhaps she wanted to talk, out of doors and without family constraints. Taking a chance, she said: 'Your daughter Caroline — '

'Stepdaughter.'

'Of course.' Many a woman would have preferred to let people know that, so far as she was concerned, her husband's daughter had by now become her daughter rather than, pedantically, a stepdaughter. 'She has her own suite on the premises?'

'Not any more. She used to have what's known as the Master's suite. Meant for the older son, but there was never any son. So she lived there until . . . '

'Until?'

Brigid shrugged. 'You may as well know. Not that it has any relevance. Last year I was close to doing a deal with the National Trust for Scotland. Letting them take the place over and pay for the upkeep, with us living in one wing.'

'It fell through?'

'My husband was none too happy, but I could have persuaded him.' Lesley had few doubts about this. 'But,' Brigid went on waspishly, 'Caroline got at him, and had a fit of tantrums, and persuaded him we couldn't let ourselves do that.'

'I suppose it would feel a bit of a comedown, squatting in one corner of what had been one's own property.'

'If they'd listened to me, we wouldn't have been responsible for looking after those paintings and all the rest of it. We wouldn't have had all this hassle. It would have been somebody else's responsibility. But they wouldn't listen.'

Lesley brought it back to the main subject. 'So Caroline moved out.'

'Very moody. You never know when she'll fly off the handle, or just go into a black mood and never show up for weeks on end.'

'Staying at home in Linlithgow?'

'Oh, she's told you. Handy enough for Glasgow and Edinburgh. But as you see, she comes back when it suits her. Says she wouldn't dream of living here any longer . . . but she can't help snooping around. In and out. Sometimes I think she's debating whether or not to move in again and bend her father's ear. Then she's off again. But,' said Brigid with sudden breeziness, 'she's not the type to steal family treasures. Wouldn't want you to get that impression.'

'Or remove them to safe keeping?'

'What d'you mean, safe keeping?'

Lesley trod warily. 'Not likely to do something impulsive, like removing family heirlooms to what she would consider a suitable place? Where she could have them all to herself rather than see them being sold off.'

'She's been complaining that I've sold things off?'

'Not in so many words.'

'As I said, she's very moody. I could go for the idea of her acting on impulse. But I don't see her having the organising ability to carry out an operation like this one.'

Lesley stopped in the entrance to the walled herb garden and looked back at the house. Someone must have cased the joint beforehand to know exactly where to go — what to choose and where it was. A very knowledgeable selection. And then get it out fast, while Mr Ross commanded the attention of Mrs Dunbar. Had the McKechnies or the authoritative Mr Murray remembered the same face or faces appearing among the visitors twice running?

A brief spurt of moisture dripped from the arch on to her shoulder. She moved back on to the path.

'The house isn't open every day, is it?'

'Saturdays from noon till five, Sundays from two o'clock, and Wednesdays from ten till five. For the time being we'll tell the tour operators to keep us off their list. After all, half the things in the brochure aren't here any more.'

Under the lee of the wall, the gravel was not so much squelching as crunching. Thinking of yesterday's newspaper, Lesley asked:

'Nothing was missing from your study — the library?'

'Not that I can see. These must be art thieves, not the sort who want to flog electronic equipment in some back street.'

'You don't suppose it's all a cover? I mean, what they really wanted was the typescript of your memoirs, as far as they've gone!'

'Nobody knew about the memoirs until yesterday, after that stupid woman had blathered to the press. In any case, by Saturday we'd taken all the stuff to Edinburgh with us.'

'They weren't to know that.'

'They couldn't even have known it existed.'

'Unless your friend Miss Vaughan-Smith

has been showing off around town before it ever reached the newspaper.'

And would any interested party then be able to hack into the Crombie computer or whatever device her ghost was using? A top operator in a top company might have ways of dialling up and getting through the protective 'firewall', or working out a devious access through a rogue program on the Internet. It wasn't Lesley's own speciality. When she keyed in to HOLMES, the Home Office Large Major Enquiry System, for a record on recent art thefts and maybe a detectable parallel *modus operandi*, she would have to ask for advice on this as well.

Or if they couldn't hack in, they would risk a raid right into the house itself.

Only they apparently hadn't touched the equipment.

'It'll be interesting to know what Gregory has to say when he gets back.' Brigid Crombie's tone was almost threatening.

Lesley wondered what it would be like to work for a woman like this; and didn't fancy the idea. Not that Brigid Crombie, or Brigid Weir, whichever incarnation she happened to be in at any given time, needed to be too bullying. She somehow had enough inner force to dominate everyone, everywhere she went. Simply a centre of human power. You

153

felt that, like a badly earthed transmitter, if you stepped too close you would reach a position when you could no longer drag your tingling feet out of the force field. By which time you didn't really want to, anyway: she had snared you.

PC Kerr appeared from the bushes. He managed to look horrified and jubilant at one and the same time. He was unsure which woman to address first: Her Ladyship, or the detective inspector. In the end he spluttered: 'Ye'd better come and see what I've found.'

On a rocky twist in the downhill course of the burn, a body lay draped half across the bank, half in the bubbling water, where a jagged finger of rock had snagged into its sodden clothes. Kerr indicated they should step carefully round the man's head, to see his profile resting on grass as wet as itself.

Brigid stooped; and gasped. 'Christ.'

'Someone you know?' said Lesley.

'You've met my first husband.'

'I don't think so.'

'Gregory Dacre. The one who's gone off to London.'

'Your ghost? I hadn't realised he was your — '

'And you've met my third.'

'Lord Crombie. Of course.'

'This is my second,' said Brigid. 'Or was.'

8

Kate was still arguing as she set the burglar alarm in the hall and went in search of her shoulder bag. 'There's no reason why I should have to tag along.'

'Moral support,' said Greg.

'Moral?' She glanced wistfully back up the stairs to the bedroom. 'Not really my role. And anyway I've got this other urgent job to attend to.'

'More urgent than my needs?'

'I've just satisfied one of your needs. Let someone else have a share.'

'Such as whom?'

'I've simply got to see Tom Archer at Schwartz's. About rights in a book on the sex life of that pop singer who died of an overdose last month. Some spicy stories are coming out in a rush. Got to get it published quickly, before some of the other roadies cash in.'

She rang for a cab. After she had finished speaking, he said: 'Some drug-sodden screecher is more important than — '

'More profitable,' said Kate.

'Only in the short term.'

'And what am I likely to get out of you,' she asked, 'in the long term?'

'All right, I'll go round on my own, without the moral backing. Mind if I use your phone and fix a time?'

'You ring the Vaughan-Smithie first,' said Kate knowledgeably, 'and she'll be in a meeting, or off to see a most important author, or something. Or down with flu. Better to go without warning and haul her out. And we'll tackle Cowan while we're there.'

'We?'

'Oh, I give in. You know darned well I couldn't let you shove your head in there alone.'

'Moral support?'

'Provided you agree not to be too morally uptight when we get back here.'

The cab arrived. The driver waited with an ill grace, raising his eyes to the heavens, as Kate went through the complicated ritual of locking the front door.

The girl at Clement & Cowan reception carried a gilt tag on her left breast identifying her as Janetta. Her hair was auburn, except where a swathe of mousy brown showed through, and she had treated her face to a chalky covering which was probably advertised in women's magazines as Natural Dusk.

She exuded courteous insincerity like a waft of over-applied perfume. 'Welcome to Clement and Cowan. May I help?'

Kate said: 'We've come to see Penelope Vaughan-Smith.'

'I'm afraid she's not in today.'

'Frightened of the backlash after yesterday's paper?' said Greg.

'Sorry . . . ?'

'The news story. The unauthorised leak about Brigid Weir's memoirs.'

'I'm afraid I can't comment on that. All I can tell you is that Miss Vaughan-Smith's not in today.'

'Can you tell me where she is?'

'I'm afraid not.' The sweeter the tone, the more transparent the indifference.

'Then we'd better see Mr Cowan. Tell him Gregory Dacre's here.'

The boss's name produced a faintly more deferential response, but there was an undertone of gloating. 'I'm sorry, Mr Dacre, but Mr Cowan's in the States, sewing up a film tie-in.'

'You're sure that's not another unauthorised leak?'

'I'm sorry, but Mr Cowan's in Los Angeles, and Miss Vaughan-Smith' — she hammered it home — 'is not in.'

'Perhaps you'd be kind enough to ring her

home number and tell her we're in town. And that it's urgent we should see her.'

In the corner behind Janetta a thin blonde girl sat at a telephone panel. She half turned, with a quite helpful and friendly smile. 'We did ring her this morning. Left a message on her answering machine.'

'And she hasn't rung back?'

'No. Probably sleeping it off.'

'Sleeping what off? Some sort of publisher's launch party?'

'On a Sunday?' said Janetta witheringly. 'No, you know her.'

'Not all that well.' Greg had an improbable vision of the scrawny Miss Vaughan-Smith getting plastered or maybe sleeping with some author desperate for her approval during a wild weekend whoop-up. It was a whole new concept which he would have found difficult to introduce plausibly into a book.

'She sometimes gets a bad migraine,' the girl at the switchboard contributed. 'She'll probably be in touch later in the day.'

Janetta fidgeted in her chair, anxious to put an end to this outflow of information. Kate sounded sympathetic. 'Poor Penelope. Look, if you could just give us her home address — '

'I'm afraid it's not company policy to

158

divulge the home addresses of our staff.' Janetta took charge again.

The girl's blank, powdery mask was beginning to irritate Greg. The only way to deal with such people, said an inner voice, was to overawe them. He had always fancied ghosting the autobiography of some leading barrister, and in private had once or twice acted out the bigger scenes in order to achieve just the right tone of voice. Now he drew himself up, the fingers of his right hand curling under his lapel.

'I am in partnership with Lady Crombie of Baldonald House on the preparation of her memoirs. She is at the moment preparing legal action against this firm and against Miss Vaughan-Smith for breach of commercial confidentiality in connection with business dealings which form an integral part of the book.'

'I don't know anything about — '

'Having collaborated on a number of Clement and Cowan projects over the years' — Greg lowered his voice a throbbing half-octave but increased the volume of the bass — 'I have established a good working relationship with Mr Cowan. In this instance I have come all the way down from Scotland in the hope of intervening in time to save him embarrassment — and considerable financial loss. If I cannot talk to him or Miss Vaughan-Smith before things go too far, I cannot be held responsible for the legal consequences.'

A light began to wink on the switchboard. The girl pressed a button, said, 'I'll put you through to Accounts,' and returned eagerly to the discussion.

Kate said: 'I think it would save a lot of trouble if you would simply give Mr Dacre Miss Vaughan-Smith's address.'

'I don't know.' There seemed to be a lot of things Janetta didn't know.

Greg cleared his throat, going a further major third lower.

The telephonist was scribbling on a piece of paper. She folded it and lobbed it expertly past Janetta.

'Emma, you've no right . . . there could be no end of trouble over you handing out — '

'There would assuredly be no end of trouble,' said Greg, 'if this *hadn't* been handed over.'

As they left, Kate took Greg's arm and looked wonderingly up at him. 'You can be really masterful when you try.'

'Serious situations call for drastic action. Many an expensive legal battle could have been averted if both parties involved could have been persuaded to effect a compromise at the appropriate — '

'All right, all right. You can drop the act now. You impressed her, and you've impressed me. Now come back up from Paul Robeson level, before you do your vocal chords an injury.'

'Paul Robeson? I saw myself as — '

'All right. Scene ended. Cut. You can be yourself again.'

Taxis cruised regularly up and down this street around lunchtime, waiting for publishers and television producers to emerge and demand to be taken to the Groucho or the Garrick. In mid-morning, it was five minutes before one dawdled round the corner and set off with them to Brook Green. It stopped in the middle of the street, so that they had to squeeze between two of the parked cars which lined the full length of the kerb.

They rang twice and had a long wait before a broad-shouldered man in a midnight blue Armani suit opened the door.

'Is Miss Vaughan-Smith at home?' asked Kate in her most genial tone.

The answer was less genial. 'Why would you be wishing to see her?'

Greg prickled. The disdain suggested that the man would waste little time before brushing them both off the doorstep like a double-glazing sales team. 'And who might you be?' he demanded.

'A friend. Any objections?'

'If you could just tell her that Gregory Dacre needs to see her. Urgently.'

'Gregory Dacre?' a voice drawled from the end of the narrow hall. 'Well, now, this could be interesting. Do come in.'

Kate said: 'Greg, just a tick, I don't think we — '

It was too late. There were two men now, out on the shallow doorstep, urging Greg and Kate indoors.

For a melodramatic moment Greg half expected to find Penelope Vaughan-Smith tied to a chair and gagged. In which case he would have to fall back on his experiences as the master spy's ghost, and do a James Bond in order to free her. Or would it be more appropriate to play a tough private eve, world-weary and fearless?

Actually Miss Vaughan-Smith was sitting comfortably enough in her own armchair, looking sulky but unharmed.

There were three men in the room. Two of them wore expensive suits, the other was heavier and had opted for black leather in which he didn't look at home.

Greg studied the weighty one. 'You must be Blake.'

'How the hell do you — '

'Shut up,' said the taller of his colleagues. He had a disillusioned drawl but hard blue eyes.

'I just want to know how he can — '

'Lady Crombie described you just the way you are,' said Greg. He heard Kate's alarmed intake of breath, but went on: 'Quite unmistakeable.'

'And just what would ye mean by that?' There was the aggressiveness of a Glasgow Saturday night on Blake's tongue.

Greg leaned against the end of the couch. He ought to have been wearing a crumpled fedora, and there ought to have been a cigarette dangling from his lip. But the only headgear he ever wore was a waterproof cap, and he had never been a smoker, so that was out.

He did his best to inject a world-weary drawl into his accusations.

For all their expensive self-confidence, the other men in the room were just like himself, playing a part. Everybody in the world had a favourite façade. Sheltering behind that was often a permanent adolescent trying to persuade himself that he was really grown up, really in the big time now.

'You're a long way from home.' Greg concentrated on Blake. 'Flown down here in a panic?'

163

'I don't have to listen to this.'

Greg studied the fingernails of his right hand. The hand crept back up to his lapel; but then he recollected that this was a different character he was playing, and he let himself slump even further against the couch.

'Correct me if I'm wrong' — he drew each word out for as long as it could be made to last — 'but didn't you start out as a bluff, tough newspaperman? Drinks in the Royal Mile, confidences to be used or misused, and then that business with the procurator fiscal? Eased your way on to a quango, then started your own placement agency to manoeuvre your pawns where they could be most useful. And not just the pawns, huh? Rose to higher things without losing your laddishness. And just what are you hoping to bluster your way out of today, sunshine?'

'I'll no' be standing for this.'

'Shut up,' said the tall man again.

Greg turned to him. 'And *you* are Matthew Hill. You slept with Brigid and thought you were using her to get a leg up as well as a leg over. Instead of which she was the one who did very well out of grooming you as bag-carrier to Veitch. Right now you're here as Veitch's mouthpiece, I suppose?'

Kate plucked at his sleeve and tried to hiss a plea.

Hill kept his cool. 'We came to interview Miss Vaughan-Smith about the chapters of Miss Weir's book so far written. It appears that in spite of what she told the Press, she has no chapters in her possession as yet.'

'Quite right. She hasn't. You really have dashed into things a bit prematurely, haven't you?'

'Since you've shown up, we're not doing so badly after all,' growled the third man.

'Mr Musgrave, I presume?'

'You can cut that clever-clever stuff out. It'll get you nowhere. We want to see whatever you've written. Before things have gone too far.'

Kate was summoning up her courage. 'My client has nothing to say. Commercial confidentiality — '

'Don't waste our time,' said Musgrave. 'There's no way we're going to let a lot of lies and libels get into print. After what we read yesterday' — he jerked a contemptuous nod at Miss Vaughan-Smith — 'we want action. Immediately. Those chapters have to be handed over.'

'They'll be handed over in due course,' said Greg, 'to the publisher.'

Blake lumbered across the room and grabbed Greg's arm, squeezing it and forcing him lower and lower over the back of the couch.

'Stop that!' said Hill.

'It's the only language he'll understand.'

'We're not in any crude strong-arm business. All the same, Mr Dacre . . . ' Hill lowered himself on to the couch and looked sideways at Greg's face, thrust down towards him. 'Let's not be silly. Do you have any of those chapters with you at the moment?'

'No, I don't.' Greg wrenched himself free.

'But you can lay your hands on copies for us. By tomorrow.'

'No, I can't.'

'I want to be reasonable, Mr Dacre.'

'I think it's time we left.' Kate walked towards the door. Blake left Greg and planted himself across the doorway.

Hill said: 'Look, let's not go O.T.T. Let's just talk sense. We were disappointed to find that Miss Vaughan-Smith had been lying to the Press. And now we're disappointed that you don't happen to have brought any pages with you. But if we have to, I assure you we can get at them.'

'I doubt it.'

'Between us we have all the expertise to hack into any databases or documents which interest us. If you don't want to come clean, we can find our own way in.'

'Not me,' said Greg. 'I haven't got a modem, any link to the web or net or e-mail or anything else.'

'A real old-fashioned hack writer,' said Hill smoothly. 'How touching. But somewhere you have the files.'

'Somewhere. And an awful lot of it,' Greg taunted, 'still in my head. And Lady Crombie's head.'

'Not a terribly safe place to be.'

'Look, if you're starting to threaten — '

'Threaten? What a crude concept.' Hill sprawled back, the essence of civilised benevolence. 'Look, dear boy, we realise now that this lady editor here has spoken out of turn. I also gather that this is not uncommon in the profession. But frankly I don't give a damn for these' — he waited a good ten seconds before launching the ultimate insult — 'amateurs. You at least are not stupid, Mr Dacre. Let's start from square one. Miss Weir — or Lady Crombie, or whatever Brigid prefers to call herself nowadays — is out to be difficult. Rather than have a public confrontation which will do none of us any good, we're prepared to do a deal. For our mutual benefit.'

'For *your* benefit,' said Greg.

'Will you convey to Miss Weir that if she wishes to come back into the business world where she shone so compellingly, we know of a consortium which would be prepared to welcome her back. And forget her rather petty vendetta.'

'She'll be delighted to hear this. But not for the reasons you think. Take it from me, she won't wear it.'

'Not even if she got the Crombie treasures back?'

'Are you telling me that you and your pals — '

'I'm not telling you anything. I'm simply *asking* you.'

'You stole that stuff?' Greg tried to hide his amazement under a grand inquisitorial expression and hoped they would look abashed. They didn't; but at least Hill looked wary and was obviously struggling to shape up other approaches. 'Even before you knew about the book we're writing? You can afford to employ a seer who told you what was in store and how best to cope with it? And this is the best you can do?'

'We did not steal any of the Baldonald House contents,' said Hill. 'Good God, man, do you think that in the circles we move in we'd lower ourselves to that sort of thing? But . . . we do have our contacts. Two of my closest acquaintances are in the auction and investment business. There are bound to be whispers. They'll hear about things being shifted, and know how to stop them being shifted . . . if the price is right.'

Musgrave straightened his tie, which had not even gone crooked. 'Look, I don't think that's the sort of deal we should be offering.'

'It's a very generous offer,' said Hill.

Kate perked up again. 'Which you can fulfil?'

'All I'm saying is that we have the contacts. And if we had Miss Weir's assurance — '

'She'd as sure as hell want your assurance first,' said Greg.

Their faces told him that he had been right. They knew her of old, and they were simply skirmishing in the dark.

'We want this whole thing settled amicably.' Hill's voice was far from amicable.

'You mean Sir Michael Veitch wants it settled amicably, so there aren't any hideous revelations before he gets his peerage.'

'What revelations? Look, all we want is an amicable write-off.'

'Tell Lord Veitch not to buy the ermine yet.'

'You'll regret this.'

'I think there's going to be a fair old share-out of regrets.'

'If we put our minds to it,' said Hill, 'we can help Lady Crombie. Or otherwise.'

'In other words,' said Kate in a thin but

courageous whisper, 'collaborate or be clobbered.'

'I would never have dared to put it into words quite that way.'

But that was what he meant. The throb of menace filled the room. Yet two of the three men were respectable, rather drab business-men. And Blake, in spite of his improbably with-it attire, had worked his way into the clan. All of them members of the right clubs, especially the most fashionable night-clubs.

In that rather tatty little room it was clear to Greg that he was dealing with people who exercised power somewhere else. And a lot of it would be deployed in roundabout ways, concealed ways, deviously organised ways. Almost everywhere else.

In spite of the suave hints, maybe they could kill. Musgrave was capable of saying it out loud, but had been quietened by his two colleagues. Of course none of them would personally be capable of stabbing or shooting or strangling or running over an obstacle in their way. But they would have, as Hill had said, their contacts.

Rubbish. Greg wasn't going to believe it, not in this ordinary room with these predictable, everyday wheeler-dealers.

Maybe he ought to start believing it.

'Unless,' he challenged, 'you're going to

170

hold us to ransom and wait for a task force to set up a siege, or Brigid to come down clutching reams of copier paper.'

Kate moved into the fray. 'There are three witnesses here. Unless you're going to kill all of us . . . '

Miss Vaughan-Smith squeaked piteously.

The three men looked at one another. They hadn't known precisely what they had hoped to achieve by descending on poor Miss Vaughan-Smith like this, and now they were at a loss.

Blake tried to bluster. 'What we want you to tell Brigid — '

'Put it in writing.' Greg was beginning to feel absurdly euphoric. He had acted them off the stage, hadn't he? 'But I still don't think she'll be interested.'

'She'd better be. Pretty soon now.'

'I think it's time we left. I recommend you do the same.'

Greg had said it very firmly, and Kate took her cue by walking towards the door.

Blake said, 'Oh, no, you don't,' and grabbed the strap of her shoulder bag, wrenching her towards him.

Greg launched himself across the floor, swinging a punch into Blake's flabby paunch. Blake doubled up, retched for a moment, then steadied himself. He took two paces

171

towards his attacker.

'Any more of that, and things could get ugly.'

'You're ugly already,' said Greg in a delirium of recklessness. 'Your gut's too big, yet you haven't got any real guts.'

Blake took a wild swing at him. Greg punched again. This time Blake let out a little wheeze like a punctured balloon, and went down on Miss Vaughan-Smith's threadbare Indian carpet.

His two colleagues stared; Hill took a step forward, then looked at Musgrave for support. Moral or physical support, thought Greg rapturously: neither would be forthcoming. They couldn't possibly keep him or Kate here, or mount a permanent guard on Penelope Vaughan-Smith in her own home. They hadn't decided even among themselves what their tough strategy ought to be. They had come round here in the belief that three of them could frighten the daylights out of a woman and be given the papers she had boasted of having. It had all fizzled out.

Soft Marzipan Layer, he thought.

'Very well,' said Hill, trying to sound menacing. 'We'll leave. I suggest you and Miss Vaughan-Smith here come to a sensible decision, and relay it to Miss Weir.'

Blake was clawing his way upright with the

aid of a chair arm. 'Oh, no, we're not just going to creep out of here.'

'Oh, but yes, you are,' said Greg.

Blake tried to keep up the heat, but had a hiccup which rather spoiled the effect. 'You'll be hearing from us. Don't think you won't.'

The other two closed in on either side, and steered him out into the street.

Greg said: 'Now, Miss Vaughan-Smith.'

'Oh, no, please. After all that, you can't start on me. I've had enough.'

It was deplorably enjoyable to see her cowering, twitching, thinking up excuses but losing the thread of them halfway through.

'I think you're safe now, Penny.' He had never thought to hear himself use that name, and she didn't even blink a reproof. 'But don't talk a load of tosh to the Press ever again, right?'

'Mr Dacre, I was only trying to set up — '

'I advise you to keep a low profile from now on. If you think that little gang of would-be thugs was frightening, wait until you encounter Brigid Weir in top form.'

Outside, as they walked arm-in-arm towards Hammersmith Broadway in hope of finding a cab or, more mundanely, going back to Kate's place by Tube, Kate said: 'All right, calm down.'

'Huh?'

There was a buzzing in his ears, a sizzling flow of adrenaline.

'Come back and lie down,' she said. 'For goodness' sake, cool off. You've been overdoing it. I could have sworn that was Robert Mitchum in there.'

'Oh. I thought of myself rather as Humphrey Bogart.'

'Miscasting. But they must have seen you were bluffing.'

'What do you mean, bluffing? That one I landed in Blake's gut wasn't bluffing, was it?'

'Knight errant,' she said. 'I loved it. Robert Mitchum plus Errol Flynn plus — '

'*They* were the ones who were bluffing. Pathetic.'

'I still think you ought to lie down. All that exertion, for one in a sedentary occupation — asking for trouble. You know how to let yourself in, while I go off and make some money to pay the rent.'

'I'm in a mood to lie down. But not to calm down.' He ran his fingers along her arm.

'A change is as good as a rest. But when I get back, don't pretend to be Clark Gable.'

'I'm told he had bad breath. And unlike him, I do give a damn.'

'For what?'

'For you,' he said; and found, to his own alarm, that he meant it.

9

Reporters flocked in through the open gates. 'Any statement, detective inspector?'

'When there's anything definite to announce, a statement will be issued. Now, if you'll just let me get on — '

'I thought paintings and porcelain pisspots were more your line than murder.'

The Chief Super had already insinuated a similar opinion, making what he obviously regarded as the poor best of a bad job. 'You'll have to run the show for a while. I'm sending you two WPCs to hover over the telephones and collate info. You *can* get phones and a VDU link-up?'

'I'll see to it, sir.'

'Cope until we can get a qualified SIO to you. Right now we're badly stretched. Detective Superintendent Tranter, DCI Rutherford and the Serious Crime Squad are tied up with those multiple killings at Eyemouth.'

'I can cope, sir.'

'And you'll have to make your own decisions about an incident room. Can't spare a mobile room at the moment. One's

175

needed at Eyemouth, and the other's got a bug in its keyboards.'

'I can cope, sir,' Lesley repeated.

'Yes, well . . . it'll be interesting,' said the Chief Super silkily. 'See how you do shape up, eh? Until we can sort things out and add a bit of muscle, let's see how you hold the fort.'

Hold the fort, thought Lesley. Hold the castle. Hold the bloody stately home. Until they send in the Marines.

She knew what the old fox had meant by seeing how she shaped up. She was in line for promotion. Here was a nice test of her capabilities. Let's see how DI Gunn copes with *this* one!

There was only one possible place to set up an incident room. It had to be near the scene of the crime, linked by compatible computer technology with HQ and between different Forces where necessary. If this case and that of the burglary showed signs of spreading south of the Border, there would certainly be an overlap with English constabularies. A lot depended on the skill of the indexer at HQ cross-referencing information into categories and sub-categories, and reporting back when some significant tie-in was spotted and could be retrieved.

The Baldonald House library, converted by

Brigid Crombie to an office fitted with faxes and a VDU, already had two telephones and could accommodate another. The Chief Super might be none too happy about establishing an incident room on the actual premises, among people who might have to be regarded as suspects. And Brigid Crombie might be expected to jib.

She did. 'Where am *I* going to work? How do you imagine we're going to be able to get on with my book?'

Lesley supposed she ought not to be surprised. The woman had shown little emotion over the loss of her husband's family treasures. She was equally unmoved by the death of another of her husbands.

But where else was there to operate from? All the facilities were here, and the scene of the crime was near to hand. The library simply had to become the incident room. If Lady Crombie was determined to argue, Lesley was prepared to appeal to Lord Crombie. She found there was no need for this. Brigid Crombie looked resentful, but she knew this was the only logical place. Having, as a matter of principle, made her resentment clear, she raised no further objections.

An uneven pentagon of phosphorescent tape had been strung between posts around the corpse. As the police surgeon completed his examination and drew back, the photographer ducked under the tape, leaving plenty of space between himself and the corpse so that his feet would not smudge any significant marks. After a brief consultation with the surgeon, two SOCOs in crackling white suits drew on surgical gloves and bent over the body.

Lesley waited for their report.

How had Simon Pringle been killed? And where? Time of death?

When the forensic team had straightened up for a breather, they could announce three things with confidence, confirming the surgeon's first diagnosis.

'He was strangled. By someone wearing gloves. But not here.'

Detective Sergeant Cameron, a lean young man with greasy black hair pulled back into the beginnings of a ponytail, set off upstream with a constable dog-handler, checking every inch of the banks.

Twenty minutes after setting out, they summoned DI Gunn.

Grass had been crushed beside the burn where the body had been forced down in the lee of a blackthorn, or had simply dropped after being strangled. The heavy rain which followed made it difficult to decide which, at this stage. Electrostatic and adhesive lifters would have to be used to recover foot and hand prints, and what might be fibres and human hair. Nobody, as Lesley had told Mrs Dunbar about the thefts from the house, could pass through any area without leaving some traces of their passage.

The corpse might have lain half-concealed by the bush, in the lee of the bank, for some time if the waters of the burn had not risen and dislodged it, not so much washing it along as pushing and bumping it along in fits and starts. The damage done as it was torn by rocks and overhanging brambles would make conclusions about the death even more difficult.

'Time of death?' asked Lesley.

The police surgeon sounded fairly confident. 'Three to four days ago. I'll confirm after we've done the PM.'

Simon Pringle was removed to the mortuary in Selkirk.

Three to four days ago? Within that range, it was necessary to go through the routine of establishing the whereabouts of possible witnesses and relations at that time.

★ ★ ★

There could be no question of who came first on the list of interviews. What had Pringle been doing in the grounds of Baldonald House; and what relationship still existed between him and his ex-wife?

'None whatsoever,' said Brigid categorically.

'You weren't expecting a visit from him?'

'I was not.'

'Can you give me some idea of the part he played in your life? In the past, and recently. Anything which might be relevant to his death.'

'His murder,' Brigid Crombie corrected her.

They were sitting facing each other in her cosy sitting-room to which a tape recorder and some of Brigid's personal files had been moved. In the library, WPCs were settling in at the phones and video links.

Brigid glanced at the machine. 'Wouldn't it be a good idea to make a recording as we go along?'

'We usually do that only when we're making a specific charge against somebody, and then it's done formally at the station. Which hardly fits *you*, Lady Crombie.'

'I was thinking of my book. Since Simon will have to feature in it somewhere, it'll save time if we tape the whole story right now. Then I won't have to go over it all again with Gregory.'

Cool bitch, thought Lesley. Cool . . . no: icy cold.

The story of her marriage to Gregory Dacre and the part played by Simon Pringle came out with impersonal detachment, like bored gossip about acquaintances only half-remembered from the distant past.

'It was one of those silly youthful marriages. We were both far too young. And Gregory was no great shakes as a breadwinner. I stood better prospects of employment than Gregory did. I tried to make the best of it, but it was hard going.'

'And Simon Pringle?' Lesley tried to steer her quickly on to the essential matter of the murdered man. 'Where did he fit into all this?'

Brigid's lips twisted faintly. 'He was Gregory's closest friend.'

'Friend?'

'Yes. A pretty peculiar one, as it turned out. Old school pals, both mad keen on cycling. Though not by the time I got to know him.'

'Your husband — your first husband, that is — introduced Pringle to you?'

'Stupid thing to do. He didn't have a clue. I knew right away that Simon was a shit. Got more fun out of double-crossing a friend than facing up to a rival.'

'But you went along with the double-cross?'

Brigid eyed her for a moment as if to object to this line of questioning. Then she shrugged. 'He was a smooth talker. Knew how to get under a woman's skin. A great . . . ' She weighed the word carefully before coming out with it: 'A great sniggerer. Knew what sort of prattle people liked to hear. Especially women. How to denigrate their husbands or lovers, and encourage them to confide in him and share the sniggers. Knowing just the moment when his victim would be ripe for him to crawl into her bed.'

'So he helped to break up your first marriage.'

'Made the break-up inevitable.'

'And marriage to him just as inevitable?'

'I was making real headway in my work. Things really began to fall into shape once Gregory was out of the way.' She was assessing memories as she might have assessed the CVs of candidates for a top job. 'And Simon was always good at persuading you that his own ambitions ran parallel with your own.'

In the same month that she became Mrs Pringle, she learned of a boardroom battle in an Anglo-Scottish Information Systems group. She knew who was likely to win, and 'impartially' recommended Simon as an independent troubleshooter, known as a Strategy Consultant, making sure that he was on the side of the winner.

Lesley wondered if a grudging admiration for Simon still lingered. Anyone who could be as sly and self-centred as she had painted him must appeal to her. Ambitions running parallel to one's own, she had said.

'But in the end that marriage broke up, too,' she prompted.

'He couldn't help himself.' It was contemptuous rather than pitying. 'He couldn't keep his hands off other women. He thought it was funny, gradually letting me know about it. I soon showed him it wasn't funny.'

However bitter some of her memories of Simon Pringle might be, she was beginning to look back on this stretch of them with some relish. She told how she had thrown him out, and planted a company doctor in his firm with instructions not just what to look for but what to find. A clear case was established that Simon had learned all that was advantageous from his present employer, and was proposing to use it in a new combination with a major rival. Brigid personally apologised to the company for having shoved him on to them in the first place, and promised to find them a worthier replacement. 'Without my usual finder's fee, for once,' she smiled at Lesley. 'I did it for sheer pleasure. And made sure Simon got no chance of replacing anybody else, anywhere else.'

She had summed it all up in a matter of minutes. Now she sounded tough and dismissive about the whole episode, but Lesley was beginning to suspect that even with a cynical, knowledgeable woman like this there were hidden weaknesses. By her own admission she had been ready to fall for a smooth tongue, for a man who knew how to play on her prejudices and above all on her vanity. Lesley was left with a nasty taste in her mouth. She wondered how this woman could allow herself to record all these details in that half exultant, half sardonic tone of voice, in the knowledge that her first ex-husband and literary ghost would have to listen to every word on the tape recorder and relive a humiliating past. Was the recording in fact aimed maliciously at Gregory Dacre rather than at the solving of a mystery?

She began to feel sorry for Greg Dacre.

And for Hector Crombie.

And for anyone else who might have suffered at this harridan's hands. 'You talked about other women,' she ventured. 'Anyone in particular? Anyone who took over from you, as it were — and might be involved in his death?'

'Nobody,' said Brigid flatly. 'Once I'd washed my hands of him, that was it.'

'Look, do you suppose Pringle could have been involved in the robbery? Maybe wanting to get his own back. Did he ever visit here and have a chance of wandering around and sizing the place up?'

'When I first met Hector, I was still married to Simon. We did visit here, together.'

'How did that come about?'

'In his work, Simon had met Hector's daughter Caroline. At the television studios. Tried to wangle some free publicity out of the company, and wheedled his way in here a couple of times. I wouldn't have put it past him to fancy his chances with Caroline and see what was doing there. But I came along with him.'

'And in the end you stayed on.'

'You could put it that way.'

Harking back to her promising idea, Lesley said: 'So he might plausibly have had a finger in the robbery. Until maybe his accomplices caught him out, bungling it, or somehow cheating on them?'

'Wouldn't put it past him,' said Brigid. 'Especially the bungling and the cheating.' She glanced at the plastic window of the recorder, as if to make sure that the spools were turning and clearly putting that particular bit on the record.

Lesley tossed out another notion. 'Would either your first husband or Lord Crombie be jealous of the second one?'

'Hector wouldn't dream of lowering himself to cheap emotion of that kind.'

'Not even if he found, or suspected, that Pringle was implicated in robbing his family home of its treasures?'

'Hector,' said Lady Crombie decisively, 'will happily shoot any winged or four-legged creature that dares to move across the heavens or the landscape. He wouldn't deign to shoot or stab or strangle someone like Simon. Horsewhip him, maybe — and then rely on one of his magistrate cronies to get him off any charge of GBH. But not this. Not Hector's scene, I do assure you.'

'And your first husband? Gregory Dacre. Could he have hated your second one enough?'

'Oh, Gregory hated him all right. Nothing like the treachery of a dear old pal to brew up hatred. But I can't see him as a killer.'

'He's played a lot of different characters in his time,' Lesley pointed out. 'Sunk himself into a lot of different personalities.'

'Mm. A talent I never suspected. If it is a

talent, and not just escapism. Maybe I underestimated him,' said Lady Crombie with a hint of what in any other woman might have been wistfulness.

'But you were both in Edinburgh that whole week? You're sure of that? He didn't take time off at any point — even half a day?'

'No. I kept his nose to the grindstone.'

'But you did spend some time at that exhibition, and he wasn't with you there.'

'A couple of hours, that was all. And he'd got work to show for it when I got back to the flat. Anyway, haven't you established that the murder took place some days before the robbery? During the week we were working in Edinburgh,' she emphasised.

'You can't think of any reason why Pringle should have come here in your absence?'

'Not unless you're right about him being mixed up in the robbery. Coming here on a recce, or something.'

'That's only a vague idea.'

And I could do with a much better one, a more solid one, thought Lesley. She would have to question members of the staff all over again. Though if they hadn't got a clue about the robbery, they could hardly be expected to have noticed anything connected with a murder.

Mr McKechnie, shown a photograph, thought he remembered seeing Simon Pringle among a batch of visitors not long ago. No, he didn't remember seeing him visiting the house as a guest. But somehow he had a feeling of having seen that face somewhere, though he couldn't swear to it.

Had Simon really been in with the thieves — casing the joint for them? — or hoping to creep back and get round Brigid in some kind of deal: begging forgiveness, or pleading for help in finding another job, any kind of job?

Where had Greg Dacre been at the time of the killing? Lady Crombie had placed them both in Edinburgh; but there were questions to be asked when he got back from London. Once you could lure witnesses to contradict one another, you opened up the useful possibility of transforming witnesses into suspects.

As she went back to the house, Lesley heard voices raised on the half landing. Caroline and her father were standing in the doorway of his snug.

'Had your damn boss on the phone,' Hector Crombie was growling at his daughter. 'Damned impertinence. Thought it'd be more tactful coming from him than from you.

Tactful? Telling me who I ought to have on the premises to suit *them*.'

'Oh, dear. I didn't realise he'd be going behind my back.'

'You knew about his plan?'

'He was on the phone to me first thing this morning,' said Caroline. 'Wouldn't it be a great idea for me to be their on-the-spot reporter? Use my old room, and stay in the middle of it all. Our own reporter in the thick of it, member of the family, exclusive coverage. Take a cameraman on a conducted tour of the empty spaces, dig out some photographs of what used to be there. And clinch it all with a juicy murder story.'

'Bad enough to have those scunners trampling all over the place. I'll no' be having your cameras and nosey parkers as well.'

'And about the murder, could I ask the police to let me make an appeal to camera, direct from the house, right from the heart, for any information the public can offer?'

'I've told ye, I'll no' be standing for it.'

Caroline put her arm round him. 'And I've already told them, there's nothing doing.'

'That feller thought all he had to do was butter me up and — '

'Nothing doing,' Caroline repeated gently.

She caught sight of Lesley, and was relieved to join her and lead the way upstairs to what had once been her own room.

'Which I have no intention of ever occupying again,' she announced, pulling an armchair away from the window for Lesley, while she sprawled on the bed. 'I imagine you want to ask me some questions.'

'The usual things, which I hope you won't take objection to.'

'Such as, where was I at the time of the murder?'

'Exactly. Where were you?'

'Exactly,' Caroline parried, 'what time did it take place?'

'We estimate about three to four days ago. Maybe five. All that dragging downstream hasn't helped.'

'Meaning it could just about tie in with the robbery?'

'Or a short time before it. That's what we'll have to establish.'

'If it's around that time, then I was in the recording studio, doing a couple of voice-overs.'

'A whole day? Or over a couple of days?'

Caroline pushed back a strand of hair above her ear. 'In and out. The ordinary routine. I can probably work out the exact hours. And they'll be logged in the studio.'

'You knew Pringle before Lady Crombie . . . that is, before Mrs Pringle married your father and became Lady Crombie?'

'Oh, indeed I did.' It came out bitterly. 'He was a pest round the studios. Forever shoving himself in, trying to get references to his company — and himself — on air, pretending a plug was a news item.'

'You didn't much care for him?'

'No, I did not. Crap with legs.'

'And . . . ?'

'His wife came along. Brigid Pringle. Only she insisted on being called Brigid Weir. Coming along just to see if Simon was living up to the big business expectations she had promoted for him, maybe. And my father was there one day, and they met. I was the one who introduced her to my father.'

'You mean you already had a steady job with the company before Mrs Pringle, or Miss Weir, or whatever, came on the scene?'

'Of course.' Caroline stared. 'Now, just a minute — has she been saying something?'

'I got a vague impression that she might have been influential in furthering your career. That sort of thing was up her street.'

'Not bloody likely. As you said, I was already there before she ever showed up. Bad enough, people thinking I'm only there because of my family background. That's been an impediment rather than a help. And on top of that, Brigid . . . no, no way.'

191

Lesley steered them back to the main subject. 'So it wasn't until *you* had introduced them that a relationship began?'

'*She* began it.' Caroline blurted it out; then adopted a more measured tone, holding herself in check. 'She expressed interest in our family and the estate, and must have done some reading up on our traditions. Then, when she'd divorced Pringle, she just happened to meet my father again, and just happened to find that they had . . . a lot in common.'

'You don't know the circumstances of the divorce? Your father wasn't involved?'

'He certainly was not.'

Caroline had said that she was the one who had introduced her father to Brigid. Lesley suspected that she had never forgiven herself for it.

'You can't think of any reason why Pringle should have come back into the grounds? He couldn't have expected much of a welcome. And he didn't get one.'

'It looks to me as though he got the welcome he deserved,' said Caroline quietly.

From *you*? thought Lesley. Aloud she said: 'Thank you, Miss Crombie. Perhaps you can think back and see if anything significant occurs to you. Things do swim up out of one's memory, you know.'

'Yes, I do know.'

'You did say you're definitely not moving back in here?'

'Definitely not.'

'May I have an address and phone number where I can reach you?'

Caroline handed her a card, with a Linlithgow address and phone number on one side, and the studio number and an extension number on the reverse.

The questions she had raised with Lady Crombie went on fermenting in Lesley's mind. Had Brigid had specific reasons, or even just an accumulated hatred, strong enough to drive her to kill her treacherous second husband? Or to hire someone to do the job for her? Because he was up to something again? And if so, what?

Or was her best line of enquiry the one about Simon Pringle being one of the thieves, who had fallen out with the rest of them because he was, as usual, playing some kind of double game? Just how much useful background could he have contributed about the layout of the house?

And if Lord Crombie had come across him skulking in the grounds . . . ?

In spite of what Brigid had said, wouldn't an ex-soldier and game sportsman be capable of ridding himself of a pest who threatened the even tenor of life here? Possibly, even, suspecting his wife of backsliding and being ready to do some sort of devious deal with her ex-husband, provided the terms were right? Worrying about the threat to the tenor of his life here . . . deciding to remove the canker before it could take hold.

This was getting too theoretical. She would have to sort out the separate strands and avoid letting them snarl up into misleading patterns.

From outside there came the faint sound of tyres on the gravel. Lesley reached the top of the steps in time to see Greg Dacre getting out of his car. She hurried down to intercept him, ready to fire a few questions before he could brace himself to contrive a defence.

And behind her on the terrace, Brigid Crombie was saying in a voice clear enough not to need raising to a shout: 'Right, let's have it: just what did that ridiculous woman have to say for herself?'

10

Sullen darkness had settled down on the afternoon long before the real dusk. Late summer lightning flickered along the ridges like strobe lights in a faraway disco.

Greg supposed that he ought to be flattered by the eagerness of two women each wanting to claim his undivided attention. But between them they had all the menace of two key figures on a selection board who proposed pinning him down in their crossfire until he admitted he wasn't up to the job. And he was still trying to cope with the news that in his absence they had found Simon murdered. He ought to be given time to work out his own thoughts on that death. He had long ago learned to associate any number of unpleasant things with his one-time friend, but never anything quite so unpleasant as his manner of departing this life. Simon, beaten at last. Somehow taking that one final step too far, and getting his comeuppance. You couldn't feel sorrow, not after all this time and so many dirty tricks. But still it was one hell of a shock. Simon, out of the picture at last.

Over Brigid's protests, DI Gunn insisted

that legal necessity gave her the right to fire the first salvo. In what Greg had known as the library and main workroom for Brigid and himself, she set him in a corner some way away from a screen whose writhing shapes kept plucking at his attention, and said: 'I'd like you to tell me anything you know about the late Mr Pringle. Anything that might explain why somebody wanted to kill him.'

'Plenty of scope there.'

'Please, Mr Dacre. This is serious. We do need a lead.' She waited a moment, then fired it at him: 'I gather that Lady Crombie, your ex-wife, was also Pringle's ex-wife. Would you have any reason to believe that she wanted him out of the way?'

He wasn't going to tell her that this was the first thought that had crossed his mind when he heard the news on the radio this morning. Not that Brigid would have strangled Simon with her own hands, but she would certainly have known exactly where to go to hire the necessary executioner.

And laid herself open to blackmail?

Or was Simon himself already in the blackmail business, and that was why he'd met his end in the Baldonald grounds?

'Mr Dacre.' DI Gunn dragged him back to the present.

Greg stared around the room. He was sure

he could contribute nothing. The flickering of the screen was irritatingly hypnotic. But she was expecting some response. 'My ex-wife is, as you say, also Simon Pringle's ex-wife. From what I've gathered, she had good reason to leave him, and good reason to detest him. But that was quite some time ago. I can't see why she should suddenly up and clobber him one.'

'And your own experiences with the late Mr Pringle were so far back that you no longer felt any violent antagonism, either?'

'So Brigid's been filling you in on that? Much embroidered, I imagine. Not that Simon's activities needed much embroidered, to bring them out in their true colours.'

'You do sound as if you still dislike him. Quite a lot.'

'He was a nasty little creep, and I'm not sorry he's out of this world now, but he was nothing to do with me any longer.'

'And you can't think of anybody else who might want him dead?'

Like a kick in the groin came the thought of Ishbel. His daughter, whom he hadn't seen over all these years, but who had fallen like her mother into Simon's clutches. Where was she? If they were still living together, why hadn't she come forward the moment that news of his death reached the papers and the news bulletins? Maybe she had, and the detective wasn't telling him. Or maybe she was already on her way. Or maybe not. She might have good reasons — or very bad reasons — for not wanting to show up.

'Mr Dacre?' said DI Gunn sharply.

Until he knew just how much Brigid had told her about Simon and Ishbel, he had to stall.

'Has it occurred to you,' he improvised, 'that Simon might have been a ringleader in the robbery? Or at any rate an essential part of it. Slinking into the grounds to make a last-minute appraisal. Or even . . . ' The euphoria of his confrontation with Blake and the others came surging back, and he let the ash from his nonexistent cigarette drop on to his lap, while breathing smoke languorously out through his nose and narrowing his eyes in thought. He went on earnestly: 'Or even jumping the gun, getting here early and trying to set something up for himself. Only — yes, this could be it — they didn't trust him, and had him followed, and realised he was going to ruin the whole project. Because if he was here before the exact date and time they'd planned, he — '

'Mr Dacre, could we please do without the Belgian accent and the leetle grey cells? I'll do the questioning, if you don't mind, and

198

then make the theories fit the answers. Not the other way round.'

He waited for another question which might provoke the same crazy suspicions in the detective's mind as were already seething in his. How much had Brigid told her about the relationship between Simon and Ishbel? And how much might she infer from that?

He could hardly repress a gasp of relief when they were interrupted by a man in a white coat, peeling off plastic gloves and laying them carefully in a tray on one of the trestle tables. 'Inspector, sorry to interrupt, but I think you'd better come and see this.'

'Can't it wait ten minutes?'

'We'd rather you had a look right now.'

They went out, and Greg could give vent to a shaky expulsion of breath. But there was no respite. Brigid was impatient to pounce into the gap the detective inspector had left.

'Come upstairs and let's have it.' She urged him up to the half- landing and into Hector's snug, where Hector and Caroline had obviously been going over and over the events of the last couple of days. 'Now, for God's sake' — Brigid overrode everybody and every other consideration — 'just what did go on in London?'

★   ★   ★

Greg told of the deal that Hill had suggested.

'Rubbish,' said Brigid.

Hector Crombie cleared his throat. 'Should no' be dismissing it out of hand, m'dear. If there's a chance of getting things back — '

'No chance whatever. We don't compromise with folk like that.' Brigid smiled conspiratorially at Greg. 'We've really got them on the run, haven't we?'

A contest was more to her taste than any compromise.

Throughout Greg's summary, Caroline had been sitting very still, sheathed in tight black trousers and a black blouse buttoned up to her very white throat. Now her voice was as tight as the fabric down her thighs. 'You mean you'd put your nasty little book before any chance of recovering our family belongings?'

'It's rubbish,' Brigid repeated. 'They don't have any of the pictures or anything else, and they wouldn't know where to start looking. They're only bluffing. They don't hold any cards.'

'You can't be sure of that.'

'They wouldn't know where to start. They're crooks and shysters, each and every one of them, but not in that particular field.'

'They may have useful contacts.'

'I'm the one who gave that lot all their

200

contacts. I know them. I know their capabilities, and what they're not capable of.'

'You thought highly enough of them once,' Caroline pointed out. 'Top quality executives, wasn't that your line?'

'Not top. Just the Marzipan Layer.'

'If they're prepared to play along — if you know them so well, surely you could use them — '

'I'd rather destroy them. And the best way to do that is finish the book. Light the blue touchpaper and retire immediately! Only I'm not proposing to retire.'

Hector Crombie appealed to Greg: 'Look, old chap, would you say they could be dangerous? I like to know in advance which flank to defend.'

'They can't be dangerous.' Brigid, too, was looking at Greg. 'If they were serious, they'd have killed you. And Miss Vaughan-Smith. Bang goes the ghost, bang goes the editor. But me — I'd still be around.'

'For as long as it takes them to get to you,' said Caroline.

'Gregory, if they had any real organisation at all, they'd have found a way of getting you accidentally run over when you'd left the house. Or boobytrapped your car on the way back from the station. They had plenty of time, if they'd had any coherent policy.'

201

'You sound disappointed.'

'No, just contemptuous of the lot of them.'

'*You* would have set it up somehow!' said Caroline. 'Without wasting one moment on compunction?'

Brigid smiled but didn't consider an answer worthwhile. Looking at her, Greg knew she would have been capable of doing just that. Just as well they were on the same side — for the time being, anyway.

'And that's all you can think of at a time like this?' Caroline was still on edge. 'With all this going on here — '

'Exactly. We can't possibly work in an atmosphere like this. Gregory and I must go back to Edinburgh. Concentrate. Speed things up.'

Greg shared Caroline's disbelief. 'You seriously think we can continue as if nothing has happened?'

'How else do we spend the time? I've told them all I know. Or all it's good for them to know. And I suppose our sonsie little copper's put you through the wringer as well? And found you could tell her as little as I could — I hope.'

Greg said: 'Just how much did you tell her about Ishbel?'

He was aware of Caroline's fingers clenching over her knee until the pale skin over her knuckles went quite white. Hector, puzzled, looked from his daughter to his wife.

Brigid said: 'How much did *you*?'

'There was nothing to tell. Not so far as I was concerned.'

'Good. Because I never even mentioned her existence. No need to stir up false assumptions.'

'We can be sure they really are false?'

Caroline was as slim, dark and quivering as a snake preparing to strike. 'What the hell are you implying? You can't seriously imagine Ishbel would be capable of . . . you haven't seen her for God knows how many years, but you're ready to let her be accused of . . . of . . . '

'We owe it to the lass to keep her out of it,' said her father soothingly. 'She's had a bad enough time as it is from that Pringle blackguard. I'll nae be letting her be hurt any more than she already has been.'

'Understood?' Brigid was glaring at Greg. 'The police don't know about that dismal business between Ishbel and Simon, and they don't have to.'

'Sooner or later, if they keep digging — '

'Let them do their own digging. None of us is going to plant crazy suspicions in their mind.'

'And when they ask us why we never

mentioned Ishbel before? Our own daughter?'

'We tell them it never occurred to us. We'd both of us lost touch, and we couldn't imagine how she could be concerned.'

'Not one word.' Caroline ground it out syllable by vehement syllable. 'Not . . . one . . . bloody . . . word.'

'Let them grub away,' said Brigid, 'and we'll get on with our own work. Preferably somewhere away from here. Impossible to concentrate with all this going on.'

'I doubt whether the police would be happy for us simply to slink off to Edinburgh,' Greg cautioned.

'Since when have I been in the habit of slinking?'

A distant mutter of voices came eerily out of the wall, followed by the squawk of a table being scraped along the floor.

'You can put those files on it, out of our way.' The voice of DI Gunn echoed up what Greg realised was the laird's lug. Then a door shut, as she and her companion must have gone back into what had been the library and was now the incident room.

'We'll go and have words, shall we?'

DI Gunn was in the library with the white-coated man, bending over a photo-graph of what looked like whorled tree rings but were more likely to be fingerprints. 'A bit wrinkled, thanks to the water. But it's safe to say that so far we can't match them with any of those from the housebreaking. And on the subject of water, once we've established whether the lungs were filled with water or not, we may find he could have been held under and drowned — and that would make a difference to the estimated time of death.' He broke off as the newcomers confronted them. 'Right, inspector, I'll go and check on what data the PNC are calling up for us.'

'We can safely leave you to it, then,' said Brigid.

DI Gunn turned. 'Leave us to it?'

'Nothing much we can do here. But we certainly can't get any work done. I think it makes sense for us to clear off to Edinburgh. I'll leave you my number. But any further questions you have to ask, I'm sure my husband and Caroline can cope.'

'Lady Crombie, you really can contemplate continuing with your . . . memoirs . . . with all these matters still unsettled?'

'All these heirlooms, dry rot and rising damp — not my scene.'

Greg could see that the detective was marvelling at what to her must look like incredible callousness. She hadn't known Brigid as long as he had: there was nothing here to be incredulous about.

'It's rather more than family heirlooms now, isn't it? Your husband — ex-husband — has been murdered.'

'As you say, my ex-husband. Ceased to be any concern of mine long before he was actually deceased.'

'I'd prefer you to remain on the premises while our investigation continues. It *is* a murder investigation,' DI Gunn stressed again.

'And you're about to charge me with complicity in this crime?'

'Of course not, Lady Crombie.'

'In that case I'm perfectly free to go where I choose.'

'That's true. But as a material witness — '

'Witness? I didn't see anything.'

'Nevertheless,' said DI Gunn very steadily, 'it would seem to me that proper procedure demands your presence here until our inquiries are concluded. It will look very strange on the eventual record — very strange indeed, Lady Crombie — if your indifference to the death of a husband so soon after a major robbery plays any part in delaying or impeding the legal process.'

Greg let the splendid phrases resonate within his head. They really were superb. And the trim little CID wench was pretty impressive — pretty *and* impressive — when

206

you came to look at her; and listen to her.

He realised that Brigid was glaring at him again, and looked away.

'In the circumstances' — good heavens, for once she was giving way to someone smaller and quieter and far less domineering than herself — 'I shall yield to your judgment, inspector. Hoping that you will conclude these investigations very speedily.' Reserving to herself, thought Greg, the right to make one hell of a fuss through police complaints procedure and any other available channel if things dragged on too long.

The sitting-room would have to serve, with the tape recorder and files which had been shifted there.

'And,' said Brigid, regaining her authority, 'I'd be obliged if you'd not interrupt while we're working.'

'Unless I have some urgent question on a matter of life and death, I'll try not to disturb you.'

Greg enjoyed the steely sarcasm in the voice, and thought that Brigid could hardly have missed it.

'Well?' Brigid swung towards him. 'Are you ready to continue earning your percentage?'

From the corner of his eye Greg was aware of Caroline coming downstairs and standing briefly in the doorway, studying the two of them. He was unable to make out her expression, and thought that perhaps this was just as well.

They had only just closed the door to the small room when there was a peremptory tap on it. A WPC was outside.

'Lady Crombie, we've got a phone call through for you in the incident room.'

'I said I wasn't to be disturbed. Your detective inspector promised me — '

'I was told it was rather urgent and you'd want to know before you went any further.'

'Any further?'

'I gather it's your publisher, Lady Crombie.'

Brigid was back in two minutes in a mood of raging exultation.

'That call was from that creep Cowan.'

'Back from his American fishing trip?'

'Do you know what he's decided?'

'Not to publish the book.'

'How did you guess?'

Greg tried to assume the suavely modest expression of a world-weary adept who foresaw every eventuality. A more vulgar gesture would have been to wink and tap the side of his nose with his forefinger. 'The obvious next step, after that meeting,' he pronounced.

'He's been got at, of course. Change of editorial policy, says Cowan the craven.

Doesn't think my book will quite fit their new image. I'll give him *image*!' Her enthusiasm was rekindled. 'We go right ahead. There'll be plenty of other publishers glad to get their hands on it.'

'You're sure of that?'

'The way this is going to work out, I'm well and truly sure of it.'

'One thing, Brigid.'

He had so rarely used her Christian name. She stared. 'Yes?'

'Just where *is* Ishbel?'

'What you don't know, you can't blab.'

11

'Inspector, there's a call for you from a Dr Smutek.'

The name was a respected one in the art world. Smutek, a D.Litt of the Charles University in Prague, had fled Czechoslovakia during the Communist days when his work in cataloguing and restoring artworks in the Hradcany collection was being officially distorted for propaganda purposes. By the time the Communist régime collapsed, he was too well established in Britain to want to return.

In London he had worked at the Courtauld Institute before marrying a Scots girl and being persuaded by her to move to Edinburgh, where he set up on his own account in an art gallery off Thistle Street. Profit always came second to the all-round satisfaction of authenticity. His judgments came to be regarded almost as Holy Writ among his contemporaries. When he spoke, people listened. When he wrote to you or phoned you, there was never any likelihood of his wasting your time. Lesley Gunn had more than once relied on his opinions on questionable artworks and the probable destination of skilful thefts.

'Dr Smutek.'

'Detective Inspector Gunn.' Over all the length of their acquaintanceship his language had remained formal, yet with a faint chuckle of personal affection. 'First, may I express my regrets at the vandalism at Baldonald House. It must have been a great blow for Lord and Lady Crombie, and is doubtless giving you a considerable headache, yes?'

'Yes.' But she knew he wouldn't have rung her simply with condolences. Smutek was invariably polite, but never time-wasting. 'You've got some news for me?'

'About one of the missing Crombie pieces, yes, I have.' His accent had softened and adapted to create a strange musical mixture of flat Czech diction and Lothian lilt. 'But it puzzles.'

'Join the club. Everything about this case is puzzling.'

'You know, of course, that my wife acts as adviser to Stephanos Souflias.'

Lesley did indeed know that Janet Smutek had a lucrative part-time job looking after the Greek shipping millionaire's collections. When he was due to spend a few days or a week in Scotland, he would ring up and instruct her to get certain pictures and pieces of porcelain out of store and instal them in his permanent suite in an exclusive hotel behind Charlotte Square.

'Also Mr Souflias consults me from time to time regarding purchases.'

With any other couple it might all too easily have been a cosy fiddle. The wife knew the millionaire's tastes, and could have steered him her husband's way. Might even have persuaded him to pay over the odds for something a bit suspect, difficult to unload elsewhere. But not with the Smuteks. They had not built up their reputation by letting themselves be tempted in that direction.

'Come on,' Lesley prodded. 'What's all this leading up to?'

Smutek laughed. 'I make it dramatic, yes?'

'Yes. Now let's have the crunch, please.'

'Something has come into Mr Souflias's hands which he wished me to verify. I am able to do so. It is the Sargent painting of Lady Arabella Crombie from Baldonald House. I saw it a couple of years ago on a visit. And it is on the list your people circulated last week to the trade.'

'And it's genuine?'

'Oh, it is genuine. Most assuredly.'

'But where did it come from? If some crook has shown up offering it around, we need to —'

'It came from a colleague,' said Smutek very earnestly. 'Not in my immediate circle, and we have dealt only infrequently with him.'

'You mean he's a bit dodgy?'

'That is not what I said. He claims that ownership is well authenticated. And I have always found him honest. But the problem is . . . ' He was tantalising her again, keeping her waiting. 'It has been in his hands now for three months. And the robbery was only a couple of weeks ago, yes?'

Lesley tried to grasp the implications. 'But someone would have noticed its absence here. Lady Crombie . . . and Caroline . . . they both confirmed it was one of the items that went missing that day.'

'Strange.' She could almost see the complacent twinkle in his velvety brown eyes.

She struggled on. 'You don't suppose that the one you saw is a fake? Someone at some time made a copy, and then eased it out into the market?'

Smutek drew a slow, indignant breath. 'No, detective inspector. I have told you. This was genuine. The canvas, the texture of the paint, the brush strokes. No, this is the real thing.'

'Dr Smutek, I'm most grateful. Truly I am. Though I'm damned if I know how this fits in. How did it come into the hands of this colleague of yours?'

'Oh, that is simple.'

'I'm glad something is.'

'I told you that title was well authenticated. It was Lady Crombie herself who put it into his hands. But asked that he should be very discreet when it came to selling it on. Preferably to someone who would keep it secure in a private collection — a very private collection. And now he reads your list, and the dates do not fit, and he is very worried. My wife, too, she worries.'

'Lady Crombie? But why on earth . . . ?'

'I think that is what you are paid to find out, yes? I have said enough.'

But somebody else, thought Lesley grimly, had a lot more to say. And the sooner it was all said, the better.

⋆ ⋆ ⋆

Greg switched on the tape recorder. The physical presence of Alastair Blake was still large and sweatily real in his mind. He felt this was a good time to add some of his personal impressions to the chapter they had already sketched out. Before Brigid could protest that she had already said as much about Blake as needed saying, he spoke to her across the microphone. In his head he was

214

not so much consulting her as embarking on a political column for a newspaper exposé.

'One-time placement guru Alastair Blake has come a long way from his days as an Edinburgh journalist, and right now is in bullish mood. There have been times when rivals predicted that his move into executive placement would overstretch his resources and he would come down heavily. But he is a heavyweight in every sense of the word, not just bearing testimony to the lunches and dinners which he is known to have shared with every aspirant to power in the forthcoming Holyrood assembly, but — '

'What on earth are you on about?' said Brigid. 'The man's no guru. And there's no such thing as a placement guru. All right, so everybody in the business knows he's fat. What's that got to do with anything?'

'In a book of this kind the reader does like to get a physical impression of a character. And now I've actually met him, I can flesh him out.'

'He doesn't need an ounce more flesh. There's already a surplus on that slob.'

'That's just it. The comparison needs bringing out.'

'All right, all right. But do cut out the gossip column style. We belong in the financial pages.'

'I thought this was to be a book of gossip.'

'Revelations, not gossip.' But Brigid was in benevolent mood. The death of her second husband had cast no shadow. Rather, she was hyped up and eager to use every minute to its full. 'Nasty, discreditable facts,' she said with relish.

Greg wondered if she was in a mood to turn her attention immediately to the chapter concerning Simon Pringle. At least she could dictate what she liked now, with no fear of comebacks. But at the same time no scope for hurting, the way she wanted to hurt the others, savage them. Simon was beyond revenge now.

Instead, she went on: 'Now, since you've made his acquaintance as well, what about Hill? Time we took the business of asset management apart. And he's a good target. After that time he overreached himself securitising a bond of copyright between a record company and a pop star — and cheating them both — the regulators put him on a sort of parole for a couple of years. But now he emerges again all squeaky clean. They're letting him play games with corporate mandates all over again. But one more black mark will finish him. And finish the regulator who wangled things for him. And I know exactly where to place that black spot.'

'Hold on a minute. Before we switch to Hill, let me wrap up a few things about Blake in my own mind.'

'There's not a lot more to say.'

'Between ourselves, it was this Holyrood business he wanted to lure you into, wasn't it? Not just a consultancy, or a placement agency, but setting up a new lobbying organisation ahead of everybody else, ready for the new Scottish parliament?'

'He could never have handled it.'

'Not on his own. But that's why he wanted you and two of your top staff in, right?'

'Right. But it wouldn't have worked. He hasn't got the style for it. He'd already jumped the gun. I knew it. That's why I refused to go in with him.'

The recollection made her look even more feral and greedy than before. Greg suspected that even more than launching her missile of a book at her enemies she was itching to get back into the real cut and thrust of her old world. She had scorned Hill's suggestion that she might be taken back in if she dropped the whole idea of the book. When she did go back in, it would be on her own terms.

'You know,' she said, obviously half in that other world of hers, 'there could be a job for you in the new set-up. You'd make a far shrewder lobbyist than blunderers like Blake.

Capable of adopting whatever face is the current one, the way you've been doing it as a writer. I know exactly where I could place you.'

He couldn't resist it. 'Knowing what's happened to the last husband you found a placement for, I think I'll give that a miss.'

She laughed. Her enthusiasm embraced him, the way she hadn't embraced him since long, long ago.

'Now Simon's gone, how do we deal with him? Make a much more topical chapter after what's happened.' She got up and paced about the room. As she passed close to Greg, a warm smell came off her — a smell he suddenly remembered, at its most intoxicating in the nape of her neck. Turning at the window, she said: 'It wasn't you, was it? You didn't kill Simon?'

'How the hell could I have done?'

'If it was you, I'd forgive you. Come on, Gregory, tell me how you did it. I'll offer you an alibi if necessary.'

'We already have an alibi. We were in Edinburgh together.'

'Yes, but they only have our word for that. My word, your word. At the crucial time, either of us might have slipped away.'

Dizzily he tried to recall the exact timing of a couple of her absences, leaving him in the flat alone. No, he couldn't see that she had ever been away for long enough at any one time.

'Nonsense,' he said. 'You don't believe for a moment that I had anything to do with it.'

'Pity.'

She could not stay still. She made another circuit of the room, and stopped this time by the door. She was wearing white linen slacks and a white jacket over a crisp, turquoise blouse. Her eyes shimmered as brightly as the blouse.

Greg said: 'Did you ever go to bed with Blake?'

'Certainly not.' She leaned back against the door with her hands behind her head, tightening the blouse and jacket over her breasts. 'Look, forget Blake. Let's just talk about you for a while.'

'I don't fancy ghosting a chapter about myself.'

'You're so good at being other people. Easing your way into their skin. Under their skin. Can't you see you have the perfect qualifications for a lobbyist? Not just smooth talk, but genuine stuff from the nerve endings. No more waiting for commissions, arguing advances and royalties. Name your own price.'

'For what?'

'For introductions. For deals. Never mind the likes of Blake. He's not even Marzipan Layer. Never make it above the currants and the candied peel. Whereas you . . . I mean, that London business. Quite heroic. Didn't know you had it in you.'

'Heroic? Life's mainly plausible pretences, not heroics — wouldn't you say?'

'No, I wouldn't.'

'As a matter of interest, why did you marry Hector?'

'We get on very well together.'

'Security? Another step on the social climb. Moving ever upwards.'

'If you're classifying Simon as a step up . . . '

'You fell for him at the time. This time you've gone for dull stability, right?'

'Stability?' she snorted. 'If you could have seen the state of the finances when I first got to this house. He really didn't have a clue.'

'Dull,' Greg repeated. 'Easy to take for a ride.'

'And just what do you mean by that?'

'Persuading him to sell things off. Or leaving you to do it for him. Right? Taking over his library, stripping it, altering every-thing in the house to suit your own taste.'

'You've been listening to Caroline.'

'No, just observing.'

Perversely she was relishing his every word. Her lips parted a fraction of an inch. 'You've really come a long way, haven't you? Really, Greg, if only . . . '

'Let's get back to business,' he said. 'Keep Simon to one side for the time being. After Blake, we ought logically to get on to this Irvine character.'

'Oh, him.'

'Those few notes you dictated on him sounded pretty ferocious.'

'Disgusting little creep. Lost his nerve in a crisis. Get to the white knuckle phase in any venture capital ploy, and he collapsed. A let-down. And a let-down in other things.'

'You went to bed with *him*?'

'He was bloody useless at that, too. Tried very hard, because he thought it was the only way to get what he really wanted — a deal. But the story about his real love nest will make a juicy few paragraphs.'

Was she still harbouring a resentment against a petty slight of that kind? Old grudges still simmering so strongly that she couldn't write them off until she had held the man up to public ridicule?

'An affair?' he demurred. 'No great scandal nowadays.'

'Not the usual sort of affair, this one. Not seducing another man's wife. Seducing the man himself as the best chance of promotion. Imagine their pillow talk about hedge funds and futures! Very romantic.' Her fingers were playing with the top button of her blouse. 'The thought of it making you feel randy, Greg?'

'Never been tempted in that direction.'

'I'm glad. Wouldn't want you to waste yourself. You know something?' She undid the top two buttons. 'After that lot of no-hopers between the sheets, right now I feel deprived. And we *were* very good lovers, once. You and I, always good at that, anyway.'

The blouse loosened. Every one of her movements was graceful, calculated, impeccable, perfect timing in everything.

He made himself think of Kate. But that did make him randy. It was always too easy and inevitable with Kate. Perhaps he should have fought more for Brigid, instead of fighting with her: too often letting her choose the ground and start the fight.

Without turning round, she slid her hand down the door and turned the key.

'Come on, the couch is quite comfortable. Unless you'd prefer the floor. More room to move about.'

'I don't need every move demonstrated,' he said as steadily as possible. 'I can write all the necessary details from memory.'

'Memory. Yes.' She ran her hands over her hips. 'We were very, very good. Don't tell me we weren't.'

'Past tense.'

'Don't look so apprehensive. You haven't forgotten what to do about it, have you?' Her hands stopped moving. He wondered how many men had enjoyed this lead-in and the bonus of what followed, a touch of icing on the cake she was offering them.

Kate was whispering in his ear from far away. *If that woman decides you're going to go to bed with her, you'll go to bed with her.*

'I thought you'd settled for a different way of life. Dignified lady of the manor.'

'Oh, come on, Greg. Hector's a sweetie. But you don't have to feel guilty about him. He's too thick, bless him, to notice anything going on around him.'

'You mean too well bred.'

'Too thick is what I said. Too bloody boring. Like so many of them round here — always blathering about horse breeding, but no good as stallions themselves.'

'Maybe the mare just doesn't turn them on.'

She stiffened. 'What's the matter?' She had always been swiftly impatient. 'Lost the urge?'

'You could put it that way. This wasn't part of the contract. Nice of you, but you don't have to offer me any perks.'

The flush that spread across her throat and round her neck was beautiful. Tempting. But he wasn't going to be tempted.

'You always were undersexed.' Her fingers snapped the buttons of her blouse back through their eyeholes. 'A dead loss from the start. Think you can summon up the strength to pour us a drink?' She gestured towards the cupboard.

He poured two liberal Glenlivets. Over the edge of her tumbler he could foretell what that fading, clouded gleam in her eyes meant. Before she could shape up any more derisive remarks, he indicated the pile of print-out he had brought in. 'Has it ever occurred to you that your main motivation is dragging people down? You get more of a kick out of destroying one man rather than giving one a lift up. It's knocking somebody off his perch to make room for someone else that gives you the greatest kick.'

'It only ever happened to those without any staying power. Fit to be replaced by the go-getters.'

'Who were suitably grateful. But what about the ones you turfed *out* of jobs, to make room for your latest fancies? Don't you think there might one day be a comeback? Or several?'

'No,' said Brigid, 'I don't.'

'Still so sure of yourself. But what are you?' He felt very calm, yet puzzled that he was saying what he did. Was he, like Brigid, bent on settling an old score that had rankled without his ever facing up to it until now? 'I'm not the only one impersonating other people. You've never been anybody in yourself, either: only a manipulator of others. Living through your power over them. Nothing in yourself.'

She had ceased to enjoy his challenges. The heat of the moment hadn't led to the denouement she had wanted. 'The book's off,' she said. 'You can forget it. I'll find another ghost. Only one with a bit of flesh and muscle on him.' She wrenched the key round, but could not go out without one parting shot. 'I'll tell you one thing. Michael Veitch is the arch-villain behind a lot of this. But give him his due, as a stud he really enjoyed it for its own sake, and never mind the business deal. Once he got going, there was no stopping him.'

She swept out, leaving the door half open.

He was sure that tomorrow she would swing back again, raring to go when some other vengeful idea came into her head.

He wasn't so sure about his own commitment.

He glanced through the notes and newspaper cuttings brought in from the library and tossed on top of his print-outs. Here and there she had high-lined references to an investment consultant specialising in art treasures. One news story reported his appearance in court on a charge of resetting, but he had scraped by on a verdict of not proven. Another story, on the shinier paper of a glossy magazine, was accompanied by illustrations of some pieces he had managed to acquire for his own collection.

Presumably Brigid was lining him up for a suitably snide chapter. Or maybe there was some other reason for her interest in a shady art dealer.

He was toying with some improbable theories when there was a faint but frenzied rush of feet from upstairs. Somebody came running along the passage and pushed the door wide open. Caroline swayed there for a moment, steadying herself against the jamb.

'Where is she?'

'Brigid? She . . . she's gone off somewhere, for a few minutes.' Then he realised how stricken and tormented Caroline's face was. 'What is it?'

'My father,' said Caroline.

'What's happened?'

For a moment she seemed to have

forgotten why she had come here. Her gaze was fixed on the alcove beside the fireplace, and her eyes were widening as if some apparition from the house's past was leering out at her.

At last she said: 'He's dead. My father's dead.'

12

The call from the Chief Super was predictable. 'What the hell is going on there, Gunn? Another death, right under your nose?'

'A natural death this time, sir.'

'How can you be sure?'

'His own doctor, sir. Been expecting it one day. He's been liable to strokes. A couple of mild ones, but this was the real thing.'

'One hell of a coincidence. A burglary, a murder, and now this.'

'The family think ... ' She stopped, because she knew just how Caroline's remark would be received.

But it was too late. 'The family think what?'

She hastily skated round the words Caroline had actually used. 'They think that the losses from that burglary had a deep effect on Lord Crombie. The worry wore him down.'

'You believe that?'

'I think I do, sir. It really did prey on his mind. There must have been real anger boiling up inside.'

'Hm. I think I'd like a second opinion on this.'

Poor Crombie, thought Lesley. In any other circumstances his death would have been simply recorded, just as his own doctor wanted to record it, and there would have been no reason for extra indignities. But other investigations had been going on around him, and he couldn't be kept out with them. Nobody and nothing could be regarded as innocent and straightforward.

More paperwork. More unpleasantness for the family.

'He died of a broken heart,' was what Caroline had actually said.

Lesley's uneasiness conflicted with her sympathy for the bereaved daughter. 'We . . . well, in our line of work we don't often find cases of that.'

'You don't believe anyone could die of a broken heart?'

'Well . . . '

'I believe it,' said Greg Dacre quietly. 'Even if you don't actually die right away, you can suffer a hurt that'll fester until in the end it kills you. Unless you find an antidote to fight it.'

Lady Crombie's only comment was: 'Hector did let it weigh on him too much. Out of all proportion. They were only *things*.

I did try to get him to see it all in proper proportion.'

It was difficult to intrude on family grief — though Caroline seemed to be the only one showing any real grief. Not that she looked for sympathy. Certainly she did not want to exchange even conventional condolences with her stepmother. After that first stricken outburst, she had remained cool and practical. Offered the chance of handing over some studio commitments to a colleague who was prepared to give up free time to help out, she drove to Glasgow and then on to Dumbarton for some historical re-creation, and then was back at Baldonald to keep an eye on things.

To keep an eye on her stepmother — from sympathy, or suspicion?

Lesley found herself confronted by a tricky balancing act. She had to smooth the ruffled feathers of the doctor with a tactful request for a second opinion on Lord Crombie's death, and ease her way in and out of the funeral arrangements while still pursuing the evidence in the case of Simon Pringle.

The Chief Super might be wrong in doubting the coincidence of Crombie's death. But surely there could be no mere coincidence between Simon's death and the burglary. There had to be a link.

Lady Crombie, seizing the reins to set in motion the arrangements for a funeral announcement, positively enjoyed answering phone calls of commiseration over the next two days. Then there was the matter of death announcements in *The Times*, *The Daily Telegraph*, and *The Scotsman*. Notification of the family solicitors. Tie everything up, be done with it.

For a moment Lesley was tempted to go for her, here and now, with a blunt question about that painting which Smutek had reported. Her old bully of a DCI, Rutherford, wouldn't have hesitated. Catch 'em while they're most vulnerable, he would have snarled. But Lesley couldn't bring herself to tackle a woman so newly widowed. It would have to wait. In the meantime, she settled into a corner of the library to assemble such fragments as they had collected into the beginnings of a jigsaw which must be completed before too long.

There was news of the credit card with which the mythical Mr Ross had paid for his cottage by the Ettrickbridge road. A professional forgery, re-imbossed upon a genuine card, it had turned up across the Border in Carlisle. The man trying to use it had been arrested and was in custody. Unfortunately he was not the man they were looking for. He had found the card in a litter bin and been silly enough to take a chance on using it. He was known to the Cumbrian police as a petty crook and a clumsy chancer, but with no known connections with the shady art world. Among prints on the card were some which matched up with those found on the electric cooker in the cottage kitchen, but not with any of the prints from within Baldonald House. Not surprising, thought Lesley wearily: Mr Ross had merely been the one deputed to keep Mrs Dunbar occupied away from the premises while the actual raid took place. Once it was over, he discarded both Mrs Dunbar and the stolen card.

She went through sheets of notes and records of incoming calls. The main facts that the girls at the VDUs and telephones had to report were scattered details about Simon Pringle's movements in the weeks before his murder. Nothing out of the ordinary there. He had been doing freelance work for the computer division of an office equipment firm, his schedules and movements being left very much to himself; but had been seen a couple of times by the firm's manager in Edinburgh having what looked like rows with a fair-haired girl who had apparently been giving him a lift in a hire car.

His home address at the time of this

employment had been traced to a bed-sitter in a back street between Musselburgh and Leith. The landlady there was reluctant to talk about any of her tenants, whom she referred to as 'guests', and when it was revealed that the questions she was being asked were connected with the murder she had avidly read about in the papers, she tried to make out that there had been a mistake and it must be a different person, and she made it a rule never to accept rent from a murderer or anyone of that ilk.

Gradually she was persuaded to speak more freely when it was made clear that the police were not blaming her for not spotting a born killer, and furthermore that they were not interested in what rents she charged or declared to the taxman.

The main thing she contributed was that for some months he shared the bedsit with a blonde girl who he said was Mrs Pringle, though the woman hadn't believed this for a minute. It was often the girl who paid the weekly rent, nearly always in cash. Again the informant slowed down at this stage, obviously thinking again of a tax vulture swooping on payments in cash and just what records were kept, or not kept.

No, she didn't know where the girl had gone. Both of them had left at the end of last month. She thought they had quarrelled, and that didn't surprise her. It wouldn't have been the first time she'd heard a row going on. Nasty, sneering type that Pringle fellow had been. But at least they'd paid up before they went, even if they didn't give a week's notice as they were supposed to do.

Who on earth was the girl, and where was she?

Overlapping the matter of Simon Pringle's death — and Lesley was convinced there had to be overlapping and interweaving between the two — were inconclusive bits and pieces about the burglary.

There was still no trace of the van which had been seen here on the day of the thefts. Not surprising, with so little identification to go on. Two vehicles which had been stopped on suspicion within the first twenty-four hours had yielded no stolen artworks, though the Strathclyde police weren't displeased to find that one of them contained a load of drugs smuggled in through Stranraer. No whisper of any artworks slipping out on to the market, except that one puzzling item reported by Dr Smutek which must have been removed before the burglary. Removed and replaced by a fake? Or had Lord Crombie known about the sale, bitterly as he might have regretted it? There was no chance of asking him now.

And as to Pringle's murder, could a lover's tiff with some blonde girlfriend have blown up into a crime of passion?

It was time to go looking for that girl, whoever she might be.

Lesley felt wretchedly that she needed help: someone to bounce ideas off. And she knew who she wanted it to be.

If he was prepared to listen.

She had no intention of letting the two WPCs in the incident room hear her appeal. There was a phone in the sitting-room where Brigid Crombie and Greg Dacre, banished from the library, had worked. After one interruption, Brigid had apparently locked the intervening door to keep any of the incident room staff blundering in on the two while they were working. Lesley went out into the corridor to use the outer door.

Halfway down the main staircase was Brigid Crombie, smartly dressed in black: suitable mourning attire ready and waiting in her wardrobe, one felt. Always prepared for any occasion, was Brigid

Weir cum Lady Crombie.

'Back to bloody Edinburgh,' she announced.

'Lady Crombie, I don't think you ought to — '

'There are things that simply have to be done by someone who knows how to do them. Got to see our solicitors, and Hector's broker, and the chairman of his club. They'll probably want to send some sort of solemn delegation to the funeral. *When* we're allowed to settle the date,' she added heavily. '*Somebody* really does have to cope with all these matters, inspector.'

'Couldn't you send your daughter — your stepdaughter, I mean?'

'She's got another of those pathetic weekly television chores to go through. Couldn't get out of it at short notice, but she'll be coming back via Selkirk to have a word with the minister.'

'He'll be holding the service in the chapel?'

'God forbid. I simply won't have that. The chapel's a wreck. And a dangerous one at that. The family vault's for worms and rats. Hector always said he'd prefer to be cremated. Scatter his ashes along the loch — that's the way he'd have wanted it.' She eased her way politely yet forcefully past Lesley. 'And now, if you'll excuse me, I really must be on my way.'

Lesley dialled the Black Knowe number from memory.

'Torrance.'

'Sir Nicholas. Detective Inspector Gunn here.'

Why hadn't she just called herself Lesley Gunn? There had been a few days when she had thought there might be something between them. She had helped him solve the mystery of a missing quaich, and between them they had exposed a sheet of music as a forgery and an historic legend as a mockery. They had drawn very close together, hadn't they? With a shiver of chagrin she admitted that she wouldn't mind having an excuse to be close to him again.

'Hello there, detective inspector.' Just as solemn yet jocular as Dr Smutek.

'I need your help.'

He must have remembered at once the way they had solved the problem of that supposedly traditional song which had been a contrivance. 'Don't tell me somebody's threatened to reveal that all Rabbie Burns's songs were really written by William McGonagall?'

'Right now I'm at Baldonald House.'

'Isn't that where they've just discovered a chunk of Roman pavement?'

'Glad you're still in touch with real history.'

'Someone's lifted the lot and flogged it to the Americans?'

'Nothing to do with the pavement.' She was in no mood for banter, though the mere sound of his lighthearted, laid-back voice could almost persuade her that seriousness was a mug's game. She decided to lead into the problem gently. 'You're a bit of a wine expert.'

'I wouldn't say that.'

'Knowledgeable enough to help me in a problem I've got.'

'What sort of problem? What to order early for Christmas?'

'Nick . . . ' She had no right to use his name so fondly, with such a rush of memory. It made no sense. But she had said it and there was no taking it back. 'It's a matter of a cellarful of vintage stuff, or what was a cellar, till most of it was nicked. They must have had a large delivery van to shift the stuff. Belting up the A1 and cutting across the Merse, it's all too easy nowadays.'

'I'm flattered, but — '

'And I'm puzzled by the labels on the bottles that are left.'

'Labels?'

'I'm sure there's something odd. Oh, and,' she added, 'there's been a murder.'

'Count me out.' He sounded very firm. 'Never mind the cellarful of wine. Or cellar half full. Or a quarter full. Me, I've had a bellyful of murder, thanks very much.'

'Please, Nick.'

'And in any case, I've been thinking of spending a couple of months in the south of France. Wallowing in wine, since you mention it. Recuperating from all our own melodrama here. Maybe even composing a masterpiece.'

His own melodrama, she thought wryly. She would concede that it had been weird enough at Black Knowe, but when it came to melodrama, could it hold a candle to Baldonald?

'When would this be?'

'As soon as I can get packed.'

She couldn't restrain herself from asking: 'With anybody special?'

'Haven't got as far as thinking about that.'

'I'm sure,' she said despondently, 'you can find plenty of volunteers.'

So that was that. Daydreams down the drain. And technical assistance swirling away down the same plughole.

She went upstairs, hooked now on this irritating business of the wine labels rather than on the decease of Simon Pringle — certainly no fine vintage year himself. There had been a bottle in Lord Crombie's snug. Not his usual tipple, but perhaps he had felt in the mood for a change from the malt.

She had not expected to find Gregory Dacre there. Nor had she expected to be greeted with such a questioning gaze, as if he knew something she didn't and was wondering whether to tell her, or wanting to sound her out.

She picked up the bottle. She was no expert, but she was sure this vinegary smell was no recommendation for the contents.

From out of the wall there came a sound like a door slamming. As its resonance faded, she knew it must come from downstairs. Yet it had been immediate, echoing into this room. She stared at him, and in a flash of wild guesswork said: 'As a matter of interest, when you and Lady Crombie were working together in the Edinburgh flat, did you go to bed with her?'

'What's that got to do with you? Or anybody?'

'So you did.'

'No, I didn't.'

'Or here? In this room?'

'This is bloody monstrous. What the hell has this got to do with anything that . . . I mean, with anybody who's been disillusioned enough once — '

'Once your successor was out of the way, old mistakes could be corrected. You'd both made a mistake, but once you'd got together again you found that — '

'Look, if you're trying to set me up as

240

being jealous of bloody Simon — '

'Weren't you?'

'Once upon a time. I grew out of it.'

'And it didn't start nagging again when you were with your ex-wife?'

'I've told you — '

'She *is* your ex-wife. I thought maybe, with you ghosting her memoirs and sort of getting to grips with her in a very intimate fashion, one might imagine you could be drawn closer again.'

'That's what I'd call a lively imagination.'

'You didn't even consider it?'

'I did not.'

Something in his tone jogged her attention. 'Did *she* consider it?'

'Not in Edinburgh.'

'Here, then?'

Instead of dodging the question or indignantly asking what the hell this had to do with anything, he rose to the bait. Old rancours died hard, if ever. 'She could never bear to take no for an answer.'

'That figures. But this time she got a no?'

'All those reconciliations, way back. When Brigid wanted it, and only when Brigid wanted it. Gushing on about how silly we'd been — meaning how silly *I'd* been — and come on, let's make beautiful music again. To her tune, of course.'

'She wasn't pleased when you turned her down this time?'

He was putting the brakes on, a bit late. 'Who says anything about turning her down, or not turning her down? And what's it got to do with Simon's murder? Or Hector's death, or any other damn thing?'

'You're still going ahead with the book?'

'She keeps changing her mind. Maybe I'll change mine.'

'What might influence her? Whether you were in the mood to satisfy her in every particular, or whether your — um — prose style wasn't quite as poetic as she'd have wished?'

'You've got her wrong. Whatever you gave her, physically or mentally, it had to be exactly the way she had decided it ought to be. Nothing poetic. No reservations. Just get at the fundamentals when you're ordered to.'

'Which you rejected.'

It dawned on him that she was staring questioningly at that gap in the wall — the laird's lug. Wretchedly he said: 'I've been wondering. You don't suppose Hector could have heard?'

'Heard what?'

'Enough to give him a stroke.'

'Can you tell me exactly what you and Lady Crombie said? Or what you were doing that might have hit him that hard?'

'We weren't doing anything.'

'But what you were saying. Can you recall that, word for word?'

'I'd rather not.'

'Mr Dacre, I may have to insist.'

'What good will that do now? We don't know for sure that he did hear.'

And there were no other witnesses. When Caroline Crombie found him, her father was already dead. Even before rushing downstairs to tell the others and then calling the doctor, she had been quite sure of that. And whether he had heard it or not, the conversation of his wife and Gregory Dacre, no matter how inflammatory, didn't constitute a criminal offence. Not in any category so far established. ABH — Actual Bodily Harm. GBH — Grievous Bodily Harm. UMH — Unprovable Mental Harm?

Lesley Gunn was in a bad mood as she got ready to drive back to the *Tam Lin*. Somebody had to pay for all this. Somebody had to help her prove to HQ that she was capable of solving a mystery on her own, wrapping it all up, fingering the villain. She would show them.

On impulse she took the exit road past the west gate. She slowed as the lodge came into view, and found herself stopping on the level stretch of tarmac beside it.

Mr Murray kept her waiting a few minutes before answering the door. He was profuse with his apologies. 'I'm sorry. Keeping you on the step. So sorry. I was playing about with the scanner, and had to close it down safely. Wouldn't want to lose my designs, you know.'

She followed him into the main room. Through an open door she could glimpse a pattern of coloured cubes and parallelograms flicking and interlocking across a screen.

'Designs?' she queried.

'A new brochure for the house, purely tentative. Skating round the missing items, you understand. But now, with Lord Crombie dead, one wonders what the future will be.' Murray raised his large hands in a splayed gesture of grief. 'I'm sorry. So sad. So very, very sad. Poor Lady Crombie.'

Lesley recalled that on her first interview with Mr Murray she had sensed her old colleague and antagonist DCI Rutherford standing at her shoulder, eager to strike rather than discuss. She had balked at the idea of tackling the bereaved Lady Crombie, but right now she was in a mood to emulate him.

'Designs,' she repeated. 'Including some wine bottle labels?'

Murray's hands descended slowly, one

plucking at his beard as if to steady his head and stop it wagging to and fro. 'I'm sorry?' Same words as he had used a minute ago, but with a very different, shaky inflection.

'Who asked you to forge those labels for a load of inferior wines?'

'Inspector, I don't know what you're talking about.'

'I assume we could call up all the individual specimens you've got lodged in that machine? Just out of curiosity, I'd like to run through them.'

'This is outrageous!' Murray eyed the door to the next room.

'Don't try it,' said Lesley. 'Don't try wiping it all.' She slipped her mobile from her bag. 'If you're not prepared to co-operate, I'll get one of our girls down from the library. They're both dab hands at this sort of thing.'

He went on tugging at his beard, and still his head went on shaking in hopeless denial.

At last he croaked: 'It was only a joke.'

'On whom?'

'It was a challenge to design the labels, find the right paper, run them off. That's all, truly it was.'

'And who issued the challenge?'

He gulped. 'It was Lady Crombie's suggestion. The original wine tastings had cost too much to set up. Tutor's fees, cost of

245

selections of good wines, and so on. So Lady Crombie suggested cutting out the frills and substituting a sort of . . . well, cut-price function.'

'And people were easily fooled?'

'The Crombies' friends just enjoyed the socialising. Their palates weren't exactly on connoisseurs' level. Socialising and drinking just for the fun of it. No harm in that. And the police are too busy in the towns to do much breathalysing round these parts.'

'So you forged some impressive labels,' Lesley summed up, 'and conned the Crombies' acquaintances into paying through the nose for cheap plonk.'

'It was a bit of a joke between us — Lady Crombie and me.'

'And Lord Crombie was in on it?'

'Oh, no. Lady Crombie felt he wouldn't countenance it.'

'No. I don't imagine he would. But didn't *anybody* ever complain they were getting rot-gut?'

'It wasn't all that bad. Just a bit cheaper than what the lecturers had been giving.'

'Just an excuse, in fact, for a piss-up.'

Lesley let him stew for a minute. He had another tug at his beard, spread his large hands on his knees, then glanced desperately at the sliding patterns on the screen beyond the doorway. If some telepathic remote control had been available to switch it off, he would have blanked out that geometric shuffling in the hope that every other shred of evidence would miraculously disappear with it.

At last she said: 'Lady Crombie has quite a hold over you?'

'She's been the one who's kept me going here.'

'She'd have thrown you out if you didn't play ball?'

'I owe Lady Crombie a lot,' he said stiffly.

She knew he had been a schoolteacher, but had not asked why he had given it up and come here. He could be old enough to have retired in the normal run of things; but on the other hand, if it was some years back . . . She wondered what had driven him here into Brigid's clutches, and why he had let himself be led into a cheap little job of forgery.

Abruptly she said: 'You taught art, didn't you?'

'I . . . that is, when I taught at the Academy . . . yes, art was one of my subjects. I've made good use of it,' he added defensively, 'in the brochures I've designed for the house.'

'And helped Lady Crombie even more? Used your knowledge of paintings, and their value, and how to make copies which would fool the ordinary viewer if hung in shadowy corners?'

'No,' shouted Murray. 'I'd never have done that. Never.'

'But were you asked? You say you'd never have done it. But were you ever *asked* to do it?'

'No.'

'Would you have been surprised if it had been suggested to you?'

He looked more and more unhappy. 'I don't know anything at all about the pictures.'

'You couldn't have set them up on that machine of yours?'

'Of course I couldn't. It's too small. It would take a much bigger scanner to produce a template to work from.'

'But then the forgery would be simplified?'

'Painting by numbers,' he grinned feebly. 'Yes. But I never had any part in anything that big.'

'You knew Simon Pringle, the dead man?'

'I just may have seen him. But I don't see what that's got to do with wine labels or paintings.'

'Neither do I. Not yet. But somehow it's all tied in with everything that's been going on. Forgeries, robberies, deaths . . . '

'Lord Crombie's death.'

'What about it?'

'That's the worst of it. A great gentleman. I'd never have wanted him to be hurt.'

Hurt by finding out that his wife was flogging off the family heirlooms, wheeling and dealing behind his back, and when the going got sticky was having forgeries made to replace the genuine stuff she'd flogged off without even letting him get a glimmer? 'Using your own knowhow' — she came back to worry away at that nagging notion — 'to put a proper value on the real paintings, and help her to contrive replacements.' Inspiration struck breathtakingly. 'Replacements,' she said, 'which had to be stolen when some items were due to be loaned out on international display, to hide the fact that they were fakes.'

'I've told you, I don't know anything about that. It's all too incredible.'

'Incredible? Oh, and while we're at it, you wouldn't be a dab hand at forging credit cards, would you?'

'Credit cards?' He looked genuinely perplexed.

'*They* wouldn't be too big for your scanner.'

But she couldn't really believe he was any more than a minor player in a devious and growingly dangerous game. She also believed, though, that in that minor way he had been used, and that other men had been used in a major way. Why had Brigid been so sure, after being told by Greg Dacre of the cabal's threats and offer of help, that nothing could be done about it? Very quick to poohpooh the remotest possibility of their having any way of getting to the loot and restoring it on their own terms.

Because she already knew where it was?

A lot of things were shifting to and fro in DI Lesley Gunn's mind like the interlocking patterns on Mr Murray's screen. Most of them were edging in to close around one woman in particular. She ought to have tackled that woman head-on; ought not to have let her swagger her way off so easily.

When Lady Crombie got back from Edinburgh, she would stay right here until she had answered a lot of questions.

13

Duncan McIntyre was a man with a wide, flat face and a chin so shallow that it looked as if someone had sliced a few inches off it with one clean stroke. The sag of his lower lip, so close to the chin, gave all his pronouncements a melancholy droop of their own, and his shiny black suit was at odds with the teak and rosewood modernity of his office furniture. Brigid had always suspected that he kept himself looking so seedy and olde-worlde in order to impress old-fashioned clients like Hector and his contemporaries, while holding in reserve a character in keeping with the fixtures and fittings.

Today he had better be bang up to the minute and ready to tackle immediate concerns.

She said: 'What about our unfair dismissal case? You've had time enough to get a boot up Sandy Cameron's backside. What sort of squeal have you had back?'

'Lady Crombie, one has to work in reasonable consultation with your old company's legal advisers. One tries the reasonable approach first.'

'Carpet slippers make no impression on shysters like that.'

McIntyre appeared shocked by her priorities. 'Surely,' he said in the tone reserved for clients of an older, more courteous tradition, 'it's more important at this time to settle the problems of your late husband's estate? I need hardly say how distressed we've all been here by the news, after all the years we have had the honour of — '

'Naturally I'm here to discuss that as well. But it shouldn't take long. I don't envisage any major problems. Knowing my late husband, I'm sure everything's straightforward.'

McIntyre cleared his throat apprehensively. 'Well, yes, Lady Crombie. Of course. Very straightforward.'

'Well, then. You've got the will here?'

'Er . . . yes.'

'Come on, man, what's wrong? Don't tell me Hector forgot to get it properly witnessed, and you let it slip?'

'Certainly not. We do not make errors of that kind in this establishment.'

'No, of course not. And anyway, I remember just after we were married he sorted out every last little detail, and I think it was the chairman of his club and the secretary who witnessed his signature. Both still alive, so they can verify that if they have to.'

McIntyre seemed to have a further obstruction in his throat. When he had cleared it, he said: 'There has actually been a later will, Lady Crombie.'

'What? He never mentioned it.' She brought the full power of her gaze to bear on the man. 'There can't have been any major alterations. No reason whatsoever why there should have been.'

McIntyre summoned up the courage to adopt the sharper, more aggressively modern image with which he overawed clients of a more recent generation. 'Not to put too fine a point on it, Lady Crombie, your husband did change his mind on several particulars. We may as well face it.'

'We may as well face it?' she snapped. 'Face what?'

Rather than continue meeting her gaze, McIntyre looked down at the document on the desk before him and recited at high speed the salient points.

Hector, Lord Crombie, being of sound mind and hereby revoking all former wills and testamentary dispositions heretofore made by him, hereby declared this to be his last will and testament. To his wife Brigid, Lady Crombie, he bequeathed five thousand pounds and any two paintings of her own choice — 'from such as remain of those

which my dear wife has not already sold off,'
quoted Mr McIntyre: 'that's the exact
wording.'

'I don't understand.'

'I think it is expressed without ambiguity.'

'And the rest?'

'The rest' — he was still not daring to look
at her, yet seemed to be taking a malicious
pleasure in his own sing-song delivery — 'to
be divided evenly between Lord Crombie's
daughter Caroline, and — ah your daughter, I
believe, by a previous marriage? . . . Ishbel
Dacre.'

Brigid could not believe that all this was on
the document in front of the man. Yet he was
hardly capable of making it up as he went
along.

'It makes no sense. He can't do that. After
all I did for him, livening the place up,
putting it back on its feet.'

'I got the impression that Lord Crombie
felt your own business interests would
provide you with a more than adequate
income. And that it would be unfair to
saddle you with the burden of caring for the
estate.'

'And who's been saddled with that burden
these last few years anyway?' Brigid tried to
keep her voice steady. 'When was this absurd
will drawn up?'

'Three months ago. There has been no revision since.'

'Three months ago. *Before* I retired from those so-called business interests, to devote myself to my husband and the maintenance of his property.'

'Since he made no move to alter the terms of the will in these altered circumstances, one can only assume that he still felt it would be unfair for the estate to continue being a drain on your resources.'

'And what resources are those two girls supposed to have, for goodness' sake? Look . . . somebody's been going behind my back. Those two . . .'

'I am sure Lord Crombie meant everything for the best.'

'I shall contest it, of course.'

'On what grounds, Lady Crombie?'

'Obviously the balance of his mind was disturbed.'

'Not so far as I or the witnesses observed at the time of drawing up this will.'

'Witnesses? And who were they?'

'Clients of my partner's. A doctor and his wife who were on the premises at the time. Quite impartial. Nothing in it for them, you understand: witnesses cannot be left anything by a testator.'

Brigid could not bear to sit here any longer

being condescended to by this grisly little pipsqueak. She got up and turned towards the door.

'You'll be hearing from me.'

'I shall be getting in touch with you very shortly, Lady Crombie, to give you confirmation of — '

She did not wait to hear the rest of the mumbo-jumbo.

As she stormed along the street, she ranted to herself. How the hell would that dismal mausoleum have survived without her? And all the time she was doing her best for him, Hector must have hated her. Hated her for opening up the house and grounds to the public, and selling off some of his crummy pictures? There had been no other way of keeping up with the running costs. He ought to have been grateful to her for shielding him from reality. Poor Hector. Stupid old creep. He had always been too naïve and unobservant to realise that even more of his belongings had disappeared than he had been told about.

If only he had known the full story behind those disappearances, leading up to the culminating robbery! In spite of her rage, she could not suppress a smile.

Her next call had better produce more satisfactory results.

She went down the area steps to a window dark with paintings of seascapes, and through the door beside it.

'Lady Crombie, I was wondering when we'd have the pleasure of meeting again.'

She was in no mood to waste time on pleasantries. 'You know of my husband's death, of course.'

'Of course, Lady Crombie.' Kevin Murdoch had the long, yellow face of an unctuous kirk sidesman, with a faint twist of his lips to the left of his mouth, suggesting hypocrisy rather than devotion. But he was not hypocrite enough to pretend any sympathy over the death. 'This will mean an alteration in your plans?'

'I'm no longer prepared to wait for the money. We shall have to conclude some deals fairly sharply. You can dispose of the authentic ones before it's safe to leak the others out gradually?'

'We do know our business, madam. Everything is as we agreed. And we've established contacts with willing buyers. We can crate and despatch the half-dozen we have here, and spread the others gradually just as soon as you . . . um . . . release the material from storage.'

'It'll have to be immediately after the funeral,' said Brigid. Already she was working

257

out timetables in her head. She visualised the cortège, the to-ing and fro-ing, the winding up afterwards, the exchange of condolences ... And herself out of the house, handing over to those ridiculous girls. She would fight the will, of course. It couldn't be allowed to stand. She wouldn't let herself be insulted like that. But for a while it might mean going back to the Leith flat and the world where she could make herself at home again. A lot of confusion for a time, a revision of her working schedule, a brief period of readjustment ... but yes, it could all be tied in satisfactorily. 'After the funeral,' she repeated. 'I would suggest two weeks on Friday. I'll confirm by our arranged signal. Otherwise no contact. Understood?'

'Quite understood. That's how we've operated so far, Lady Crombie.'

Murdoch half bowed as he held the door open for her to leave. It was a disdainful gesture rather than a deferential one.

She had reached the corner of the street when a tall figure cut across from the narrow pavement opposite to intercept her.

'Lady Crombie. What a pleasant surprise.'

For Brigid it was a surprise, but not pleasant.

'Visiting the Murdoch establishment?' he asked blandly.

'I have a lot to do today, Sir Michael.'

'We never used to be so formal, Brigid.'

Brigid shook her head. 'I have rather a lot to do today. You'll have heard of my husband's death, of course.'

'Of course.' He sounded as little regretful as Kevin Murdoch had done. And suddenly, lethally, he added: 'I trust you had him fully insured?'

Brigid had an angry feeling that somehow everyone today was laughing at her — at her and certainly not with her. She wasn't used to it. She longed to shake them all off and finish her programme here as swiftly as possible. And then sit and think about the full significance of Hector's appalling will.

'There's a nice little French restaurant just round the corner here,' Veitch persevered. 'However much you had to get through in a day, you always used to appreciate a good meal.'

'Right now I'm not hungry. And I really do have to get round an awful lot of places.'

'An awful lot. Yes. But it might clear your mind to have a nice informal chat about the arts in general. Books — like the one you're writing. And paintings — like the ones on which you're hoping to make a double profit. Insurance money plus what you can flog them for overseas.'

'I don't know what you're talking about.'

'Brigid, you've always had some damn good contacts. And some very dubious ones. So have I. It was inevitable that sooner or later we should meet at a crossroads.'

His drawl grew more and more affected. She knew it had been laboriously acquired, and that he had lost his own real voice long ago. He had made a better job of it than, say, Alastair Blake; and had also managed to acquire an infuriating self-confidence.

Hoping to dent it, she said: 'As a matter of interest, were you behind Simon's murder?'

'Simon?'

'You know perfectly well. Simon Pringle. Killed on our estate.'

'Ah, yes. Do you really suppose I could have done that?'

'Not personally. But if in some way he had let you down, you'd have known who to employ.'

'Funnily enough,' said Veitch, 'we half suspected it might have been you. Very much within those same parameters.'

'What reason could I possibly have had?'

'Plenty, from what we heard. Not the most desirable of husbands, was he? Or the most desirable of exes, either. What was he up to near your home? Might he have been involved in the theft of those pictures, and let *you* down?'

'Pure fantasy.'

'Far from pure. Really, Brigid, we ought to talk about these things. In a civilised fashion. Rather than let it get unpleasant for you. Or for any of us.'

What Veitch had said about her usual working day was true. Even during the most tense business battles, Brigid had always been able to eat with a good appetite, adapting the pace of a meal to suit her conversation and plans. But today, in a secluded corner of the restaurant, she studied the menu without interest, ordered automatically, and waited for him to pour her a glass of the Meursault he remembered she liked. Michael Veitch had learned the importance of a good memory when it came to dealing with potential allies and potential enemies, potential backers and potential back-stabbers.

'Now.' He lolled back in his chair, all smiles and goodwill. 'In the first place, if we're going to strike a mutually satisfactory bargain, let's agree that your silly little book has to be scrapped.'

'I think not.'

'Little Murdo Cowan has seen the light. He realises there's no market for such a book, and the deal's off.'

Brigid began to cheer up. So they really were getting the twitches! 'Yes, I realised who had to be behind that. Change of editorial policy, the imbecile says. Doesn't think my book will quite fit their new image. I'll give him *image*!' Her enthusiasm was rekindled. 'You may have bullied him into withdrawing, but there are plenty of other publishers. As you'll discover. A pity to deprive the reading public of something so entertaining.'

He stopped lolling and leaned forward. 'And a pity to deprive them of the full story of your substitution of certain pictures in Baldonald House with fakes? And the removal of the anamorphosis and the Stewart paintings before they went to Canada for this forthcoming exhibition and then were discovered to be fakes. Who did get the real things in the end — and how much are you collecting for them?'

'You're groping in the dark.'

'Poor Crombie. How you cheated the old lad.'

'And where have you dug up all these delusions?'

'As we've agreed, we do both have our contacts.' He nodded towards the window and the street outside. 'And some of them turn out to be the same contacts.' His smile grew more and more inviting, without any hint of sincerity. 'All right, Brigid: where have you hidden the ersatz pieces?'

'Oh, so none of your so-called contacts have come up with a plausible story to back up that fantasy? How naughty of them.'

'It's only a matter of time. And a matter of who can offer the most substantial investment.'

'Bribe, you mean?'

'I'm talking about investment . . . diplomacy . . . Come off it, Brigid. You'll never make a fortune out of that junk, except by bumping up the insurance claim. And that's going to be risky.'

'You used to be so level-headed. Where does all this nonsense come from?'

'Brigid, let's talk sense. It's time you were back with us, instead of against us. Your old acquaintances. Friends. I think a position as a corporate client on a very respectable quango could be yours for the asking.'

'You wouldn't dare push that too far. Not right now. One false move, and everything goes wrong for you. It's a dithery time, isn't it, *Sir* Michael? One false move now, one breath of scandal — '

'There isn't going to be any breath of scandal.'

'You've seen to that, have you? All so praiseworthy. Putting all your financial muscle behind a vast investment in biotechnology, putting Britain in the forefront of food additive research. And ensuring that much of the production is centred in key areas where, surprise surprise, three Cabinet ministers have their constituencies.'

'There's nothing shady about that. Nothing underhanded.'

Her taste buds were back to normal. She finished a mouthful of roast duck, then said: 'But your price-fixing cartel doesn't come out quite so sweet-smelling. One of my nominees was at that meeting last year. All agreed to jack up world prices by thirty per cent, right? And adjust distribution to keep the prices up there.'

'What's known as rationalising output. Every big firm does it when it can.'

'Until it gets caught. Or until competition watchdogs get a sniff of something nasty, and your government contacts are suddenly out of contact . . . and bang goes any hope of Lord Veitch of Ecclefechan, or wherever.'

This was her world, her real world. The cooking of books was a much more interesting subject than writing them.

'You really are malicious, aren't you?' He looked almost admiring; but coldly calculating at the same time. 'If you can no longer pull the levers of intrigue, you're equally happy throwing a spanner in the works.'

'Which I have every intention of doing.'

'I thought we might have had a sensible discussion.'

'We have had just that,' said Brigid. 'And now you know what the outcome is.'

She finished the main course, and waved away the dessert menu.

'Coffee, madam?' said the waiter. 'Sir?'

After he had poured the coffee, Brigid leaned across the table with an intimate smile which might have suggested to a casual observer in the restaurant that this was a lovers' tryst and they had skipped the dessert in order to hasten off and spend the rest of the afternoon together.

'The collapse of two major woollen mills in the Scottish Borders, and two hundred workers out of a job,' she murmured. 'Nothing to do with you?'

'Nothing to do with me, personally, no. I had a hand in raising the venture capital for a takeover, but when it went wrong I was perfectly within my rights to recommend a reappraisal. Commercial rationalisation, the details entirely in the hands of the local managers. If that sort of petty whine is the best you can come up with — '

'Those so-called managers don't simply do as they're told after your meetings in New York last February?'

The muscles in Veitch's face did not

265

tighten even a fraction, yet he had somehow become more alert and less complacent. He said: 'You of all people should hardly need telling that international retrenchment has had some unfortunate side-effects on individual companies. Any investment counsellor has to take the long-term view.'

'The long-term view being,' said Brigid remorselessly, 'that it pays US fund managers to invest in Scottish manufacturing, win large enterprise grants from the Government, and promise a bright future for the local workforce. Then when you've creamed off all the best ideas, products, and European contacts from these firms, you announce that economic rationalisation regrettably means that the Scottish factories will have to close and all production will be shifted to the States.'

'I wasn't solely responsible for those decisions.'

'Not nominally, no. But whoever carries the can in public, you were the one who told him where to rattle it. It's all there, for anyone who cares to look.'

'Nobody has — '

'Nobody has looked? Not so far. Not when the financial correspondents have been wined and dined by spin doctors from your very own personal health service. And especially when fed on glib jargon that makes them feel they're connoisseurs of the diet at the top table. But there are some honest ones who won't be corrupted, and who'll wake up when prodded.'

'Meaning you intend to prod?'

'Don't buy your ermine yet.'

'You wouldn't risk libels on that scale.'

'I intend to publish and be damned — or rewarded.' As they left the restaurant and reached the corner where he had met her, she added graciously: 'Oh, and thanks for the lunch . . . which failed to corrupt me.'

'You know' — his tone had changed, he had assumed the charm she well remembered — 'it didn't used to turn out like this. We used to follow a good meal and a good argument with a leisurely hour or two in your flat.'

'Not so leisurely, as I recall.'

'So you do recall some of the more agreeable things in life.' He took her arm easily, casually, as if to stop her slipping off the narrow pavement in front of a delivery van. 'You know, I believe I still have the key to the door. A sentimental sort of chap, me, as you know.'

'I know just the opposite,' she said, 'which is why I had the locks changed long ago.'

'Brigid, for the last time, do see sense. You don't imagine we'd let you finish that book?

It's simply not going to happen.'

'And what exactly is going to happen?'

'Oh, I'm afraid you'll find out.' He released her arm. 'You'll find out very soon.'

She strolled in search of a cab, musing over that parting threat. There had been a lot of talk about contacts. She didn't doubt that if he wanted to kill, he would know how to contact a professional killer without ever risking his own involvement. But it was too melodramatic, inconceivable in a city like this, walking along familiar streets like this.

After a few hundred yards she found a cab to take her to Hector's club, to agree the wording of an obituary for the notice-board. She accepted condolences with becoming gravity while waiting for another cab to be called.

Back in Leith, she let herself into the flat, kicked off her shoes, and padded into the kitchen. She was ready for another cup of coffee, even though too much coffee tended to produce prickly heat along her throat and neck.

She couldn't help thinking about Veitch in this flat. He had been one of the best. They could have been two of a kind; but she had shied away, sensing his potential as a rival rather than a colleague.

Brigid laughed quietly, remembering the

truth of that remark of his about a good meal, a good argument, and a leisurely hour or two in the bedroom a few yards away; then choked off the laugh as there was a footstep behind her.

She turned, catching her breath, then demanded indignantly: 'Just a minute. How on earth did you — '

The gloved hands closed round her throat.

14

Detective Chief Inspector Jack Rutherford looked Lesley up and down and smirked. 'Hello, Lez. So we meet again.'

It might amuse him, but it was a meeting Lesley Gunn could well have done without. She had had a bellyful of the DCI on previous cases, and could predict exactly what would happen here. The Eyemouth killings had been settled to his satisfaction — the killer had in fact slit his own throat, which saved the police a lot of paperwork and time wasted in court — and now he was ready to trample through the investigation of another case.

'All right.' He had taken command of the incident room with his usual assertiveness. 'You seem to have let two murders occur within much the same family, and in between them a death which you don't think is suspicious. Quite a score!'

'This last one wasn't even in this neighbourhood.'

'Bloody inconsiderate, I'll grant you. But don't worry your little head. I'm briefed to work in Edinburgh with the Fettes Avenue team, and the high heidyins are already having fun arguing who'll be liaising with who, and whose toes mustn't get trodden on. So I'll be up there, and you'll be down here.'

That at least was something to be thankful for.

'But don't tell me,' Rutherford ground on, 'there isn't some connection with this stately pile here, and that earlier murder. Too much of a coincidence, these bodies lying around.'

'Just who did find Lady Crombie's body?'

'The family solicitor's clerk. The boss had tried ringing her about some legal wrangle they'd been having but couldn't get any reply. In the end, he sent his clerk around. Found the door open. The medic reckons she'd been there a couple of days.'

'With the door open all the time, so anyone could walk in?'

'How the hell should I know? Now, just to start up this great liaison of ours, can I be having your rundown on what's been going on here, and who smells suspicious?'

From the moment she had heard that Rutherford was moving in on this case, Detective Inspector Lesley Gunn had hastened to memorise all the people and issues involved so far, and fit them into the categories she knew Rutherford would want them slotted into. In a corner of the incident room she began her summing up. He listened in his characteristic posture, his right shoulder hunched as if frozen in the middle of a disdainful shrug.

'Both the dead people must in some way be linked with what brought me here in the first place,' said Lesley: 'the theft of paintings and *objets d'art.*'

'Hold it a minute, Lez. Word was that you hadn't made much progress on that front. Why are you trying to manacle 'em all together now? You been holding something back?'

'I was just about ready to ask some awkward questions. Only the person I wanted to get into the interview room is the one who's just been rubbed out.'

'Look, let's get the punters in the right order, shall we? From the first murder. Put 'em through their paces.'

Lesley set about running through the cast list in the nearest she could manage to a logical order. Starting with Gregory Dacre, the dead woman's first husband, who had been invited here to ghost her memoirs. No criminal record, not even a minor offence.

'Ghost?' queried Rutherford.

She explained. His shoulder hunched higher in a twitch of incredulity. It was yet another freak to add to the bulging category of oddities he had encountered in the course of duty. He found it easier to cope with razor gangs and demented husbands wielding blunt instruments or wives putting kitchen cutlery to lethal use.

Then she trotted out Simon Pringle, the second husband, who had been strangled and then, fuller investigation revealed, had had his head held under water. 'To make sure, I suppose,' said Lesley. 'And there was a smaller intake of water when he was being washed downstream and deposited where we found him.'

'We?'

'Lady Crombie and myself.'

'She led you there?'

'We were going over the ground of the burglary. Just strolling. And then PC Kerr called us over to see what he'd found.'

'Just strolling,' Rutherford echoed sceptically. 'By pure chance, close to her dead husband. Did she look surprised? Upset?'

'That's hard to say.'

'Not hard at all. Did she or didn't she?'

Lesley was being made to feel that she was under suspicion herself. It wasn't the first time she had been subjected to Rutherford's heavy-handedness; she must simply refuse to be ruffled.

'She's a very tough lady.' She shivered at

273

the faint echo of what Brigid Crombie herself had said at first sight of the corpse: 'Or was. Once she'd recognised him, she seemed rather amused.'

'Amused? For Christ's sake. And she didn't look particularly surprised?'

'I've told you, she was a very tough lady.'

'Do you or don't you suppose she had a hand in the killing? Maybe hand in hand with that first husband — this Dacre character. I mean, he lets himself be brought here by his ex-wife, comes under her thumb again, could be jealous of the one who hopped into bed after him, and she could have played on that to get him to — '

'If the medic's assessment is accurate, even with some leeway either way, both Lady Crombie and Dacre were in Edinburgh at the time of the killing.'

'And in their absence, if it really was in their absence, just what might Pringle have been doing in the grounds here?'

'That's what I'd like to know. Creeping in to ingratiate himself again, maybe. Because everything I've heard suggests he was a wily little creepy-crawly just like that. Or — '

'Seem to be plenty of folk who'd be happy to remove Pringle from this world. Including the Crombie woman herself. But then, who decided to eliminate *her*?'

'And strangle her,' Lesley commented, 'just as Pringle was strangled.'

'You're with me, then. Not two separate murders?'

'If it all ties in with the thefts — '

'Which we don't know it does.'

Lesley had always prided herself that she never got headaches. Problems could prove stressful. Witnesses and suspects could prove stressful. Colleagues could prove even more stressful when you found that instead of working as a team you were engaged in some mutual showing-off or rivalry. Still you coped, and didn't weaken or give in to neurotic resentments. But right now she was beginning to get a headache. There were too many balls to be juggled here; too many strands like the wires of last year's Christmas tree lights, obstinately snarling up into ever more complicated knots when you tried to reassemble them.

'And this Lord Crombie himself,' Rutherford was saying. 'This woman's third husband, right?'

'He was her third, yes.'

'All these men. She must have had something. You met her. What was it? Sexy? Rich? Dominating — whips and leather?'

'She didn't need whips and leather to dominate. She was always in charge.'

'So she could have ordered her third husband to get her second one out of the way when he proved troublesome?'

'Not from what I saw of him,' said Leslie with a spontaneous glow of respect for Hector Crombie's memory. 'No, it's not on.'

'Or got the first one to do it for her?'

'But then,' said Lesley, 'who disposed of Lady Crombie herself?'

'Any more bit-part players you haven't wheeled out on stage yet? Members of staff with a grudge? Other relatives?'

'There's a daughter.'

Rutherford pounced. 'Whose daughter?'

'Lord Crombie's. By his first wife.'

'Who hated his next wife?'

'Caroline certainly didn't appear to like her,' Lesley admitted, 'but I don't see she had any reason to rub her out.'

'Where was this Caroline when Pringle was killed? And when her stepmother copped it? Hey, how do you grab this, Lez — wicked stepmother? Real fairy-tale country, now. And how does this local princess spend her time?'

'She works in television. Flits in and out of here. Devoted to her father, but never seemed much concerned with anybody else.'

'Married?'

'Nobody quite in her class. That's the way

it is in these hard times. And a region like this.'

'Oh, is it now? The Morningside meritocracy nae good enough for her?' The rasp of his always smouldering peevishness grew more pronounced.

'She's not married,' said Lesley flatly.

'And you've written her off as a likely killer?'

'I've written nobody off,' said Lesley.

'Good girl. You'll make a good tough lassie yet.'

Phones had burped and tinkled through the entire conversation, interrupted only by the crisp, courteous voices of the women officers thanking the caller, asking for details — 'Slowly, please, madam . . . now, what was that address again?' — when one of the operators stood up above her VDU and waved to Rutherford. 'A call for you, guv. From Fettes Avenue.'

Rutherford jolted his shoulders into line and groped round the maze of tables. He listened, grunted, and was back within two minutes. Some tasty ingredient had been added to the simmering pot in his mind.

'Right, those boys have been hard at it. You'll have to put on a good show at this end to match them.'

'They've found some prints?'

'Plenty. And also that there was no forced entry into the flat in Leith. Her ladyship could have left the doors ajar when she went in — I mean, both the downstairs entry and her own flat door — but that's difficult, since the ground floor one shuts automatically the moment you're indoors. Or somebody else had keys for both.'

'Maybe a cleaner?'

'Maybe. You think that if she was away a lot, like down here at Baldonald, she'd have let a cleaner have a free run of the place?'

'I think she'd insist on it being cleaned only when she was in residence.'

'So who else? Her husband?'

'I'd think so. I gather that when she was working — with Gregory Dacre, for instance — Lord Crombie stayed away from the premises. But they must have gone to a number of formal occasions in Edinburgh and used the flat. So he'd have had a key.'

'But you say that when this chap Dacre was there, his lordship stayed somewhere else?'

'At one of the Scotch Malt Whisky Society's flats in Leith. And I believe he had a club in the New Town as well.'

'You suppose this laid the way clear for her ladyship to get laid again? Happy reunions with one of her assorted husbands?'

Remembering the laird's lug, Lesley trod

278

warily. 'Literary collaboration, yes. But I'm pretty sure Dacre at any rate wanted no other kind of reunion. That's not how I see it.'

'I've seen so much that I'm prepared to see anything else if it's shoved under my nose. Like this Dacre character being egged on to get rid of Pringle, because Pringle had somehow become a pain in the arse.' He let it stew for the larger part of a minute, then grimaced. 'But how could he have known Pringle was going to be in this neighbourhood at just that time? The Crombie woman herself knew, and instructed him? Some deal that had gone wrong between them, maybe.'

'But then who killed Lady Crombie?'

'Dacre again? Because he was in it up to his neck by now.'

'Into what?'

'Some scam that misfired.'

'I still feel,' said Lesley, 'that it's all tied in with the thefts from the house, before Dacre ever came on the scene. Brigid Crombie had been flogging family treasures openly to start with. Everything points to her getting rid of a lot more without her husband knowing. Maybe replacing a few with convincing forgeries. And then instigating a theft to clear the place out and claim insurance on the lot. Cashing in twice over.'

Rutherford nodded, less sceptical this time.

'And somebody in the scam got alarmed? Wanted her out of the way before she talked too much — to this Dacre character, maybe?' Before Lesley could interrupt, he hurried on with that greedy snatching at ideas which she remembered so well. 'Dacre himself, getting close to the truth and spilling the beans to someone who decided she had to go?'

'Dacre was here on the premises at the time of her murder.'

'But he could still have leaked some nasty information.'

'He'd hardly want her murdered, when he was hoping to make money out of ghosting that book for her.'

'But what part did Pringle play in this? One ex-husband up to no good, the second one commissioned to stamp on him and her other enemies. Which one of them decided Lady Crombie's usefulness was at an end?'

'We can't grill her,' said Lesley glumly, 'or Pringle.'

'And this Lord Crombie — he really did die a natural death?'

'It's my belief that it was a natural death, but caused by the behaviour of somebody else.'

'Such as?'

She had half hoped to protect Hector Crombie's dignity, but the truth had to come out. 'Could have been what he heard his wife saying through the laird's lug.'

She took him to the little sitting-room and then upstairs to the snug, explaining what Crombie could well have overheard.

'I think I'd like a bit of a crack with this Dacre character. He could be in it a whole lot deeper than you've cottoned on to.' Rutherford led the way out of the snug, looked down the stairs, then up the few steps from the half-landing, and opted for the first floor corridor. He strolled along the corridor, opening doors without knocking and peering in. 'As a matter of interest, where are you based, Lez? Risky to be too close. I've already got the vibes of you going native.'

She explained the *Tam Lin*.

'Even more dangerous, maybe. The evil distortions caused by alcohol, hey?' He was making decisions off the top of his head. She must move to police quarters in Selkirk. 'And now there's a mobile incident room free, we'll have that brought in sharpish. Park it in the grounds — but keeping a healthy distance.' He went to issue instructions to one of the telephonists, then swung back, seething with enthusiasm. 'And now, before I go off to the big city, let's get to grips with this Dacre character.'

* * *

Greg had to face up to the fact that he was well and truly out of a job now. The only thing that made sense would be for him to call it a day, pack his bags, and head home, perhaps via Kate's flat to discuss where his next chunk of income might come from.

He was packed and ready to go when he was summoned to the interview with the DCI which could surely be only a formality.

He found that it wasn't.

And yet again he found himself in the library from which he and Brigid had been driven. Rutherford had dragged one of the tables end on to the wall, and indicated that Greg should sit opposite him, on one of the less comfortable chairs which had been installed for the VDU operators.

'I need hardly tell you, Mr Dacre, that you're an important factor in this investigation.'

'Is that what I might interpret as a caution?'

'By no means, sir. Have you any reason to suppose that we have reason to suspect you?'

'Suspect me of what?'

'At the moment nothing, sir. Let's just say that you're a material witness.'

'I can't say I recall having witnessed anything.'

'Nothing whatsoever? And you being a writer? I understand you *are* a writer?' It was said without any flicker of respect.

'Not of murder stories.'

'But you must have more than an inkling of the ins and outs of these unfortunate events. You must,' Rutherford fished, 'have some theories of your own. Ideas of how you would handle a situation like this if you were writing a book about it.'

Greg tried to maintain a cool detachment, but Rutherford had prodded the right nerve. How, indeed, would he tackle such a subject? Either as a sleuth or a master criminal? The criminal element was the more challenging. As a serial killer, how would he have coped with this interrogation? He narrowed his eyes and tried to look tough and invulnerable.

'Why are you squinting at me like that?' demanded Rutherford.

Greg switched to being cool and mysterious as they ran through the events of these past few weeks.

Yes, he had disliked Simon Pringle, but not enough to commit murder. And in any case — how many more times was he going to have to point this out? — he and Lady Crombie had been in Edinburgh when Pringle was killed.

'And when your ex-wife, Lady Crombie, was killed?'

'I gather that she was in her flat in Leith. And I was here.'

'You know the flat? You've been in it?'

'Yes. Doing some background work.'

'Often?'

'Just the one week or so.'

'And you have a key?'

'I did, for a few days, but it was Lord Crombie's, and I gave it back to him when we left.'

'You got on well with your ex-wife?'

'Very few people got on well with her for long. This latest business was just a professional working relationship. And I was here,' he emphasised, 'working on our notes, when she was killed.'

Rutherford sighed. He was not satisfied, but obviously he had nothing tangible to chase after at the moment.

'You're not planning to leave the neighbourhood, Mr Dacre?'

'There's nothing more for me here. I'm only in the way. And I do need to get back to work.'

'On those memoirs you and Lady Crombie have been working on?'

'Of course not.'

'I'd have thought you might have cooked

up something juicy and saleable on your own. She won't be expecting a cut now.'

Greg lost his cool. His own opinions of Brigid might have slid downhill over the years, but he wasn't going to stand for a grubby little copper enjoying himself with grotty remarks of this kind.

'You're talking about my wife,' he snapped. 'The lady who was my wife.'

'Quite so, sir. I was hoping you could help us get at the truth.'

'You'll get nowhere near it by speaking disrespectfully of the dead.'

'Sorry, sir. I didn't get the impression you retained much respect for your ex-wife yourself.'

'She's dead now, and I'd prefer to forget any personal problems. And get on with my own life, if that's all right with you?'

'It will be perfectly all right, sir, once we've completed our enquiries. As I've said, we'd prefer you not to leave.'

'But you can't expect me to hang around here. I mean, the work we were doing — it's all over, there's nothing to keep me here.'

'I'd like to have you close at hand until we can eliminate every improbability and see what we've got left. Your willing cooperation' — the politer Rutherford's words, the worse the discord of an undertone — 'would be far preferable to any awkward legalities.'

'I can leave you my address in Norwich.'

'I'd prefer you not to be so far away.'

'But I can't stay on here,' Greg insisted.

'There'll be a room vacant at the *Tam Lin*. Very hospitable little inn, I believe. And within easy reach.'

'How do you know there'll be a vacancy?'

Rutherford grinned a knowing grin. 'I've arranged for one to be empty as from this afternoon.'

'But how long am I expected to mess around here? I mean, I've got work to do.'

'Have you, sir? You've just admitted it's come to a dead end, if one may put it that way in the circumstances.'

Greg decided it was time to go on the attack. 'You won't object to my ringing my agent?'

'To get something else set up for you? No objection at all, sir. Provided she doesn't want you to flee south too soon.' As Greg got up and began heading for the small sitting-room, the DCI barked: 'Just a minute. You can make any call you like from here. What d'you suppose all these phones are for?'

'I wouldn't want to block any crucial incoming calls for you.'

Greg tried a twist of a sneer himself. 'And in any case I prefer a little privacy when discussing my business affairs.'

'Please don't touch anything in there, or anywhere else, until we've finished with it.'

Greg half expected Rutherford to veer suddenly in the direction of an outright prohibition; but at that moment DI Gunn came in, murmured something urgently, and made a brief gesture that the DCI should come with her. Greg made his escape.

To his relief, Kate was at home, but did not sound terribly sympathetic about his woes. 'You really have a knack of landing yourself in it, haven't you?'

'Obviously there'll be some delay in my getting away. While I'm stuck here, maybe you can rustle up some commissions. I'll need to make up for what I'll not be getting from the Brigid project.'

'You mean you've already switched your mind off that whole thing? You can actually contemplate plunging into something else without batting an eyelid?' she marvelled.

He could visualise her perched on the end of her desk, the phone tucked under her left jaw, rhythmically tapping the pile of manuscripts which seemed never to diminish on the desk; or was she in the bedroom, sprawled on the edge of the bed, languidly stretching herself as she talked, and stroking the pillow?

He said: 'To be honest, I just needed to hear the sound of your voice.'

There was the rustle of her breath in the receiver, gasping and unsteady. 'You really mean that?'

'I wouldn't have said it if I didn't.'

'Oh, I don't know, it depends on who you're impersonating at any given moment.'

'There's nobody to impersonate right at this moment. Just me being me.'

'Not sure I recognise that one.' She still sounded dazed and uncertain. 'But by the time we do get to meet, I'll probably have found you someone else's skin you can slither under.'

His gaze had been wandering as they talked, conjuring up more and more enticing visions of Kate. Abruptly it came back into this room as his eyes picked out a small black rectangle on the table where Brigid's whisky glass had so often stood.

It was her PDA address book. Still talking automatically, he flicked it open and pressed the initial 'I'. Maybe Brigid had a secret code, or maybe she hadn't even bothered to contact Ishbel recently. But there it came up: Ishbel. Alongside it, the address of a garage, and a phone number.

He closed the palmtop, slid it into his jacket pocket, and heard Kate saying: 'Greg, you're rambling. What was that last bit about?'

'I've got to go,' he said. 'The cops are getting restless. I'm being ordered to stay in a pub called the *Tam Lin*.'

'Oh, my God. Ghosting the memoirs of a fairy queen?'

'Not me. Not this time. Bad casting. Look, I'll let you know when I'm settled in, and when they're likely to let me leave.'

'If they do let you leave. More likely you'll be arrested and sentenced to life imprisonment for being a ravening serial killer and a menace to society.'

'Kate . . . '

'Yes?' she said hopefully.

'Oh, nothing. I'll tell you when we meet.'

'I bet you won't,' she said. 'I bet you just somehow don't get round to it.'

He hurried upstairs to collect his bag and the briefcase with his own copy of the Brigid Weir story as far as it had gone. He wasn't ready to relinquish the project entirely. Not yet.

He had every expectation of being intercepted by Rutherford and given veiled and not so veiled warnings about not straying too far away. An incitement to stay in the bar of the inn and get permanently plastered, to loosen his tongue? But in the hall DI Gunn was busy introducing the DCI to Caroline Crombie.

Greg quickened his pace. 'Off to the inn, right? Following instructions.'

Rutherford nodded brusquely, his attention already elsewhere. DI Gunn glanced at Greg and seemed about to say something, but was dragged back into the conversation with Caroline.

Greg slowed at the main gate. The *Tam Lin* lay five or six miles to the right.

He hesitated only a few seconds, then turned left, and put his foot down.

15

The WPCs in the incident room were busy assembling notepads and equipment on a trestle table near the door, ready to transfer ongoing records to the mobile room when it arrived. Rutherford had commandeered the more civilised end of the library, where he chose the larger armchair for himself and indicated to the Hon. Caroline Crombie that she should perch herself on one of the more basic office chairs. Lesley Gunn could have predicted that Rutherford's blustering style of interrogation would put Caroline Crombie's back up. It showed in the stiffness of her neck as she sat bolt upright, and in the cold, starchy replies she offered to his questions.

'Right, Miss Crombie. To start with, where were you when your stepmother was murdered?'

'Do we know the exact date and time?'

'Let's say two days before the body was found.'

'I've been in and out of the studio most days. Out on location last Thursday, doing a shoot on flood defences at Berwick. And Friday morning I called in on one of my father's old friends, just to chat to him for ten minutes. I was certainly just wrapping up a voice-over in the studio when news of the murder came through.'

'How exactly did you hear about it?'

'I was told she'd been found by Mr McIntyre's clerk.'

'Mr McIntyre?'

'The family solicitor. The young man was still away, helping the police with their enquiries, when I went round to the office.'

'You went round to the solicitors?' Rutherford contrived to make it sound the most heinous thing she could have done in the circumstances.

'To take up where Brigid had left off. She had been in town to arrange my father's funeral and see if there were any urgent legal problems.'

'And that was your first thought — to pick up the routine as if nothing had happened?'

'Somebody had to take over. I owe it to my father's memory. He hated people hanging about and not getting a job done.'

'You were very fond of your father?'

Caroline's head tilted back a fraction. She was looking down her nose at Rutherford as if he were some baffling alien species. 'I see nothing unusual in that.'

'Och, now, it's not all that usual nowadays. Children fall out with their parents, leave home, couldn't care less.'

'In the circles you move in, perhaps, chief inspector.'

Lesley detected the same inflection which Caroline had used when referring to '*Lady Crombie*.'

'And fond of your late stepmother also?'

'We found a *modus vivendi*. I wouldn't put it any stronger.'

'You mean you couldn't stand her.'

'I mean that for my father's sake I made an effort to get along with her.'

'You wouldn't have gone so far as to kill her?'

Most women would have flown off the handle at that, but Caroline's cold distaste for the questioner was more than a match for his suggestive jab. 'He wouldn't have wanted that.'

'But then, after *his* death . . . ?'

'What would have been the point of killing her then?'

'And the earlier death — Simon Pringle?'

'On the few occasions I met him, Pringle struck me as an exceedingly unpleasant person, and the world is better off without him. But why should I have had anything to do with him?'

'Why, indeed?'

'I still think,' Lesley interposed, 'it all has to

tie in somehow with these business types Lady Crombie was going to write about. She aimed to show them up. They wanted her silenced.'

Rutherford glowered. 'And I think they're all separate. Or the murders are, anyway. But it's time to give Fettes Avenue a nudge. Ask them what progress they're making — whether the local crime squad saw anybody with the Crombie woman that day in Edinburgh. Or heard even a whisper of anything out of the ordinary.' He swung back towards Caroline, still pursuing some vague hunch of his own which made no sense to Lesley. 'As a matter of interest, Miss Crombie, where were you at the time all this was going on?'

'I've told you. Mostly at the studio. Several days on the trot. The Edinburgh police didn't waste any time: got in touch with me at once. They're pretty familiar with our programmes, and where I'm likely to be found. I couldn't offer them any explanation, any more than I can offer you one.' She gave Lesley a vaguely friendly nod, which she would certainly not have offered to Rutherford. 'Though I think all the probabilities are in that theory of yours. A lot of powerful businessmen were known to be targets in her forthcoming book, and they might have wanted to silence her.

And since I've told the police in Edinburgh everything I know' — she turned back to Rutherford and became imperious again — 'there's little point in my going over it all again. I didn't come here for that.'

'What *did* you come here for, Miss Crombie?'

'To continue with arrangements for my father's funeral.'

'You do realise, of course, that Edinburgh won't be releasing Lady Crombie's body until forensic tests are complete. And until we have more evidence to lay alongside it and see what gels and what doesn't.'

'I don't see what relevance that has.'

'I thought possibly you were considering a joint ceremony for Lord and Lady Crombie.'

She stared at him in mounting disgust. 'That's not my intention. Brigid said my father would have been in favour of cremation. I don't agree. He should be laid to rest in the family vault.'

Laid to rest. For all the taut, aggressive modernity of her appearance, Caroline spoke in the language of old, sentimental tradition.

'Alongside the rest of our family,' she finished.

'Including your own late mother, no doubt,' said Lesley respectfully.

'My mother died in a plane crash on a

charity mission to Ethiopia.'

'I'm sorry. So she's not buried in the vault.'

'No, even though she belonged there. And nor will Brigid be. When you do get round to releasing Brigid, she can be cremated, since I assume that's what she would have preferred.'

Lesley said: 'One thing, Miss Crombie. On the subject of family, you say you went round to see your family solicitors as soon as you heard the news. Was there any particular reason for that?'

'I'd have thought that would be obvious. To see how far Brigid had got with the funeral arrangements, and invitations to my father's club members and other old friends. And to stop any steps she might have taken towards his cremation.'

'And was there anything else while you were there?'

All at once Caroline was less haughty. On the surface her manner did not alter, but she was bracing her right foot against the floor as if her chair had become unsteady. 'The usual drab legal jargon. Wringing of hands, expressions of deep distress. Mental arithmetic, summing up the balance between lost income from the deceased, and charges they could reasonably make for getting probate and spinning out administration of the will for as long as possible.'

'Now that both your father and Lady Crombie are dead, you will presumably inherit the estate?' said Lesley.

'Actually' — she might have been picking her way very carefully over loose stones — 'it's between two of us.'

Rutherford thrust his meaty neck forward. 'Two of you?'

'Myself and Brigid's daughter Ishbel.'

Rutherford shot Lesley a baleful glance. 'You never said anything about the woman having a daughter of her own.'

Lesley glanced at Caroline, and was sure that Rutherford, like herself, must have smelt that almost rancid tang of fear. 'She doesn't seem to have played any part in anything around here for a long time,' she excused herself as smoothly as possible. 'Lady Crombie mentioned her when I first interviewed her, but I got the impression they didn't see much of each other any more.'

'You *got* the *impression*,' Rutherford mocked. 'But now it looks as if her mother did still think very well of her indeed: well enough to — '

'It was in my father's will,' said Caroline, 'not Brigid's.'

'He split the lot between the two of you? After his wife's death, that would be.'

'No.' Caroline's head went even further

297

back, so that now she was staring at the ceiling. 'While she was still alive, she'd get only a small legacy. The property is for Ishbel and myself. I fancy that my father thought we'd make a more dignified job of running it than Brigid would have done.' A touch of gentleness crept into her voice. 'He grew very fond of Ishbel when she did come here.'

'Just a minute. You say this girl is Lady Crombie's daughter. But she's not your sister?'

'No.'

'Then *her* father . . . ?'

Lesley knew the answer to this one. 'The first husband. Gregory Dacre.'

Rutherford was for a moment out of breath. Caroline took the opportunity to stand up and move towards the door. Rutherford gulped and waved a threatening hand. 'Miss Crombie, you can't just walk out until we've finished.'

'If you'll excuse me, I'll get on with what I came here for.'

'I've got a lot more questions to ask.'

'Think them over while I cope with the task in hand. I'm not likely to leave for quite a time yet.'

She was scarcely out of the room when Rutherford slammed his fist down on the table.

'Looking down her nose at me, and asking why we could suppose she might want to get rid of Lady Crombie after old Crombie's death! Knowing she was in line for that much money! What better motive?'

'But did she know beforehand?'

'The old man could have told her, just to spite his wife or maybe to . . . oh, hell, this'll take some working out.'

'But she made it clear that Lady Crombie inherits precious little. So if the bulk of the legacy was all for the two girls anyway, there wouldn't be any motive for either of them to murder the widow.'

'You've met that woman. I haven't. But from what I've heard, she doesn't sound the type who'd let the two girls get away with that sort of share-out. Maybe she was already stirring it up, and they had to remove her. Two girls,' he repeated. 'Just what do we know about this daughter of Dacre's?'

Lesley tried dredging up from memory the first interview she had had with Greg Dacre and with his ex-wife. Had neither of them let slip any reference whatsoever to a daughter? Halfway through her apologetic summary, Rutherford exploded again.

'Not one single bloody mention of her by her father or her mother?'

'You said yourself, only few minutes ago,

that families today — '

'All right, inspector, don't quote me as a defence witness. Just where is this interesting female right now? And just what might the two of them be up to? This bloody place is overrun with some very weird families. And I want two of the members right here, just as fast as we can lay hands on them. And especially I want to meet this Ishbel Dacre.'

'We could ring her father where you sent him — at the *Tam Lin*.'

'And give him warning, and the chance to do a runner, or tip her off?' He glared at Lesley. 'Have you shifted your things out of there yet?'

'You haven't given me time,' she protested.

'Go and get them now. And get the girl's address. And bring Dacre back here with you.'

It was only ten minutes' drive. There was no other traffic on the road, and no movement on the hillsides. The stillness was threatening rather than peaceful. Although there was no wind, the surface of the loch was fretted by little ripples fidgeting, flattening out, and then bunching into wavelets which rose, fell back, and then waited for another thrust of energy. The light on the white-harled wall of the inn as she approached was ominously rusty rather than golden.

The landlord greeted her with his usual brief nod and a 'There'll be a regular smirr brewing up out there, miss.'

'Mr Dacre's booked in? We did ring through, and I understand you agreed he could have my room.'

'Aye, but he's nae showed up yet.'

Lesley's first thought was of Rutherford's fury when he heard this. Not showed up yet? When it was such a short drive, and he'd been gone for quite a time. And there had been no sign of an accident on the road — the only road which came in this direction.

She collected her things and piled them in the car, then nerved herself to ring Baldonald House on her mobile. To her cowardly relief, the DCI was outside in the grounds, supervising arrival of the mobile incident room. 'We're all geared up to shift everything out there,' said the WPC resignedly.

It was only postponing the evil moment, but Lesley hurried to say: 'I won't disturb him. When you see him, tell him Dacre seems to have done a runner. And I'm on my way back.'

As she drove in through the gateway, a long trailer was being manoeuvred into position close to the wall of the refreshment room. Rutherford, not content to leave the operation to the seasoned driver and a uniformed constable signalling a hard left, back, right hand down, forward and line up here, was jerking his arms about and jabbing his right thumb first in the air, then downwards. The driver was glad to see Lesley approaching, to distract the DCI. Lesley was less happy.

'Never showed up?' Rutherford blew his top. 'I knew from the start that we shouldn't have turned our backs on any of them. Not for a minute. I'd like to have the whole shower of 'em in custody.'

'We can put out a call — '

'We'll do more than that,' raged Rutherford, without specifying what, 'before the two of them get up to whatever it is they have in mind.'

'They're hardly likely to flee the country. Not with their inheritance coming up like that.'

Rutherford did not reply. His attention had been distracted by the sight of Caroline Crombie making her way down the path towards the chapel, with a large key dangling between her fingers. 'Just a minute,' he yelled. 'Miss Crombie, just where are you off to?'

She did not disdain to answer, but disappeared round a sprawling copse, kicking aside a tangle of brambles.

Rutherford stormed after her. What he hoped to achieve, Lesley could not imagine. When he was like this, he would pick on the nearest possible victim and hammer away until he got what he wanted — or found he was getting nowhere near what he wanted, and so was plunged into an even worse temper.

Lesley followed him, taking care not to catch up.

Caroline had reached the abandoned hulk of the vault beside the chapel. It must once have been an imposing, heavily ornate tomb, with coats of arms at each corner and wrought iron initials in the grille strengthening the oak door. One felt the grille was there to prevent the inmates returning to this world rather than to keep intruders out. Finely chiselled stonework was largely obscured by tentacles of ivy winding round it. Lesley conjured up a vision of knights of old within, each with a stone head on a stone pillow, hands clasped across the breast, a faithful hound at his feet.

Probably eroded out of recognition by now. Maybe cremation was, after all, less demeaning in the end. Yet those symbols and formalities, no matter how cobwebbed, were more to her own taste.

Caroline was having trouble with the key.

She tried pushing it harder into the massive lock on the door of the vault, but it would not engage. She held it up to the light and shook her head.

Rutherford reached her. 'Think some noble cadaver's put a curse on the place, miss?'

'It's the right key. Always been kept by the cellar steps. I know it's the right key. But it won't fit the lock.'

'Maybe your stepmother fitted a new one. She seems to have done a lot of shifting things around and altering them.' He bent over the lock, patronising rather than helpful. But then Lesley, from where she was standing, saw his shoulders hunch. He fingered the heavy lock and inspected the end of his forefinger. 'This is a newish lock. But it's been deliberately covered with gunge. Anyone strolling casually down here — '

'Which we don't encourage,' snapped Caroline.

'To anyone not examining it close to,' Rutherford finished complacently, 'it wouldn't be noticeable. But someone's been here not so long ago.'

Caroline gripped the old key like a weapon. 'I've got to get inside. We've got to open this place up.'

Rutherford took his phone out. 'Sergeant, have you opened up the mobile room yet?

Right, well there should be some bolt cutters in the kit under the end bench. Get them down here at the old chapel right away. And send them with somebody strong enough to use them.'

They waited in silence. Lesley was doing her own guesswork, and was sure the other two were doing the same, but she doubted if the outcome would prove to be the same.

The uniformed constable who had accompanied Lesley on her first encounter with Baldonald House arrived with the cutters.

He got one blade under the hasp of the door, bent over it, and gripped fiercely. His face went so red that Lesley was afraid he might have a stroke. Then, with a final squeeze and a savage twist, he wrenched the metal apart. When he reached for the edge of the door, it creaked and sagged ominously.

Inside there was fetid darkness, breathing a rank smell of years of neglect.

Caroline stepped impetuously towards the opening.

'Hold it,' commanded Rutherford. 'Just stay there a minute. We wouldn't want the roof coming in on top of you.' He looked at the torch Caroline was carrying. 'I see you came prepared. No electricity for the departed?'

'Hasn't been any in the chapel for ages, let alone the vault.'

'Might I have that?'

For a moment Lesley thought that Caroline might refuse to hand the torch over; but she held it out, the way one would hand over a knife, with the handle towards Rutherford.

He stooped and went very slowly in, a step at a time. Lesley heard him curse as his feet scrabbled on fallen masonry. She saw the beam of the torch waver and describe a wild parabola along the far wall. Then it stopped, and turned in a slow, steady arc.

'Well,' said Rutherford. 'Well, now. Lez, you'd better come and have a look at this. Mind where you tread.'

With unusual courtesy he trained the light on the floor and sketched out a safe path for her. When she was well inside, he said: 'Stop right there. Now tell me what you make of this.'

She was in darkness again as the beam made its way along the edge of a high stone tomb.

Propped against the stonework, obscuring most of the pious lettering, were a number of paintings. Herself framed in the doorway like a portrait against the daylight outside, Caroline let out a snarl of anguish.

'What are they doing here? Our pictures. Father's treasures . . . shoved in here to rot away. What the hell . . . ?'

'You're the expert.' Rutherford handed Lesley the torch. 'Take a closer look.'

She played the light slowly across the surface of a portrait she recognised as undoubtedly one of the earlier Crombie ladies. Then there was a soldier who could almost have been Hector Crombie himself. And then a landscape. Caroline, edging in, cried: 'The Grey Mare's Tail! I've always loved that.'

Very carefully Lesley said: 'I think you probably loved the original.'

'What do you mean? That's the picture I — '

'Indoors, in not too good a light, you wouldn't think of inspecting it detail by detail, every day you passed it. You were used to it being there, like all the others. Part of a familiar background. Once we get them out of here, I'll have a closer look. But I'm already willing to bet that they're all fakes.'

'But who'd have put them here? And why?'

'They certainly wouldn't be any good to anybody anywhere else. Unlike the originals — wherever they may have got to by now.'

Rutherford waved them peremptorily out into the open air. 'All right, inspector. This is

307

what you came here for in the first place. I'll leave you to it, while I concentrate on — '

He was cut short by the bleeping of his mobile. 'Well,' he said. And then: 'Is that a fact, now?' When he turned back to them he was clenching his fingers like a man warming up for a fight. 'I'm sure you'll be happy to hear this, inspector. Someone helping to bolster up your theories. On the day of Lady Crombie's murder, Sir Michael Veitch was seen having lunch with her. And leaving with her. The waiter says they seemed to be having an argument. And there's a suggestion of further sightings later that afternoon. I've asked them to hold their fire till I get to Edinburgh. I've just got to sit in on this.' He glanced at his watch. 'And while I'm there, maybe I can set them on to finding out just where this Ishbel Dacre has got to.'

Lesley turned towards Caroline, waiting for bewilderment and anger at the discovery within the vault. But Caroline, who had been so staggered by the first glimpse of those pictures, was transfixed, her face paler than ever, staring after the DCI as he headed off towards his car.

16

The board stretching above the wide main entrance in Musselburgh framed the name of *Ritchie's Transport* in large letters between sketches of a lorry and a minicab. In the cramped office behind a wide glass window, a screen was fidgeting with patterns of black and green. They were everywhere nowadays: Greg was distracted for a moment by a gloomy calculation as to how long he might survive before books disappeared altogether and gave way to these collections of circuitry and visual declamations.

James Ritchie was a podgy little man so anxious to give the impression of swift efficiency that he kept scuttling to and fro within that confined space, darting and dabbing in such non-stop attentiveness that he really ought to have shed a lot of that surplus weight.

'Right, sir. What can we do for you?'

'I was looking for Ishbel Dacre.'

For a moment Greg wondered if Ishbel had used another name — at any rate a different surname — but Ritchie replied at once. 'Nae, she's nae here. But nae hassle. Standby driver's just back in.' He bit off the end of every remark like a would-be sergeant-major. 'So where'd ye be wanting to go?'

'It was Miss Dacre I particularly wanted to see.'

Ritchie was studying him with a mixture of apprehensiveness and defiance. 'I was wondering when somebody was going to show up.'

'Show up? Why should anyone show up here?'

'You the police? Or a reporter?'

'Neither. Why should I be?'

'Wi' all that about her mother. Being murdered. I wondered when someone would come asking questions.'

'So you knew her mother?'

'Only on the phone. She'd ring up, ask to be driven somewhere. Very condescending. Doin' a great favour, putting work the girl's way.' He stopped, still peering warily at Greg. 'But what would it have to do with you?'

'I'm her father.'

'Her faither? Well, na . . . '

'What exactly does she do here?'

'She doesn't. Nae more. She left a few weeks ago, wi' precious little warning. A pity. Up till then she was a reliable lass.'

'All right. What *did* she do while she was here?'

'Regular minicab work. Valeting hire cars.

310

Delivering them to Waverley Station or the airport. Collecting from wherever. Any hour of the day or night. Could handle the heavy stuff, too. Take a lorry to Inverness, deliver a new truck to a client in Carlisle. A tad too intense, if ye ken what I mean. But anything to keep the money coming in.'

'And from time to time her mother would call on her?'

'Aye. Rang and asked to be picked up and driven places, sometimes.' Ritchie's gaze became curious rather than apprehensive. 'That'd be your wife, then?'

'It would.'

'But she called herself Lady Crombie. Made a gey big thing of it. Only ye wouldnae be Lord Crombie?'

'No, I wouldn't. We were divorced years ago. And Lord Crombie's dead.'

'I didna ken.'

'So is she, now.'

'Aye, shocking business. No' that many miles from here.'

'Did Ishbel hear about it here, before she left?'

'I told you, she was awa' some weeks back. I thought maybe that feller of hers had taken off somewhere else. Found himself a job somewhere else, maybe.' But that last barked sentence had acquired a sceptical snarl.

'What fellow would this have been?' Greg had a prickling awareness that he almost certainly knew the answer.

'Ach, I think ye'd no' be wanting to know his sort.' Ritchie turned away dismissively, but bobbed round again immediately. 'Some lasses, they do pick the bad 'uns, don't they?'

'You knew his name?'

'Nae. Just used to appear — come and pick her up here. But I know a skellum when I smell one. Reckon she took on all that work just to keep them going. She'd hand over money to him — he'd be asking for it the moment he got here. Times I thought she'd sooner he didnae show up here like that. But he was that type. Wasnae going to give her a chance of getting rid of any of her money before he got his hands on it. A lot older than her, and bossy. Bad as a pimp.'

'Look, if you're suggesting — '

'Ach, that wasnae what I was saying about *her*. She was a fine lass. But him — couldnae keep his eyes to himself. Or his hands.

'He tried to rob the till?'

'Nae, not that. Hands on the women, that's what I'm saying. Tried to get himself in wi' our office girl. Thought maybe she'd earn more for him than Ishbel. Marie wouldnae have him, Ishbel had had enough and decided to ditch him.'

The tiny office was overheated, but Greg felt very cold. *Ditch* him . . . He thought of Simon Pringle lying dead in the burn, well and truly ditched.

'And where's she gone to now?' he demanded.

'Used to have a place in a back street off the Portobello Road. But she seems to have left it once he was out of the scene.'

'And now where is she? You must have some idea where she went to. She must have left a forwarding address.'

'I don't know that she'd want me to — '

'Look, I've told you. I'm her father. I've got to get to her.'

'Before the police do?'

The chill intensified. Greg hadn't put it to himself in quite such words. But yes, he did want to get to Ishbel, fast.

'Right at this moment,' he said shakily, 'I think she needs me.'

'Ach, weel.' Ritchie still looked unsure, but said: 'I did have some back pay to forward to her.' He reached for a scrap pad and flicked fingers across the keyboard below the screen. 'Aye, here we are.' He scribbled, and tore the sheet off the pad. 'Once you're there, ye'll have to find the street yoursel'.'

Greg looked down at the scrawled lettering. It was an address in Linlithgow. He

313

had never seen the address before, but had a creepy suspicion that he knew whose it was.

★ ★ ★

Ishbel opened the door to the ground floor flat, and looked blankly at her visitor.

She was slender, just escaping thinness. Long blonde hair drifted across her face and down to gaunt shoulders. Her eyes were wide and questioning. You got the feeling she was always questioning.

'Yes?'

'You don't remember me.'

'Should I?' Then she leaned forward, pushing her hair back in a way reminiscent of Caroline, but more wildly, shaking her head the moment she had done it so that the long strands fell back across her forehead again. 'No,' she breathed. 'It's . . . Daddy . . . '

'So you do remember.'

He wanted to throw his arms round her, kiss her, but sensed her bracing herself against the possibility, ready to push him away.

'What . . . ?' It was a whisper, fading away as she agitatedly ran her right hand down her left arm, then reached for the edge of the door as if to slam it against an unwelcome tradesman.

'May I come in?'

'I . . . don't know. I don't think I ought to — '

'I do have to talk to you, Ishbel.'

'After all this time?'

'Please.'

She stood back and let him pass. Mutely she gestured towards a door on the left. He went into a room with a settee, two armchairs and a coffee table littered with magazines. The settee and chairs were drawn up in a huddle to face a large television set.

Ishbel waved him towards the nearest armchair, then stumbled past him and wavered in the middle of a dark woolly rug, like a stranger uncertain about her own choice of a seat.

Those wide eyes were very pale eyes, but he was sure that when she became interested in something the colour would flood into them just as it had done with her mother's.

She said: 'How did you find me? And why?'

'I went through Mr Ritchie. But don't blame him. I told him who I was, and he agreed that I really did have to get in touch with you.'

'Why?'

'You know that your mother's dead?'

'I read about it, yes.' She shivered in a

convulsion that shook her whole body. 'It's horrible.'

'And you know about Simon's death?'

'I . . . yes, I . . . heard about that, too.'

'But you didn't show up — didn't come to find out what had happened, or what questions people might be asking?'

She shook her head wildly to and fro, then let herself collapse on the settee. 'I don't know anything about them. Nothing to do with me, either of them.'

'But they *were* something to do with you. In a big way, from all I hear.'

'And where did you hear it?'

'Your mother told me how Simon got up to his old games.'

The nails of her right hand scrabbled at the arm of the settee. Her lips were trembling, but not in any readiness to talk.

'All this business with Simon.' He got it out in a rush. 'How could you ever have let yourself get involved with him?'

'I thought you said that mother had filled you in on that.'

'But when things started going wrong — really wrong. Your mother, Simon, and all the rest of it . . . God, I could have told you — '

'Told me? Could you? When we'd never spoken a word to each other for years. Never

316

even seen you.' It had triggered her into a burst of retaliation. 'Daddy, where *were* you? Mother would never tell me. I always got the impression you couldn't be bothered, anyway.'

'That was your mother's story?'

'Whenever I tried to ask about you, she'd tell me how . . . well, how . . . useless you were. Never cared about me, or you wouldn't just have gone off and left me. Couldn't have, if you'd cared tuppence.'

'And you believed every word of that?'

'What else is there to believe, when you're a kid?' She was holding back tears. 'And when you weren't there, just the way she said, what was I to believe? You never did get in touch.'

'Because we agreed . . . she made me think it was better that way.'

'And you went along with it, just because she said so.'

'I'm sorry, Ishbel. Really I am. It was bloody ridiculous. But this business of Simon. If only I'd been around — '

'But you weren't. And now that you are, it's a bit late.'

'You hate me, don't you?'

'I used to wonder where you were.' The tears had failed to come. She had stopped scratching the arm of the settee. She was

317

quite calm and collected. 'And then I learned to hate my mother.'

'You can't really feel that. I mean, she was there and I wasn't. I wasn't much use, I wasn't there to — '

'No,' whispered Ishbel. 'And that hurt, you don't know how far down the misery went. But she *was* there, and she taught me to hate her. Building it up gradually. When I was old enough, she'd take me out to dinner — big treat, she made it sound — and I'd find there was some sleazy tycoon on the scene, giving me the eye. And I was supposed to be nice to him. 'But you don't have to keep it up,' she told me. 'Once we've hooked him, you can get out.' She thought I'd find it amusing. But she wasn't amused when I fell in love with Simon.'

'Love? Simon wouldn't know the meaning of the word.'

'He was very plausible. About everything. As a stepfather, he was . . . oh, for a while he really did seem very kind. And somehow we . . . it built up into something different, and I hadn't meant it to do that, but there it was.'

And how much of that had been a deep-seated urge to rebel against that hated mother? Who had then turned on the two of them and destroyed Simon's job, and destroyed any hope of a high ranking

318

appointment anywhere else. That much he had been told in no uncertain terms by Brigid. And then Ishbel couldn't help herself: pride demanded that she go and live with him. She supported the two of them by working for the firm in Musselburgh, driving delivery vans, occasionally taking Simon for job interviews in the Borders, away from his usual haunts. Anything to keep them going.

'And you were still living together until . . . ?'

There was a long pause. Then Ishbel rushed on again. 'He went off. Maybe because I'd told him I was getting fed up. He wasn't ever going to get a job, was he? Wasn't really trying. Just leaving it to me to keep him. So he said he'd . . . show me.'

'Show you what?'

'I don't know. I think it was just one of his boastful remarks.'

Words stuck in his throat like vomit. 'Some other woman? Next one in line?'

Ishbel gave a parched sigh. 'Could have been. Maybe found someone with better prospects. So he just wasn't around any more.'

Just not there. Like her father, just not there any more.

'Not getting back in touch with your mother for some reason?'

319

'What reason would he have for that?'

Anything to keep the money coming in, Ritchie had said. In spite of her story, could Ishbel and Simon Pringle have been together in the robbery? Simon either crawling back to Brigid . . . or deciding to rob her. Which way had it been? And could Ishbel, so good at handling any kind of vehicle, have been the getaway driver?

Unthinkable. Utter bloody rubbish.

As she began scraping the settee again, more slowly this time, he changed tack suddenly. 'After all that sleazy two-timing, you don't suppose your mother could have killed Simon? Could have met him in the Baldonald grounds before I came with her to Edinburgh, or came back without my noticing, and . . . ?' He left it dangling.

'If my mother wanted to dispose of anybody, she certainly wouldn't have done it herself. She'd have known exactly the top man in his field, and hired him to do the job for her.' Without warning, Ishbel demonstrated that she too could change tack when it suited her. 'Daddy, just what brought you into this part of the world?'

He told her. Her eyes widened. Instead of brimming with tears, they were filled with incredulous laughter.

'Ghosting *her* memoirs?'

'It seemed an interesting idea. Your mother was most insistent.'

'Insistent. Oh, dear, yes. Daddy, how could you have let her exploit you all over again?'

So she had learned, over the years, that her mother had been the exploiting kind. He put out a hand towards her, wanting a contact, wanting her hand in his.

She dodged at once, got up again. 'Would you like some coffee? Or we've got a bottle of white wine in the fridge. Would you like a glass?' Without waiting for him to say yes or no to either offer, she went out.

Greg glanced at the VCR clock. Just about time for the early evening news. He found the remote control under one of the coffee table magazines, and flicked it on.

There were some lurching scenes of people running in a street somewhere in the Middle East, and men firing guns into the air, followed by a steadier picture of two men in dark suits shaking hands in the Foreign Office. Their faces gave way to those of DCI Rutherford and a uniformed superintendent seated beside him, facing a cluster of microphones on the table before them.

The superintendent spoke gravely of two brutal murders within such a short space of time — that of Simon Pringle, in the grounds of Baldonald House in the Borders, and then, so tragically soon after the death by natural causes of her husband Lord Crombie of Baldonald House, the murder of Lady Crombie in Leith. His summary was slowly and ponderously paced, in rolling sentences which joined seamlessly on, one after the other, until the general sense was camouflaged.

Behind him, Greg heard a faint gasp. Ishbel had come in with the glasses, but instead of handing one of them to him she was focusing on the screen.

'He was talking about mother, wasn't he? Daddy, what's going on?'

'Press conference. The usual appeals for witnesses, I'd guess.'

He guessed right. The superintendent had handed over to Rutherford, who enjoyed such occasions. He was not one for obliquely framed subsidiary clauses and public relations pussy-footing. With a determined thrust of his chin he spoke masterfully to viewers, not so much soliciting their help as demanding it. There had been two brutal killings, and somebody must have seen something. It was their public duty to come forward. In confidence, of course.

'Investigations into the Baldonald House killing are proceeding satisfactorily. New evidence this very day means we hope to make a public statement within the next couple of days.' Rutherford sounded as confident as he always did when there were so many loose ends to be tied up. 'But the police will still welcome any reports of Pringle's movements between the 18th and 24th of this month, in or around Edinburgh and in the Selkirk and Baldonald region.' The phone number came flashing up in large numerals across the bottom of the screen. A disembodied voice read it out slowly and heavily for the benefit of those more used to watching television pictures than reading.

And then, linked with the first murder on the Crombie estate, there was the matter of Lady Crombie's murder in her Leith flat.

'Anyone who can offer any sightings in Edinburgh should get in touch with the police at this number.' Again a line of figures, and a background recitation. 'We know that Lady Crombie visited the family solicitors, and that she returned to her flat in Leith, where she was murdered. Anybody who saw her in or around Thistle Street, or Heriot Row, or entering her flat, *especially* if she was accompanied at any stage, can help us settle this distressing case. We are already working towards an arrest, but confirmatory evidence would be a great help.'

What he meant, thought Greg, was that

they did not yet have a really solid lead, but that Rutherford would be happy to accept anything that would build up his image.

'At the same time' — Rutherford had reserved his safe boast till the end — 'I am happy to announce that we have solved the mystery which brought us to Baldonald House in the first place. Thanks to the skills of our specialist technical staff, we have recovered a large number of the artworks stolen from the house.'

Without taking her eyes off the screen, Ishbel handed Greg a glass of wine. 'Is that true, Daddy?'

'It's news to me. Not a word about it before I left.'

Rutherford was lying: 'An arrest is imminent. It now appears that the gang which broke into the house had hidden their loot in the disused family vault to be recovered later.'

'No,' said Greg softly. 'Oh dear, no, I don't think so.' He glanced up at Ishbel as he sipped his wine. 'I think your mother was behind it all. Stowed them away in the hope they never would be found, or not until she was ready to do with them whatever she had in mind.'

'Why? Daddy, what are you on about?'

The DCI's voice was going on about a

possible linkage with the two murders and repeating his appeal for members of the public to come forward with what, he implied, would be the last nails in the coffin of certain villains. Over his bombastic tones. Greg said: 'The only thing that makes sense is that she'd already sold the really valuable ones off, and replaced them with fakes. She was bound to know somebody who'd do that for her. But in any exhibition, someone would have spotted they were fakes. And an exhibition of several of the more historic pieces was coming up. So the lot had to be shifted. Fake a robbery of the fakes! Get the stuff out of the way . . . '

'In the vault!' breathed Ishbel. 'If Hector had ever found out — oh, how could she?'

'Collect the insurance,' Greg went on, 'thereby raking in the money twice over, allowing for the original sales, and later choose a moment to burn them, maybe.'

Telephone numbers were flashed on the screen again, before the pictures changed to those of a pile-up of two transits and an artic hit by sudden gusts of gale force on the A7, followed by a weather forecast of increasingly high winds and rain squalls over the next few days.

Ishbel gulped at her wine.

He looked around the room, at a few media

magazines on the coffee table, and a painting of a waterfall. 'This is Caroline's flat, isn't it?'

'She invited me to stay. For as long as I like.'

'Hiding you away?'

'I've got nothing to hide from.'

'In that case,' Greg said with more conviction than he felt, 'you'll be perfectly safe if you come back and tell the police all you know.'

'But I don't know anything.'

'Then tell them that, so that they can eliminate you from their enquiries. Unless . . . '

'Unless what?'

'Unless you want me to help you get away. Edinburgh airport, say. Got your passport?'

'Daddy, you're not thinking I could have murdered them? Both of them?'

'I'm thinking of what they might think. I mean, if you were to tell them what you've told me — how much you'd grown to hate your mother, and hated Simon too. Both murdered. They could jump to the wrong conclusions. And they'll give you a rough old time anyway.'

'Let's go.'

'To the airport?'

'No.' She had put the glass down and was waving her arms, her hair flying. He got up and at last threw his arms round her, holding her until she stopped threshing to and fro. 'Back to Baldonald,' she sobbed. For a moment her head sank into the crook of his arm; then she was on her way to pile a few clothes into a holdall.

It took her a very short time: she gave the impression of having been travelling light over recent times.

'And I must tell Caroline.' Again she was shaking her hair impatiently, muttering quickly into the phone before slamming it down. 'Her mobile's switched off. Had to leave a message on it, saying I'm on my way.'

★　★　★

As they approached Baldonald House down the side road, gusts along the valley smacked hard against the side of the car. Along one bank of the loch below, in the shelter of the hills the water was ruffled by skittish ripples as if someone were blowing lazily along the surface. Further out the whidders were fiercer, whipped from above, an inland sea growing more boisterous by the minute. The sky was a sullen bronze, heavy behind the ridges.

The trees creaked and leaned over the path towards the chapel and vault. Caroline was standing at the end of the path, and DI Gunn was a few hundred yards behind her, talking to a uniformed constable.

Without warning a cock pheasant shot out of the rough grass like a jet fighter taking off at a steep angle. The thump of its body against the radiator jarred the car more fiercely than the wind. There was a flutter of wings and torn feathers. The bird hit the far side of the drive and twitched in a terrible ballet of convulsions.

Even before Greg had stopped, Ishbel was wrenching at the passenger door and stumbling out, just as Caroline strode across the drive and stooped over the pheasant.

'No, Caro! No, you can't!'

Caroline took the bird's neck and wrung it in one expert twist.

'Don't be so sentimental, Ishbel. Kindest this way. No use to itself or anybody else in that state.' She wiped her hands on her slacks, and stared an accusation. 'I've been trying to ring you back. But you'd already left.' Now the accusation was turned on Greg. 'Just what the hell are you playing at?'

'Caro . . .'

Ishbel took a step forward, and was all at once in Caroline's arms. Stroking the tangle of blonde hair, Caroline said: 'I told you to stay put until we knew exactly what was going on.'

'Caro, Daddy's right. I had to come.'

Caroline stared over Ishbel's shoulder at Greg. 'Couldn't you have stayed out of this?'

'Since I was able to find her,' he pointed out, 'the police would have done so as well, very soon.'

DI Lesley Gunn was picking her way over the unevenness of the path and brushing aside a windblown branch.

Caroline released Ishbel as Greg got out of the car. Close to his daughter, he said: 'So that's how it is. You and Caroline — what's known, I believe, as an item?'

'Yes,' said Ishbel defiantly. 'Does that disgust you?'

No, it didn't disgust him. But he did wonder, dazedly, just how this fitted in with the Simon Pringle interlude; and who had found it expedient to dispose of Simon.

DI Gunn was saying: 'I presume this is your daughter, Mr Dacre?'

'It is.'

'I'm glad she's put in an appearance at last. Perhaps you could come into the cabin and answer a few questions, Miss Dacre.'

And that was something else to wonder about: had the detective also seen the two young women for a few moments in the same light as Greg had seen them, and begun asking herself the same questions?

17

Before DI Lesley Gunn could settle down to questioning Ishbel Dacre, there came a phone call concerning a stolen credit card. Police in Galashiels were holding a man attempting to use the card in a local supermarket. He was known to them for petty crimes, always on the coat-tails of heftier villains.

'We've checked the dabs on the card against the National Index, and we think you'll find they tally with some of those you collected in that rented cottage. Only we can't hold him for long on a lowgrade charge like this without granting bail, unless we can make the charge more serious.'

'It could be a whole lot more serious.'

'You'd better get over here quick, inspector.'

Before leaving, she had to know where Ishbel Dacre was proposing to stay. No good pursuing one promising trail, if another prey slid off while your back was turned.

'She stays here, of course,' said Caroline Crombie.

'Can I rely on that?'

'I did come here of my own free will,' Ishbel pointed out. 'I'm hardly likely to flit off into *that'* — she waved towards the door of the trailer as it vibrated and produced a strangled gulp in the wind.

'I'll be responsible for her,' said Greg. 'I'll book her into the *Tam Lin*, and I'll be responsible for her.'

Lesley studied him suspiciously. 'There's no vacancy there at the moment. We both know that.'

'In any case' — Caroline overruled any other possibility — 'she stays here. In her own home. *Our* home from now on.'

There was another phone call to hold Lesley up. Rutherford was on the line, rejoicing that he was on Ishbel Dacre's trail. The local lads had traced her to a car rental firm — 'And, would you believe it, her father showed up there and went off in one hell of a rush after her.'

'Yes,' said Lesley, 'I do believe it. They're both here right now. Her father's just brought her in.'

Rutherford was not going to admit to being deflated. 'Right. Don't let them out of your sight. If that girl tries to do a runner, bung her into a cell somewhere.'

'On what charge?'

'Use your imagination, Lez.' He switched to another accomplishment where he was on firmer ground. 'We've hauled Veitch in. After

331

leaving the Crombie woman, he was traced to a security firm. A dodgy one, run by two ex-coppers. Both known by their old colleagues to be bent.'

'Capable of hiring out as contract killers at short notice?'

'Take it easy, Lez. I'm with you on that, but the timing's a bit tight. I aim to find out just what they've all been playing at. But as of this moment he's not in any mood to co-operate. Playing the high and mighty. Refusing to answer a single simple question until his brief shows up. But we'll break him. And then I'll be back to see this Dacre girl. Nothing like getting all our suspects into the same shopping trolley, hey?'

★　★　★

The High Street in Galashiels was being dug up, so Lesley had to weave her way round back streets to find the police station above the Gala Water, swollen and tumultuous with storm water coming down from the hills.

She was greeted by a middle-aged inspector who eyed her appreciatively but then stiffened into formality and spoke crisply and impersonally. Somebody must have been delivering lectures about sexual harassment in the Force. 'His name's Fenwick. Jackie

Fenwick. Came onto our manor from Gateshead five or six years ago after a career of petty crime along the Tyne.'

'Another forged card, like the last one?'

'Oh, no, this is a genuine one. Nicked this very morning in the hope of putting it to immediate use. But the owner noticed within minutes that he'd lost it, and notified the card protection company. Fenwick's been trying it on in a small supermarket, one of a local chain. Cramped space, like so many wee stores nowadays. Haven't quite got the hang of it yet. Our little weasel hoped to catch them on the hop and slip through. Nice full basket at their checkout, and then at the last minute he wanted a bottle of Bell's and twenty cigarettes from the shelf behind the girl, so that she'd get confused when punching the codes into the machine, and he added to that by chatting her up and distracting her. Fancied himself as a ladies' man, by her account.'

'But she didn't fall for it?'

'She's the daughter of the owner. Scared stiff of what her father would say if she let someone get away with a fast one. She had the door shut on him and the phone ringing a whole lot faster than she rang up his kipper paste and haggis.'

Lesley was given an interview room, and a

uniformed constable brought the suspect in. Peeling off the wrappings from a cassette, he started the machine and ran through the familiar routine of date, time, and those present.

Fenwick was a wiry, lean-featured man in a lumberjack shirt, black leather jacket, and frayed jeans. He was goodlooking in a raffish kind of way, and had what he himself would doubtless have described as a roguish twinkle in his eye. He smirked as he perched on the uncomfortable metal chair. I've been through all this before, his attitude proclaimed: it's small beer, a petty offence, I know the score. Maybe a couple of months. Might even get away with a fine, the prisons being too full to take me. Probably not, but nothing to get het up about either way.

Lesley said: 'You realise that you are still under caution, Mr Ross.'

The constable blinked at her. 'Inspector, we've just put his name on tape — John James Fenwick.'

'That's me,' said Fenwick jauntily.

'Also known as Mr Ross, though. To Mrs Dunbar, that is.'

'I'm not acquainted with any Mrs Dunbar.' Fenwick's Geordie accent was also meant to be lovable, with an engaging lisp. 'Is that to be regretted, would you say, bonny lass?'

'Your prints were all over that cottage up
Ettrickbridge way. And all over this credit
card you've been silly enough to flash around.'

'Cottage, bonny lass?'

'I'm not your bonny lass.'

'More's the pity.'

'You may be interested to know that the
loot from Baldonald House has been
found.'

'Wherever that may be. I'm sorry, pet, but
I'm not with you.'

'And I imagine your prints will be on some
of those paintings as well, when you were
helping carry them out.'

'Now, look, I never carried no paintings.
Never set foot inside the house.'

'No, of course you didn't,' smiled Lesley.
'Silly of me. You were only the decoy, weren't
you? Luring poor Mrs Dunbar out of the way
while the others got on with it.'

Fenwick's jauntiness was fading. He was
looking aggrieved, his twinkle giving way to
the soulful, hurt innocence of a bullied
mongrel. 'I've told you, I don't know any Mrs
Dunbar.'

'And did you have any hand in getting
Simon Pringle out of the way as well?'

'I know nothing about that either. No way
am I going to have any murder rap pinned on
me.'

'So you know about the murder?'

'Why aye, I . . . read about it. But it didn't mean anything to me.'

'Yet the moment I mentioned it, you associated it at once with what we'd already been talking about. Because you *do* know that neighbourhood, don't you?'

'I need a brief.'

'I'll ask the duty sergeant to contact the duty solicitor. Unless you have one of your own?'

'Look, pet, you've got me all wrong.'

'And while we're sending for a solicitor, I think we'll send for Mrs Dunbar, too. To identify you. Or, of course, to clear your good name.'

It was difficult to sag on that small, straight-backed chair, but Fenwick managed it.

'Look, I'm not going to get picked on while the rest of them walk away. If you want the big boys — '

'So you do work with some big boys?'

'What's it worth?'

'No deals. But,' said Lesley very carefully, knowing the constable's eyes were fixed on her, and the tape would puritanically confirm any attempt to lean too hard on the suspect, 'the fact that you were only a small cog in a rather nasty machine might tell in your favour. If you could tell us how the rest of the machine worked.'

'Well, it was kinky, wasn't it?'

'Kinky?'

'I mean, setting up a gang to rob your own house, the way she did.'

It took a further half-hour to extract from him everything he knew. Even that was partly speculation: it was true that he had only played a small part on the fringes; but in spite of his plea to be let off lightly because of that, it went against the grain to admit his insignificance. He could not help boasting, claiming the acquaintance of the real big boys, knowing their methods, and knowing their programme for the rest of the year.

Lesley leaned forward across the table. 'Programme? What's next?'

Fenwick wavered between fear at how much he had given away and the desire to show off even further.

'Well,' he hedged, 'I do know there's going to be this funeral.'

'Is that a euphemism for a killing?'

'A you-what?'

She thought of Rutherford's suspicions about Sir Michael Veitch. 'A contract killing? Some gangland rivalry?'

'No, some big local funeral. Some big cheese.'

'Lord Crombie?'

'That'd be it. Aiming to hit the target that day, when all the nobs are at the service in Selkirk. In and out fast, sawn off shotguns, wire cutters, get the best pieces. Sod the burglar alarms. Ten minutes and they're away.'

'More violent this time?'

'Why, aye. A shot up the arse for anyone who interferes. Has to be fast, because this time they won't be getting the layout all spelt out for em by the lady of the house, will they? A commando raid, the way I hear it.'

'Taking lessons from those French steal-to-order operators blasting their way into the châteaux,' Lesley mused.

'I divva knaw about that. But it's going to be hard hitting.'

'And where will this be aimed at?'

'Look, I don't know the names of these places. All I heard — '

'Just tell us everything you heard.'

'It's got to be worth my while.'

'If you don't talk,' said Lesley affably, 'it's hard to assess just what will be worth your while.'

Jackie Fenwick sagged still further. He knew he had already gone too far. Too far, Lesley prayed silently, for him to scuttle back now.

★　★　★

Greg felt drained. He was tired, longing for bed, longing to get away from this place altogether, have a long sleep and then take up real life somewhere else.

Caroline and Ishbel were side by side on the settee in the snug together, looking unreasonably contented. Just being together was enough for them. He wanted to ask how the hell his daughter could have fallen into Simon Pringle's clutches when all the time this was her real passion. But he could predict that questions would mean getting involved in an intense discussion, and he'd had enough of intensity these last few weeks.

Time, when he could summon up the energy, to get out of here, into his car, and drive through the late evening darkness to the *Tam Lin* before they closed the doors for the night.

Caroline was saying: 'I couldn't really turn him down. I'll have to unpick things with the minister in Selkirk, but he'll probably be delighted to find himself conducting the service in the Westerlaw Castle chapel.'

'They're really going to miss your father,' said Ishbel fondly. 'Me, too.'

'Sir Lachlan wanted to take over all the

339

arrangements, but I told him that was still my job. He'll put his chapel at our disposal for the ceremony. Still in lovely condition, unlike our own. And then we drive back to Baldonald and lay the coffin in the vault. And seal it up. I don't think there are going to be any more Crombies.'

'Certainly none like your father.'

Their fingers intertwined.

Greg was getting drowsier. He tried to pull himself together. 'Look, this all sounds very decent and generous and the way it ought to be. But what about the important things?'

'What's so important?'

'Simon's death. And Brigid's death.'

'That will all have to wait.'

'But any time now they'll both be back — those two detectives, Rutherford and the Gunn girl. They'll have a lot of questions to ask. I mean, Ishbel — '

'I can give Ishbel an alibi,' said Caroline.

'Caro, I don't want you to let yourself in for — '

'You were with me,' said Caroline. 'I'm prepared to swear to that.'

'On both occasions?' said Greg blearily. 'Both murders?'

'Both. And not just then. Every night,' said Caroline ardently.

Greg stirred himself. He kissed Ishbel, who

patted his cheek with her right hand — not so much in filial affection as in vague pity — and nodded to Caroline, who said: 'Don't worry too much, Mr Dacre. I'll see no harm comes to Ishbel.'

The wind was bouncing off the gable end of the inn as he parked on the hard shoulder alongside a small car silhouetted against the pale light through the curtained window. He had hauled his bag out of the boot and turned towards the side door when it was opened for him.

'Since you were kind enough to provide me with your change of address,' said Kate, 'I thought it was high time I came up to see whether you needed bailing from some Scottish dungeon.'

'You've driven up today — all at one go?'

The wind howled through his teeth, and he clutched at the door jamb. Kate took his arm and dragged him indoors.

'After your call, I found the phone number here and tried ringing you. But you hadn't shown up. And when I tried Baldonald House, you'd dashed off somewhere in a hurry. I didn't like the sound of it.'

They went into the bar. Two regulars lingered on stools at the end. The landlord, leaning towards them, did not look round as Kate closed the door.

'Gregory Dacre,' said Greg as commandingly as possible. 'I believe you have a room for me. Sorry to be so late, but things have been happening.'

'Aye, so we hear.'

'Perhaps a couple of drams while we get our breath back?'

The landlord poured two large Longmorns.

They perched on the two remaining bar stools, and Kate took a long, appreciative mouthful.

'My friend's had a long journey. You've got accommodation for tonight?'

'There's only the one room free, and you're the one booked into that.'

'That'll do fine.'

'I'm nae so sure. We're still no' used to those ways up here.'

One of the regulars at the end spluttered over his glass. 'Och come off it, Angus. What about those twa walkers last April? Ye'll no' be telling us you thought they were rightly wed?'

'Well, that was a wee bit special.'

'And when young Roberston was trying out Susan before deciding to marry her? Man, you've done as thriving a trade as Gretna Green, wi' nae bother about a blacksmith.'

'Och, well maybe . . . '

Greg put his hand over Kate's. 'Have you had anything to eat?'

'Stopped for a quick coffee and a pastry, that's all.'

Greg looked at the landlord, who made no suggestion of providing a meal at this late hour.

'You're not hungry?'

Kate glanced towards the door at the foot of the stairs. 'Depends what you mean by hungry.'

18

During the night the wind became ferocious. Sagging roofs of old barns were lifted, shredded, and scattered over the fields. Power lines and telephone lines came down in a tangle. In the morning, Lesley Gunn arrived at Baldonald House in the company of one of the WPCs with a festoon of twigs and torn leaves wrapped into her car's windscreen wipers, and a scratch across the offside panel where a branch had lashed out as they passed. In the house there was no electricity, and daylight was too feeble to reach into far corners of the rooms. Mrs Dunbar had instructed young Drew to light fires in the library and the sitting-room, and place paraffin lamps on a table in each. DCI Rutherford phoned on his mobile to report hold-ups at two blocked roads. He would have to find a longer way round. Lesley predicted he would be in a foul temper and would undoubtedly expect a report on the Dacre girl the moment he did get through, and be in a mood to tear it to shreds.

She would have preferred to interview Ishbel Dacre formally in the mobile incident

344

room, but the gale had lifted it from underneath and tilted it so that the floor slanted too steeply for it to be occupied. It would have to be the library.

There were four of them present. Because the tape recorder was not functioning, and there was no sign of a portable recorder as a stopgap, Lesley, had settled the WPC in a corner with a notebook. And Caroline had insisted that since the detective inspector had the backing of a uniformed officer, Ishbel was entitled to a legal representative or a friend to safeguard her interests.

'It looks as if it would take time for any solicitor to get through at the moment,' Lesley pointed out.

'Then I must insist that you let me sit in. Just to make sure that Miss Dacre is not subjected to unreasonable pressure, and that her evidence isn't twisted to suit police prejudices.'

'Miss Crombie, I've no intention of fitting Miss Dacre up. We want to establish the truth, and that's the way it will be.'

Caroline sat at an angle with her elbow propped on the table, alert and ready to protest at any transgression.

Lesley aimed to keep it as conversational as possible. 'Now, Miss Dacre, you knew the late Simon Pringle.'

'Yes.'

'I understand he had at one stage been your mother's second husband.'

'That's right, yes.'

'And what precisely was *your* relationship with him?'

'He was . . . my stepfather, of course.'

'Of course. But after that — after he and your mother had split up?'

'I . . . I felt sorry for him. We lived together for a while.'

'It was an aberration,' Caroline burst out. 'Utterly stupid.' She stared at Ishbel almost with loathing, contradicted in seconds by a forgiving, compassionate smile. 'Seeking a father figure, perhaps.'

That would have made Gregory Dacre wince, thought Lesley.

She studied the two of them: just like a married couple, swinging between mutual irritation over a lingering dispute and long-standing mutual devotion.

'Stupid,' Ishbel echoed. 'Yes, it was. I soon realised that.'

'But you didn't immediately break off the relationship and go back to . . . ' Lesley hesitated, glancing at Caroline, but then amending it: 'To your mother?'

'I wasn't going to be beholden to her.'

'But you must have felt . . . how shall I put it . . . ?'

'Defiled,' said Caroline. 'What else could she have felt?'

'Miss Crombie, will you please leave this to me. Miss Dacre — '

'All right, yes. I felt defiled.'

'So badly that you were prepared to wipe him out — kill him.'

'I object to that,' snapped Caroline. 'It's grotesque.'

Lesley was beginning to share Rutherford's scepticism about the two murders being related. The girl might have killed Pringle after he had let her down and filled her with loathing; but, whatever the pressures, surely she wouldn't have killed her own mother?

Or were there dark, perverse motives that she and Rutherford hadn't even guessed at yet?

Just for once she was impatient for Rutherford to appear on the scene, preferably with some conclusive evidence about Veitch or some of his associates.

At random she said: 'Miss Dacre, did you never visit your mother when she was staying in Leith?'

'No. I've told you, I — '

'And not on the day she was killed?'

Caroline said: 'It would save time if you let me tell you one thing: Ishbel was back with me at the time of the murders.'

347

'Both of them?'

'Both of them. I'm prepared to swear to that, if necessary.'

'But Miss Crombie, didn't you tell us earlier that you were in the studio at the relevant times? How could you provide Miss Dacre with an alibi for those same times?'

'You're trying to trap us. Let me make it clear: I can vouch for all Ishbel's movements. She couldn't have had anything to do with either of those murders.'

'Caro, please,' Ishbel begged. 'Don't stick your neck out for me. Of course you weren't with me.'

'Hush, love. Not another word.'

'I was on my own. I won't have you getting into trouble by shielding me like that. You were in the studio both times. But' — she blazed suddenly at Lesley — 'I still didn't kill Simon. Or my mother.'

There was the sound of voices in the corridor outside. Before the WPC could get to the door, Gregory Dacre came in with a young woman whose olive complexion blended into the shadows of the uncertain light, but was still discernibly beautiful.

'Well, we made it,' said Greg cheerfully. 'Flying foliage to the right of 'em, flying foliage to the left of 'em, but we got here.'

He went towards his daughter and kissed

her. Lesley saw the girl flinch and instinctively draw back; but then she smiled briefly,
and touched his arm just as briefly.

'Mr Dacre, I'd rather you didn't interrupt
us at this juncture. If perhaps you and your
friend — '

'Kate Hadleigh,' said Greg. 'I think you
ought to include her in your enquiries. She
was with me at that London meeting with the
cabal. She can confirm the goings-on there,
and add a few comments of her own.'

There was to be no peace. A tap at the
door, and in came Mrs Dunbar, ignoring
everyone in the room but Caroline. 'Would ye
be wanting tea, or coffee, Miss Caroline?'

'You've got something working?' Greg
marvelled.

'The Aga is getting along very nicely. Miss
Caroline?'

Without waiting to consult Lesley, Caroline
nodded. 'A wonderful idea, Mrs Dunbar.'

★　★　★

Greg led Kate to two of the original library
armchairs which had been pushed back
against the shelving. In spite of the appalling
weather, after last night with Kate he felt
optimistic about things — about everything.

'How are we getting on?' he asked the DI

heartily, as one skilled researcher to another.

'Mr Dacre, when we've finished our coffee break — '

'If I were writing a novel,' he said, 'I know how I'd resolve this plot.'

'But you're not a novelist,' said Lesley tartly. 'You're a hack assembler of random facts.'

Kate bristled. Before she could rush to his defence, Greg waved a tolerant hand. 'Thanks a lot. But all right, I suppose there's not a lot of difference, really.' He was in no mood to be deterred. 'Now, the most plausible storyline is that Miss Crombie here was the one who killed Simon Pringle . . . ' A silly, tempting echo buzzed into the back of his mind: *Miss Crombie, in the kitchen, with the length of rope* . . . He fought it off. 'Killed Simon Pringle,' he said, 'because he was chatting her up and she simply had to silence him before it became too disgusting.'

Ishbel screamed at him. 'Daddy, you can't . . . '

Greg shook his head sympathetically. 'I'm sorry, love, but it really is a plausible hypothesis.'

Silently he apologised to the late Hector Crombie. He felt so at home here in Baldonald House, as if Hector were at his side encouraging him, though regretting what he had to say about Caroline. He would have liked to ghost Hector's memoirs — draw out of him, from depths he himself might be unaware of, the whole story of his ancestors and every development and redevelopment of the house itself over the centuries.

No need for ghosting, maybe. Hector himself would haunt these corridors without any need of outside help.

Greg waited for the old man to steer him in the right direction, even if it hurt to do so. There would be no flinching. Hector had been the real top layer. Brigid and all the rest of them could never be anything but the Marzipan Layer.

As Ishbel spluttered another protest, Caroline said: 'Your father's almost as weird as your late mother.'

'And where on earth is the evidence for all these hypotheses?' asked Lesley.

'Solid physical evidence, none. Not so far. But I do have a sort of . . . well . . . '

Kate managed to make a contribution this time. 'Empathy. Especially with the workings of his late wife's mind.'

'The murders had nothing to do with Brigid's scheme, unless maybe Simon was working with Brigid in spite of everything, and that was another reason for Caroline to hate his guts. Maybe somehow he was involved in the original recce — and when he'd disappeared, the gang wondered what had happened. But somehow I don't see it that way. I do think the robbery has to be pinned on Brigid, and it's got nothing to do with the killings. We don't know exactly what she intended to do with the stuff she'd stashed away in the vault — whether that was purely temporary and she would shift it when the hubbub had died down, or whether in the end she'd torch it and destroy the evidence of forgeries. But one thing we can be sure of: Brigid didn't murder Simon.'

'We can?' said Lesley ironically.

'Whatever her intentions, Simon's death mucked them up. I mean, with police swarming all over the place because of the murder, that could have meant a whole re-think of her plans. She'd be the last person to want a corpse on the scene while she went about her little games.'

Caroline said: 'As a novelist, Mr Dacre, you'd never make the bestseller list. The remainder counter, maybe. And with all these witnesses to your defamatory remarks, I'm wondering if I could sue you for slander.'

Kate leaned across the arm of her chair. 'Greg,' she muttered, 'do remember that you're neither Morse nor Wexford. Leave it to the professionals.'

Mrs Dunbar came in with a tray of cups and saucers, followed by Drew with another one bearing a large coffee percolator, milk jug, and sugar bowl. There was something about their stately progress that silenced everyone else in the room, watching each move as in some hypnotic arcane ritual.

The effect was spoilt by the arrival of DCI Rutherford, hard on their heels.

'Another cup and saucer, Drew.' Mrs Dunbar bobbed a curtsy to Caroline, and scurried out.

* * *

Rutherford was panting as if he had run the whole way.

'Right, inspector. How far have we got?'

Lesley summed up briefly. Before she could finish, he had interrupted, his gaze fixed hard on Caroline Crombie while he was talking about other things.

'We may have to forget Veitch, unfortunately. It seems his visit to those security cowboys was straightforward enough. Wanting to set up a surveillance operation on one of his office complexes. Doesn't trust anybody. And yet he's proposing to hire two of the most untrustworthy operators in the business.' He shrugged. 'I'm still keeping *him* under surveillance. May still have a chance of turning over a few stones. But now, Miss Crombie.'

She returned his gaze stonily.

'Inspector Gunn, didn't you tell me a few minutes ago that Miss Crombie's attempt to provide an alibi for Miss Dacre had fallen flat because she wasn't with her, but in the studio?'

'That's right.'

'But at the relevant times — both dates — she wasn't. In the first one she had supposedly gone out on an appraisal for some nature programme. Left to her own devices. No need for a minder. A trusted executive in her particular field.'

'Marzipan Layer,' murmured Greg Dacre.

'At the time of the second murder' — Rutherford might almost have been punching Caroline one blow after another rather than talking to her — 'you were in the studio early in the day, but not in the afternoon. The programme that day when Lady Crombie was murdered didn't all go out live. Your section had been recorded and edited two days earlier.'

Ishbel began a quiet whimpering as if trying to clear a frog in her throat. Caroline made no sound and no move.

'So I'd be no good as a novelist?' Greg

reached to tap Kate's shoulder. 'I was right all along. Look, the way I see it — '

'Mr Dacre, haven't we had enough of your — '

'Miss Crombie.' Greg felt his own voice going down a sinister half octave. 'You murdered Simon because he was making a pass at *you*. He was finished with Ishbel, and thought he could get round you. I don't know what he was doing snooping about in the grounds here, but you must have bumped into him and — '

'Oh, for Christ's sake,' bellowed Rutherford. 'Who let this man in here?'

Lesley said: 'The awful thing is, it makes sense. Miss Crombie?'

There was no stopping Greg Dacre — or Poirot, or Miss Marple, or whoever it was at this instant. 'And later, you had the key to Brigid's flat. Your father must have had a key. You were making most of the real arrangements after his death . . . and found the key among his belongings. Carried it around until you knew when Brigid would be in Edinburgh. And went along to wait for her.'

'Why should I want to do that?'

'Because she had killed your father.'

'My father died of a heart attack.'

'Because of what he overheard.'

Rutherford belched a protest. 'Look here,

Mr Dacre, if you'll just leave us to do our job — '

Greg went on firing words directly at Caroline, more lethal even than Rutherford's. 'Virtually killed your father,' he insisted. 'Because through the laird's lug he overheard what Brigid was trying on with me. And the things she said about him. Were you there with him the whole time, or — '

'I came in just as it was finishing.' Caroline was livid with a rage of memory. She stabbed convulsively at her hair in some attempt to calm herself down before it was too late.

'And he had a stroke, and you weren't ever going to forgive Brigid.'

'She was a bitch. And now we know she was a fraud. Sold off father's treasures when it suited her, and replaced some with fakes. And even that wasn't enough: she faked a robbery of the fakes when there was a chance of her being shown up. Just to make money. And more money.'

'So she had to be killed?' said Lesley Gunn wonderingly.

'No.' But there was no conviction in it.

Rutherford turned to Ishbel. 'So you don't have any alibis after all?'

'No. But it wasn't me. And I don't believe it was Caro.'

But every twitch in her face showed that

she did now believe it.

Cunningly Rutherford concentrated on her. Lesley realised what he was up to. You had to admire his tactics, even while you were hating him for his ruthlessness.

'You had as good a reason as anyone to kill Simon Pringle. And your mother, who might have stood in the way of your inheritance from Lord Crombie. Come to think of it' — Rutherford was positively beaming — 'you *both* had the same reason. The inheritance. Working together to dispose of Lady Crombie before she had time to start a legal battle.'

'You really are contemptible,' said Caroline. 'And incompetent.'

No, thought Lesley sadly. Contemptible, yes, but not incompetent. He would lean on Ishbel, the more vulnerable of the two, until Caroline cracked. Because Caroline, strong as she might be with her ruthless strangler's grip, was enfeebled by a hopeless, all-devouring love. She would not let Ishbel carry any of the blame.

'All right,' Greg Dacre shouted at the DCI. 'If you think it's my daughter, why don't you charge her? And then we'll have the pleasure of suing you for wrongful arrest.'

'You've been reading the wrong sort of books.' And Rutherford added with calculated offensiveness: 'As well as writing them.'

Caroline cracked.

'Let's be done with this. There's a time when you get too tired to go on struggling.'

'Caro, you can't — '

'Like putting a pheasant out of its misery,' said Greg.

'Like the pheasant, yes,' Caroline confirmed with a weary smile. 'Kinder to put an end to it quickly.'

Rutherford gave Lesley a peremptory nod. She cleared her throat and intoned: 'Caroline Crombie, I am arresting you on a charge of murdering Simon Pringle and Brigid, Lady Crombie.'

'No, no, no.' Ishbel was whimpering, rocking convulsively to and fro. Her father lurched awkwardly across the room to put his arms round her. She shook him off and went on rocking.

'You do not have to say anything. But it may harm your defence if you do not mention, when questioned, something which you later rely on in court. Anything you do say may be given in evidence.'

Ishbel flung herself into Caroline's arms.

Now that the charge had been read, Rutherford relaxed into a mellow and almost sociable mood. 'Miss Crombie, we can understand why you hated your stepmother so much that you had to kill her. But just as a

358

matter of interest, what about Pringle? Hatred because he had taken over Ishbel Dacre, and then cheated on her — was that enough to justify strangling him?'

Over Ishbel's heaving shoulder, Caroline looked at Greg Dacre. 'I must apologise for my remarks about your creative abilities, Mr Dacre. You were getting uncannily close to the truth. Only it was even more disgusting.'

Rutherford looked none too pleased at the idea of Caroline sharing information with the rest of them. 'If you'd prefer to save the details until we can record them under proper conditions, Miss Crombie — '

'I think Mr Dacre, with his connections with both Brigid and Ishbel, is entitled to a few facts. Also, my father enjoyed his company.' That was the clincher. 'I knew that father and Brigid were away in Edinburgh that week, so while I was in the neighbourhood I . . . well, I just dropped in. I meant to wander round the house while Brigid wasn't in it, pretending it was all the way it used to be.' She took a deep breath, for the moment as tremulous as Ishbel. 'I drove in by the side gate, the way I usually do from that direction. And parked near the burn and walked up the slope to a spot I'd always loved as a child. And there was Simon, slinking down from the boundary wall. My favourite spot contaminated.'

'Just a minute,' objected Lesley. 'We never found his car, abandoned by the roadside, or anything. How could he just show up like that?'

'He hadn't got a car any more,' said Ishbel in little more than a whisper.

'There's one bus a day goes along the upper road,' said Caroline. 'He must have come on that. And there he was, the same old Simon, saying that he was dropping in — *dropping in* on Brigid. No hard feelings, they were a civilised modern couple, weren't they? And there were things they had to discuss. Same old Simon,' she repeated: 'same old sly, smirking know-all.'

'And what was this discussion going to be about?'

'I ought to have waited.' Caroline sounded genuinely apologetic. 'Looking back, I'd guess he might have got on to the planned burglary through some of his shady friends. He was here to blackmail Brigid, maybe offering her a deal where he got a cut of the proceeds. I wouldn't put it past him to have suggested coming in on the actual robbery. If I'd waited, he'd have leaked a lot more. He couldn't help himself. Had to show himself as the great manipulator.'

'But you didn't give him time.'

'I told him that, whatever he was up to, Brigid was in Edinburgh. That bit he *didn't* know. He was very peeved. But he wasn't going to go away empty-handed. He started daubing his irresistible charm all over me.'

'Making a pass?'

As Ishbel nodded dismal recognition of the likelihood of this, Caroline's lips tightened almost to invisibility. 'Told me he'd always fancied me, but never dreamt of coming near me while he was still married to Brigid. And then of course he'd made a terrible mistake, been a gullible fool, falling for anyone as . . . '

It trailed away. 'Go on,' said Ishbel. 'Something about me? Go on, say it.'

Caroline's lips parted, then tightened again. 'No. It was despicable. And then, would you believe, he said that we would really make a wonderful pair. He guaranteed to give me a child. Keep on until my father got the grandson he craved. The old man would soon come round. It was nauseating. And the swine had obviously talked himself into believing it was possible.'

'And that was when — '

'Yes, that was when. I couldn't help myself. I got my hands round his throat, and I enjoyed every moment of it. I strangled him, and then held his head under the water of the burn, just to make sure. Though afterwards I hated the thought that I'd polluted the burn.'

'You left no fingerprints that we could trace.'

'I was wearing my driving gloves.'

'Where are they now?'

'Ripped to shreds, somewhere in the Forth just below Queensferry.'

'And the ones you were wearing when you killed Lady Crombie?'

'Likewise. But you won't need them. I'll give you all the supplementary details you need. I'm not ashamed of what I did.' Her poise wavered for only a moment as she held her arms out towards Ishbel. 'But I'm sorry, my darling. For us. So sorry.'

19

The stone hulk of Black Knowe tower house, at least, had stood up to the gales and destruction without so much as a scratch. Lesley got out of her car into the shadow cast down the slope, and for a moment was ready to panic. She ought to have rejected Sir Nicholas Torrance's invitation. There was nothing here for her.

Yet that was silly. She knew perfectly well that she would have been unable to resist the chance of seeing him again.

'In the first place,' he said as he held her hand firmly in his, 'I really must apologise for not coming to your rescue when you phoned. After what I've read since . . . I mean, you do seem fated to get caught up in the rough stuff, don't you?'

'Nobody could have predicted the out-come.'

'If I'd rallied round, we might have sorted matters out a lot sooner.' He smiled that half sheepish, half endearing smile of his. 'Or maybe not.'

He led her to a chair below Alma Tadema's fanciful painting of the Bareback Lass.

Although between them they had proved the whole legend of the Lass to be a fake, and although the picture owed more to the artist's voluptuous imagination than to any historic reality, Lesley was glad to see it still here on the wall. It belonged. And although Sir Nicholas had entered his inheritance so recently, his patrician features seemed, too, to have belonged here for centuries.

He was wearing mottled brown tweed slacks and a short-sleeved terracotta shirt. He must have been away for a short holiday: his face and arms were lightly tanned. Lesley was captivated, as before, by the music in his voice; and for a silent but waiting accompaniment there were the keyboard she remembered and the clarsach on its stand in the corner.

He said: 'After my being so offhanded, it was good of you to come. Because now I'm asking *you* to come to *my* rescue. And not just me, but some other needy folk in the Borders.'

'You want my department's advice on security,' she guessed. 'The Baldonald House thefts have put the wind up the lot of you.'

He was looking disconcertingly at her lips as she talked, with a touch of self-reproach for something he might have missed, all through his own fault.

'That latter bit's got some truth in it,' he admitted. 'But it's not by any means the whole truth. You've heard about conditionally exempt works of art, of course.'

'Of course. Estate owners can escape inheritance tax on any of their heirlooms if they allow the public to see them. They don't have to display them publicly, just let punters make appointments to see a particular work. And then,' she added drily, 'ensure those appointments are made as difficult as possible.'

'But legislation's on the way to compel owners to have their designated treasures on regular public display, not just viewable only after a minefield of difficulties.'

Lesley had already heard whispers of dismay across the estates of the landed gentry at the proposed strictures. There were pieces of conditionally exempt Chippendale, paintings, prints, sculpture and jewellery scattered throughout Scotland, all of them a security risk and a much more serious risk if the doors of the treasure houses were flung open. Expert thieves were assuredly already checking on the web site which listed all the paintings and *objets d'art* available for inspection. With a new insistence on public display if there was to be tax exemption, an increase in private collections being open to the public would demand much tighter security everywhere.

'Yes,' she agreed. 'I can see the problem. You're all going to have to get together and work out a mutual scheme for safeguarding your tax perks.'

'Full-time surveillance is what we're after, yes.'

'Well, that lets me out. I can't help you. The police can't offer that: not for any single building on the off-chance of a raid, let alone a whole string of them.'

'Lesley.' He had seated himself in the old oak chair below the reivers' lances forming a deadly fan on the wall. She tried to shield herself from the subtler, much more dangerous weapon of his voice. 'We wouldn't want bits and pieces of advice, the occasional consultation, someone showing up when there's been trouble and it's too late to stop it. What I'm suggesting is a fulltime job for you. In charge of five of our local residences.'

'You're suggesting I should leave the Force?'

'Police priorities rarely coincide with our own. Don't blame them. But someone like yourself, working independently but still keeping contacts with your old associates . . . don't you see, we'd all be better organised that way.'

'And it'd be my head that'd roll when a garden gnome went missing.'

'You'd have a free hand. No chief inspectors and superintendents to shove you around. You've got the whole thing at your fingertips. Set up an overall security system. And for starters, complete computer cataloguing of the contents of all the stately homes and other historic buildings in the group, a sort of aristocratic Neighbourhood Watch. And exactly what each one of us needs to do for our particular premises. Telling us what facilities you need. No,' he smiled: 'not telling us — *ordering us?*'

Lesley thought of working exclusively with things she loved, being a sort of personal guardian of great portraits, beautiful china, a custodian, chatelaine, loving helpmeet . . .

'You could have your own quarters in Black Knowe, if that suited you,' said Nick Torrance, 'and work from here.'

He sat back and waited. He was in no hurry. She longed to accept, and he knew it, and was patient . . . but too complacent, too sure of her, damn him.

* * *

Ishbel met Greg and Kate at the head of the steps, just as Caroline had met Greg when he

367

first set eyes on Baldonald House. Unlike Caroline, she did not at once look in command, a part of the house's history. The long façade was not a family backdrop, taken for granted over the centuries, but a great burden liable to weigh down on her. But she smiled bravely, and let her father kiss her.

'So you're off.'

Their two cars stood side by side on the drive. He waved towards the Laguna. 'Come back with me. For a while. You can't stay here with no one to talk to.'

'I have to stay here. For Caroline's sake. At least until after the funeral.'

'It'll be ages before the trial. And what can you hope to do after that, here on your own?'

'I shall just have to see.'

She was not waving her arms about any more. Her hair was tied tautly back.

'Ishbel, I haven't had a chance of getting to know you. I know a lot of it's my fault, but — '

'Don't,' said Kate. She wasn't talking to him but to Ishbel. 'Don't encourage him, whatever you do. Any minute now he'll be in full cry as the guilt-ridden father. He's so good at becoming other people, he'll make himself really and truly miserable.'

When Ishbel smiled at her, it was becoming a proud, self-confident smile. She took an unhurried step towards Kate, kissed her with all the grace of a hostess bidding farewell to guests at the end of a dinner party, and said: 'Look after him. If he has any sense, he'll ask you to marry him.'

'Just a minute,' Greg spluttered. 'You hardly know us, and here you go dishing out ideas that . . . I mean, what on earth makes you think — '

'Empathy?'

Even more the gracious hostess, Ishbel watched the two of them go down the steps towards their waiting cars.

Greg said: 'Look, I'm sorry if — .'

'Where do we stop for lunch?' asked Kate coolly.

'I . . . look, we've got to talk.'

'Over lunch.'

'There's that nice place in Boroughbridge. The Black Bull.'

'Meet you there.'

She got into her driver's seat and closed the door. He followed her down the drive, and waited until they were well out on to the main road before overtaking her, then wondered why he had felt it so important to do so.

His car phone buzzed.

'One thing I've been meaning to mention,' said Kate. 'You're going to need some work to keep you occupied.'

'Agreed.'

'Maybe we can think about selling serial rights in as much of Brigid's book as you can sort out.'

'And get those businessmen on my trail? I'm beginning to think I've had enough of Brigid and her marzipan sweeties.' He slowed over a blind summit and made sure she was still at a sensible distance. 'Look, don't you think that trim little detective might have some interesting tales to tell?'

'No,' said Kate fiercely. 'I've noticed the way you've been looking at her. And I don't fancy it.'

'Any other helpful suggestions, then?'

'I'd better start rooting around to find some marvellous male hunk you could ghost for. Then maybe some of that would soak off on me. Rewarding to be in bed with a macho stranger.'

'Speaking of going to bed together.' His mouth was dry. 'What do you think about that idea of marrying me?'

There was a long delay. At last she said: 'What do *you* think?'

'It would be an interesting role to play. Me, myself, just for a change.'

'Never mind taking the clothes off. Would you really take the masks off?'

He nearly grazed a tractor edging out on

the road without pausing at the junction. Although they could still have heard each other, he waited until Kate had overtaken the tractor and was in his mirror again before saying: 'I promise. I do.'

'You know, I think I could learn to love you.'

'You mean all this time you haven't?'

Her car crept closer to his, but until she was within a distance frowned on by the Highway Code, she did not reply. 'This is no way to communicate. Let's leave it till lunch.'

'Or dinner. And stay the night.'

'Somewhere.' Quite deplorably she accelerated, gave his back bumper a heavy thump, and then fell contentedly back.

★   ★   ★

DCI Rutherford was impatient for DI Gunn's return, even though she had been perfectly entitled to her day off. The moment she appeared he grated: 'You know what this bloody funeral's going to lead to?'

'An interment in the family chapel, if they've shifted the loot out of the way. What else?'

'I'll tell you what else. That other business you came up with. While all the big cheeses in the county are at Crombie's wake, one of

371

their houses is going to be targeted.'

'That's what I was told, yes.'

'But there's been this last-minute shift. The lairds and ladies won't be away at a service in Selkirk. It's all been switched to Westerlaw, isn't that right?'

'Right. I don't see that that'll make much difference, though. The gang, whoever they are, must have heard. Either they'll call it off, or — '

'Or they'll bash on regardless. And I do mean bash. And if I knew *where*, I'd have a TSG and as many SAS volunteers as I could muster.'

Lesley thought of Nick Torrance and how right he was to see the growing need for surveillance and protection. Gangs here were gearing up to emulate those in France, where raiders on the most richly endowed châteaux had violent entry down to a fine art: in and out through reinforced fences with their bolt and wire cutters, their ladders and shotguns, all within four or five minutes, stealing to order and knowing where everything was. Coping with a spreading plague like that would be a challenge. Protecting things like that would be a worthwhile profession.

Why hadn't she said yes on the spot?

'But I've got another job just for you,' said Rutherford.

'Somebody's defaced the chief constable's photograph in HQ foyer?'

'You're deputed to provide a presence at the funeral.'

'Lord Crombie's?'

'The very one.'

It was already common knowledge that, with the Hon. Caroline Crombie in custody, General Sir Lachlan McIver, Brigadier of the Royal Company of Archers, had insisted on taking over all the arrangements for his old friend's funeral. Under no circumstances should it be skimped. The Baldonald House chapel was unfit for use, and Caroline had not had time before her arrest to finish clearing out and making safe the family vault. Sir Lachlan took over all responsibility. The service would be held in the chapel of his home, Westerlaw Castle; and the coffin would then be taken to the thoroughly cleaned family vault. And Sir Lachlan insisted on Caroline being present. It was not a matter of her being concealed, allowed like some medieval leper to look upon the service through a squint. She was the late Lord Crombie's daughter, and at her father's funeral she should take the place of honour.

'And it's been made clear that a police presence will be negotiated' — Rutherford mouthed the words as in a smutty recitation

— 'on the understanding that it shall be discreet and preferably using plain clothes officers. Sir Lachlan will himself be personally answerable to the Sheriff Principal for looking after the prisoner and delivering her back into custody after the ceremony'.'

'I think that's very civilised.'

'You've been well in with the family. We'll get a policewoman in plain clothes to drive, and you and the Crombie girl's dyke can travel with her in the same car. I'm relying on you to see she doesn't make a break for it across the fields.'

'She won't.'

'We have to be sure.'

'I'm sure about Caroline Crombie,' said Lesley: 'what she's likely to do, and what she's not likely to do.'

'Fancy yourself as a psychologist, Lez?'

'And don't call me Lez.'

'It's all right, I've never really thought of you as one of those.'

'Then don't make it sound that way. And let's not allow anything to rob this funeral of its dignity. It's all a sad business, every aspect of it.'

'Then let's sort out our arrangements, and get it over with.'

20

There was a great digging into cupboards and wardrobes all over the region. In preparation for the day of the funeral there was a great sorting out of kilts, sporrans, military decorations and, in case the ceremony went on too long, hip flasks. A Rolls was wheeled out and polished ready for the day. One newly knighted whisky distiller decided it would be more fitting to leave his latest BMW in the garage and bring his father's lovingly preserved Armstrong Siddeley out of retirement. A number of estate cars went under the pressure hoses to remove a year's good honest dirt.

It was felt by many that it would be much more fitting for Lord Crombie and his lady to be buried at the same time. Yet there was also an uneasy awareness that Lady Crombie was undeserving of the honour. Hector Crombie had died as he had lived — decently, conventionally, in his home. A stroke was almost as much a part of noble tradition amongst men of his generation as being killed in action. Brigid Crombie had had the bad taste to get herself murdered, which was somehow a reflection on her as much as her killer; and in any case the coroner would not release the body until police investigations had been concluded.

The Westerlaw Castle chapel was in a seventeenth-century wing, with a flamboyant ceiling of Biblical scenes painted by two Dutch artists. The Old Chevalier had paid a fleeting visit as the true King of Scotland, despite the throne of the Union being otherwise occupied, to touch members of the castle staff and a few selected local peasants against the King's Evil. At the same time he had graciously endowed the building with a Communion table, hidden away during some contentious periods but long since restored to its rightful place.

Lesley, seated immediately behind Caroline in a pew as hard and narrow as even John Knox could have wished, spent most of the brief service unobtrusively studying the de Wet altarpiece and the walls hung with paintings of saints which had somehow escaped the Reformist iconoclasts. She wondered if Sir Lachlan was one of Sir Nicholas Torrance's beleaguered clique; and listened with only half an ear to the hymns, prayers and tributes while sizing up the problems of securing all this against brutish invasion. Today the intrusions would be quite different from those suffered by the McIvers in the distant past.

Other members of the congregation shifted in their cramped pews to snatch a glimpse of Caroline's profile and maybe detect in it all the stigma of a ruthless murderess. Some shook their heads in sympathy, having heard glimmerings of the real story.

At last the coffin was lifted by four members of Lord Crombie's club, and two of his regiment. The two old soldiers in the middle appeared in imminent danger of strokes themselves, and progress was slowed less by reverence than by lameness.

Caroline travelled behind the hearse in Sir Lachlan's Bentley, while he came third in his Jaguar. The Bentley's driver was a policewoman in plain clothes and a chauffeur's cap. Lesley Gunn and Ishbel Dacre sat in the back. A few of the women among the mourners had looked askance as Ishbel held Caroline's arm tightly all the way from the chapel to the gate and the line of cars. Their disapproval had nothing to do with Caroline's killing of two people who were, by their standards, beyond the pale — or at any rate below the salt. In the old code of the Border reivers, a family insult had to be avenged in blood feud, and nobody thought the worse of the avenger for it. But the women did flinch at the undisguised relationship between Caroline and Ishbel as the two of them headed for the same car. Still, in coming here the mourners had deferred to the dictates of Sir Lachlan, and nothing was said aloud. Not here and now.

The cortège proceeded down the main drive and out on to the narrow road covering the eight miles between here and Baldonald House. Workmen unblocking a drain jammed by pulped vegetation and mud stopped work to remove their caps as the cars rolled past.

Lesley's radio bleeped suddenly, sounding twice as loud as usual in the funereal silence.

Ishbel glared at her. 'Couldn't you have left that cursed thing at home, just for once?'

Rutherford's voice crackled into the car. 'I've had another tip-off from our pet snout. The raid's all set up, just the way Fenwick said it would be. Only now we know where it is.'

'Guv, you do realise that right now I'm — '

'It's a fast break-in and getaway. At Westerlaw Castle.'

Caroline heard it, and gasped. 'No. Oh, no. Not Sir Lachlan.'

'They'd got Westerlaw in their sights anyway, and the funeral alterations haven't put 'em off. Just the opposite. Makes it simpler, really: the moment after the procession left for Baldonald House the way would be clear for a frontal attack. Nobody of any standing left on the premises. I've had an armed response unit on standby, but now we know the location they'll have ten miles to cover. I'm on my way. But there's just been a landslip along their likeliest escape route. Roadside bank undermined by floodwater, collapsed into the road. Odds are that they'll have to try the route you're on.'

'You want us to block the road?'

'Like hell I do. These scunners are capable of pumping all your vehicles full of holes. Let 'em pass — don't risk anyone getting shot. But ring the moment you can give me a rundown — time, speed, direction . . . and if you could follow them at a reasonable distance, without getting too close and risking them blasting off at you . . . '

'The bastards,' Caroline breathed. 'Bastards. After all Sir Lachlan's done for me!'

The cortège rolled solemnly on. Lesley leaned forward to keep an eye on the rear-view mirror, trying at each bend in the winding road to see past the string of cars behind her. For an agonising ten minutes there was still no sign of any van or truck racing up and pulling out to pass them.

The hearse slowed at a T junction, swung carefully to the right, and then jolted to a stop, angled across the road, out of Lesley's view; a horn was sounding impatiently. The hearse edged a few inches further, and stopped again. Somebody, still out of sight beyond the ragged hedge, was yelling furiously. Above the hedge was the top of a large blue van.

The driver of the hearse got out, adjusting his black headgear and taking a dignified step towards whatever was round the corner.

It dawned on Lesley what must be happening. 'No!' she shouted. Not that anyone outside the Bentley could hear her. She opened the door and stumbled out. 'No, don't! Come *back*!'

Out in the open air, she heard someone shout: 'Get that bloody meat wagon out of the way.'

Rutherford's calculations had been wrong. Whatever blockages there might be on the roads heading away from Westerlaw Castle, the raiders had not chosen to avoid them by following the route of the funeral cars — perhaps to avoid that possible slow-down — but had opted for a road sweeping close to Baldonald House and then away along the valley.

Lesley clutched her phone. 'Guv, they've blocked our way. Or we've blocked theirs. At the *Tam Lin* T-junction. It has to be them.'

'Christ. Don't take any chances. Armed

support'll be heading along that road anyway. On its way right now.'

Don't take any chances, she thought ruefully. Easy enough to say, miles away.

The row was heating up. 'Back up, or you'll finish up inside your own bloody hearse.'

'I canna. Not with all this behind me. Use some sense, man. You're the one who's got to back up.'

Sir Lachlan got out of his Jag and was stalking towards the junction before Lesley could wave him back.

'What the devil's going on?'

'Stay where you are, sir. Better still, get back in your car.'

'I've asked you, officer. What *is* going on?'

'I'm sorry, Sir Lachlan. Your home has been broken into. I fancy the thieves are in that vehicle just round the corner. Armed support is on its way. They won't get far.'

'Won't get . . . ? Damn it, if I get my hands on them . . . '

There was the sudden gunning of an engine, and fierce acceleration. The hearse driver made a wild lunge to one side, flattened against his hearse, as the bull bars on the radiator of a large blue van like a Securicor vehicle bounced round the corner. Tyres slithered on the verge; lumps were torn out of the hedge.

Crazily, the thieves were trying to escape by heading back part of the way towards the castle.

Sir Lachlan McIver was lifted off his feet by the nearside wing, and thrown into the ditch on the far side of the road. He began scrambling out as the van hit the third car in the cortège, a grey Volvo estate, and itself was jarred to one side, tilting over into the opposite ditch.

The driver wrenched his door open, brandishing a sawn-off shotgun.

'All right, get back. Well back, the lot of you. And stay there.'

Take no chances, Lesley told herself. She turned to check that everyone else understood. No time for ambling about, and even less for heroic gestures. Just stay put and be ready to duck well down when the cavalry arrived.

But Caroline Crombie was out of the Bentley, with the driver groping vainly to stop her.

'No!' Lesley yelled.

Caroline wove past her like a rugger player making a last fierce run for a touchdown.

'Bastards! You filthy bastards!'

The man slid down to the ground, and fired. In court he might later say that he had been off balance, and the gun had gone off without him squeezing the trigger. Or it had been a panic reaction.

Caroline choked a cry, stumbled to a halt, and opened her arms to clutch at the air. In agonising slow motion she crumpled into a heap in the middle of the road, and blood began pumping slowly from her mouth.

Over the brow of the low hill an armed response vehicle raced down upon them. Ishbel Dacre was half out of the Bentley, sobbing helplessly. And Lesley was sobbing a call for an ambulance into her phone.

But they had only to look at that crumpled figure in the road to know that it was too late for paramedics, an ambulance, a hospital. The only place for Caroline Crombie now was in the silence of the vault along with her father.

* * *

They sat in Rutherford's drab office with a deskful of reports, an ashtray of stubbed-out fag-ends and scribbled memos between them. Lesley enunciated words which seemed no longer to have any meaning for her. 'All right, say it. I shouldn't have let Caroline get out of that car.'

'No, you shouldn't. Neither should that driver.'

'I was the senior officer there. Pin it on me.'

'Certainly nobody's going to pin a medal on you.'

'So that's it. I can pack my bags and go.'

'Go?' He was hunched up in that weird Quasimodo distortion she hated so much. 'Go where?'

She told him about the other post she had been offered. The way things were, she could obviously look forward to a better future working with Sir Nicholas Torrance and his friends than battling on here. She wasn't really equipped for this.

Rutherford heard her out, staring at her with that disconcerting intensity of his. He could make anybody feel guilty, especially his own colleagues.

'Well,' he said. 'Yes, I suppose it would be a classier kind of job than you've got with us loutish lot. Just a squad of day-to-day dustmen, aren't we? Garbage removal, trying to keep the community clean. Better for the soul to play nanny to some respectable ancient paintings than real, lousy human beings.'

'Jock.' She had never used the name before, and used it now only because she knew he hated it and she wanted to kick him out of his own bossy offensiveness. 'I do happen to think those things are important.'

'Sure, sure. Scratched-out old canvases better any day than carved-up corpses. If you have a sensitive stomach, that is.'

'I'm a specialist. This is my speciality.'

'Yes. But look at what you've contributed to your section here. You'd rather drop all that, leave us to start all over again, while you wander off into Veitch's world?'

'What's Veitch got to do with it?'

'Hiring security men. Ex-coppers. Bent ones. To protect his property and his . . . shall we call it his interests?'

'I'm not a bent ex-copper. It won't be like that.'

'I suppose not. A bit posher, protecting the knick-knacks of the very tasteful rich, eh?'

'Taste has a lot to do with it, yes. Nothing wrong with that. It's what keeps civilisation going.'

'Oh, no it bloody isn't.' Rutherford was quite frightening as he slammed his fist down on the table and dislodged two piles of paper. 'What keeps civilisation going, Lez, is sanitation. Street sweepers and clearing the muck out of the drains, scraping the shit off the streets, disinfecting the place. Helping keep your fine pictures in position, yes, fair enough. All part of the service. But only one ingredient in the same soup dish of good men, bad men, weird women, and scum who poison the soup. You belong to us, Lez.'

'I've got this chance of doing a whole lot better for myself.'

'Och, aye, all right. So you would, in some ways. But . . . just when you're in line for promotion.'

'I suppose you've been consulted on that.'

'That I have.'

'You mean you're going to recommend me?'

'No.'

'That's it, then.'

'Silly bitch. No, I'm not going to recommend you. I've already done so.'

She had shied away from Nick Torrance because of his taking her for granted. Now she wanted to back well away from Rutherford.

'I'll have to think about this.'

'No, you won't,' said Rutherford with even more insufferable complacency. 'You've already decided.'

'Have I?'

'Yes. You're staying. You can't tell me you're not.'

That was exactly what she longed to do. Tell him she wasn't staying, that she'd had enough, that she was handing in her ID card and emptying her locker and leaving.

And she couldn't bring herself to say it.